Stained with Ash

By: E. Molgaard

To my parents that read my books even though they think I should talk to my therapist about the darkness I write.

Table of Contents

Note to Readers

This is a reverse harem romance which means the female main character has more than one love interest and she doesn't choose between them. There are dark themes in this book that can be triggering such as Drug use, Grooming, Abuse, Dubcon, Graphic rape scenes, Murder, Kidnapping, Threats of rape, Anal play and Torture. Please feel free to message me directly if you have any concerns or questions.

Scarlett

Stella

Sadie

With each name, I've had a different life. The only constant is the monster that haunts me. Cyrus was the boy I fell for, but he only wanted to own me. For years he made my life a living nightmare until the night they came and helped me escape my horrible life as Scarlett.

He always promised he'd never let me go and would always find me.

He kept that promise.

My Lord has come back for me, but I'm not going back.

Running from the happy life I created in New York, I once again change my name. The only problem is my life as Stella is too hard to let go. My friends who won't let me fight alone and the two men who have slowly put my heart back together have promised to slay my monster so I can come home to them.

What if New York isn't the only place I want to call home?

What if New Orleans holds something unexpected and I don't want to leave them either?

Will being Sadie finally give me freedom and the life I want, or will he find me again and I'll have to run, leaving behind not just two but four pieces of my heart?

Chapter One

Stella

Music pulses through the speakers as I walk across the floor at Mystique, the burlesque club I manage. Every seat is filled and all eyes are on the girls on stage as they dance the opening number to *Feeling Good* by Michael Bublé with their feather fans. Walking behind the bar, I wave to the bartenders as they move nonstop around each other and head to the registers. The second show just started so it's time to pull the numbers from the 6 o'clock show.

Swiping my keycard, I enter in my code and press the drawer button. The cash drawer pops open and I grab the cash bag with the receipts and first show's cash proceeds. Locking the drawer back, I turn facing the stage, watching Nadia give the audience a small peek of her bare breasts with her nipples covered by gold sequin flowers. Monica and Carla stand behind her with their backs to us as they spin their fans around in circles only showing glimpses of their gold thongs and round asses. A smile pulls across my face as the song ends and the girls slowly strut off the stage with the crowd cheering.

The lights darken as the next performer is about to come on and I turn back towards the register to check the open tabs. Seeing that the numbers are good, a smile forms on my face. Tonight's going to be a good night. As if my happiness manifests them, my phone goes off with a text.

Tanner: Blossom, have dinner with us.

I beam at my phone. Colton and Tanner have been trying to take me out to dinner for weeks, but I haven't agreed to go yet because I like spending time with them alone. When it's just the three of us here or at their place, it's so easy and fun.

Stella: Working

Colton: We'll pick you up at closing.

Stella: I'll still have work to do.

I don't really but I know they'll show up and I'm perfectly okay with that. I bite my lip to hide my smile as I think about what kind of fun we could have in the sex rooms below my feet. We've been hovering the line for awhile, them allowing me to set the pace, but I've been ready for awhile, wondering what room they'd be into.

Colton: Give us a time.

Tanner: We can bring you dinner.

A smile pulls across my face as I sense someone's eyes on me. It seems they couldn't wait. Looking back over my shoulder, I expect to find two gorgeous twins standing at the bar, but they aren't there. Scanning the crowd around the bar, I don't find them or anyone else looking at me. That's weird. I swear someone is watching me.

The feeling gets more intense the longer I stand here and the excitement I felt thinking it was Tanner and Colton is replaced with alertness. Are we being cased? Gripping the cash bag tight in my hands, I logout of the register and wave one of the security guards over.

Carter joins me as I step out of the bar and he silently follows me as I walk across the club, scanning every guest I pass. Being robbed is the last thing I want to deal with but it would be their death wish. Riona isn't going to let anyone steal from her. Stepping into the back hall relief fills me as I smile at Carter and enter my code to access the stairs to my office. "Thank you, Carter."

He nods but doesn't move until the door closes behind me. As I get to my desk, I pull up the security cameras and look over the club. My happy feeling is gone and a feeling that something is about to happen sits heavy in my stomach. Picking up my walkie that's linked to all the security guards, I press the talk button. "Keep your eyes open tonight, guys. Something doesn't feel right. Make sure the girls stay safe."

Our staff is always our first priority. The majority of us have been rescued from a traumatic life and are just trying to find our place in the world again. I'll do anything to make sure that never happens to any of them again.

The guards don't respond but I can see all their nods. I scan the cameras one more time, not seeing anything alarming before working on processing all the transactions from the first show. I double count the cash I pulled from the register and complete the deposit slip for the bank run in the morning. Verifying all card transactions next, I input the sales into our accounting software and start adding tips to payroll. As I'm inputting the tips, a beep rings out letting me know someone's coming up the stairs.

Looking at the camera feed, I see Carter walking up with a vase full of roses. I buzz him through my office door and he beams at me. "Special Delivery!"

I chuckle at him. "Thanks, Carter." He sets it on my desk and leaves. Standing, I bring my nose to the red roses and smell the lovely floral scent. Tanner and Colton are upping their game. Good thing I'm upping mine as well.

Seeing a card sticking out of the side, I grab it, expecting to see a note from them saying they'll be by later. I slide the card out of the envelope and my whole body runs ice cold as my worst nightmare comes true.

You look beautiful tonight, Scar.

Always the leading Lady.

Your Lord is here to collect you.

Cyrus

Chapter Two

Scarlett

Past - Age 9

July is my favorite! School's out and it's warm and sunny. It's also my birthday month. But my favorite thing is I get to be with my mom.

I miss her all the time, but she lives in Las Vegas and with me living at school or with my grandparents in Texas, this is the only time I get to see her. We always have so much fun together playing with my dolls, dressing up like princesses, painting pictures, going to see the ocean, and going swimming.

She left me at my grandparents one day when I was four to follow her dancing dreams and I didn't hear from her for two years. When she finally called asking to see me, my grandparents only allowed one week. But this year, I convinced them to allow me to stay for a *month*.

I skip down the hallway leading to baggage claim holding the airport lady's hand, looking around all the tall bodies searching for her. Seeing her white blonde hair that is just like mine, I let go of the lady's hand and race toward her. My mom beams at me as I scream out for her. She crouches down with her arms open and I jump into them. "Mom, I missed you so much. I have so much to tell you. Did you know Hannah and I are best friends now? I can't wait to show you the puppy Granny and Papa got me. Her name is Star. She's not real but sooo cute. Here…" I look around for my bag. Where is it? No, I lost it. Star is gone.

Tears start forming in my eyes as someone calls out my name. "Scarlett sweety..." The lady from earlier bends down in front of me with a kind smile. "You're not going to want to leave this." She moves something in front of her and I squeal excitedly at my pink rolling bag with Star sticking out the front.

"Mom, this is Star." Grabbing the stuffed golden puppy from my bag, I hold it up above my head, showing her.

"Oh, she's so cute. Scar, tell the nice lady thank you."

I quickly turn around and hug the lady's legs. "Thank you!"

She leaves as soon as I let her go and my mom wraps me in her arms again. "Oh Scar. I'm happy that you're here. I have a surprise for you." She stands up and looks behind her, waving someone over.

I look past her, trying to find the surprise, but all I see is a man and boy walking toward us. They look identical in their fancy white suits that make their tan skin glow and their curly brown hair shine. My eyebrows scrunch together as they get closer. Who are they? They can't be my surprise. They aren't exciting.

I watch as the man reaches out for my mom and pulls her to him, kissing her. Gross. I look away from them and find the boy looking at me. He stands like a foot taller than me so I have to look up to see his face. "Hi. I'm Cyrus."

"Hi. I'm Scarlett. Why are you my surprise?"

He chuckles. "I don't think we are but I do have a surprise for you." He pulls something out from behind him and I squeal at the American Girl doll.

"Oh my god! I love her!" I take her from Cyrus, jumping up and down. "Mom! This is the best surprise." I hold up my new doll.

She separates herself from the man's lips and chuckles. "That's not my surprise, honey. That's Cyrus' gift."

I look back at the boy I just met for a second before I jump at him, hugging him. "Thank you! I've always wanted one of these. She's so pretty." I pull back from the hug and he's smiling down at me.

"She looks just like you." Looking down at the doll, I realize she does look just like me. Her hair is white blonde, straight, and cut right past her shoulders. Her eyes are blue and she has one dimple just like mine. Her outfit is just like my favorite dress. I can't wait to wear it now so we can be identical.

Fingers brush through my hair and I look up at my mom. "Scarlett, I want you to meet Franklin Cunningham and his son Cyrus." I wave hi to the man and he crouches down.

"It's nice to meet you, Scarlett. Your mom and I are so excited for you to be here on our special day."

Special day? I always come to visit my mom today. July 1st always starts my time with Mom. That's when Granny and Papa go on their cruise.

Franklin stands and wraps his arm around my mom. "Scar, Franklin and I are getting married today and I want you to be my flower girl." She smiles happily at me and I match her smile.

I've always wanted to be a flower girl. To wear a pretty dress. To throw the pedals. To wear makeup and get my hair done. My friends have told me stories of them being a flower girl and it seems so glamorous.

"Do I get a pretty dress?"

"Absolutely, honey. Come on, I'll show you in the car." She grabs my hand and we walk out of the airport.

A long black limousine sits outside the door and Mom heads toward it as a man dressed in a black suit and black hat steps outside and opens the backdoor. I try to look inside to see who's getting out. It's got to be a celebrity. Maybe Selena Gomez and Justin Bieber. I walk on my toes trying to get a look but I don't see anyone.

"Mr. Cunningham." The man looks at my mom's friend and nods.

I look back at him and he smiles at me. "Go on."

Looking between the open door and Franklin confused, I ask, "This is for us?"

"Yeah."

"Wow. So cool." I quickly climb in and go all the way to the back. As I fall into the seat the furthest in, I find Cyrus right behind me, taking the seat next to me. I watch him closely, trying to figure him out. Does he want to be my friend? I've never had a friend who was a boy before. Everyone at my school are girls. Will he play dolls with me? I don't think so. He looks like he'd be into sports or video games. I tilt my head to the side. "Are we friends?"

He chuckles. "I want to be."

"Do you play dolls or dress up?"

He chuckles again, and I feel like he's laughing at me which makes me not like him. "I'm too old to play dress up or with dolls. I do like to explore and go on adventures. Would you like to go with me?"

That seems fun. I smile and nod excitedly. "You can even bring your doll and this guy with you."

He holds up Star, and I quickly grab her and squeeze her and my doll to my chest. "Girl. She's a girl. Her name is Star."

"Oh." He leans forward and takes Star's paw in his hand. "My apologies."

I chuckle. "How old are you?"

"Fifteen." Cyrus gives me a bragging smirk.

"Wow. I'm only nine but I'll be ten in one week."

"Cool. You get to be a princess twice in one week."

"I like dressing up as a princess. One day I'm going to marry a prince." I smile brightly at him. I'm going to marry Prince Charming.

"I'll be your prince." He reaches out, grabs my hand, and kisses the back of it.

"Scar, honey. Check out your dress." I look at Mom and Franklin, realizing I missed them getting in the car and us driving away. Franklin has his arm around her and she leans into him as she nods at the garment bags. "Look in the one closest to you."

I hand over Star and my doll to Cyrus before I reach for the bag. Zipping the bag open, I gasp at the puffy light pink dress with sparkles all over it. "It's beautiful." I run my hand lightly over the tulle. "It's for me?"

"Yes. You and your mom are going to look so beautiful." Franklin leans over and kisses the side of her head.

The car slows and I look through the window to find a White Chapel that has a sign outside of it saying Vegas' #1 Wedding Chapel. We stop in the parking lot and I clutch my dress to my chest as I climb over Cyrus ready to put it on. Mom and Franklin climb out first and I'm close behind them. Cyrus is behind me, carrying the other garment bag. "Star and Lady are okay in the limo. No one will touch them."

"Lady?" Who is that?

"I hope it's okay I named the doll. She's royalty just like you."

"I love it. Come on." I grab his hand and drag him after our parents.

Once inside, I race to my mom's side and eagerly listen to her and Franklin talk to an older man dressed in a preacher robe. Reaching up, I grab her hand and she looks down at me.

"Let's go get dressed." She points to the room that says Bridal suite. Not letting go of her hand, we walk to the suite as she grabs her dress from Cyrus. As soon as the door closes behind us, she starts talking a mile a minute. "I know this is a shock, but Franklin will take care of me. Take care of us. He has a huge white mansion that he runs his business out of. I'm no longer going to be alone."

Looking up at her confused, I squeeze her hand. "I'm here. You're not alone."

She places her hand on my cheek. "He'll be here when you aren't. He'll be my family. You, me, Franklin, and Cyrus will be a family."

I bounce up on my toes, excited. "Granny and Papa too!"

"No, honey. They can't know about Franklin." I sink back on my heels deflated. Why not them? "You have to keep him a secret."

My smile brightens. "A secret for just you and me?"

"Yeah. Pinky promise to seal the secret." She holds out her pinky, and I wrap mine around hers. I love it when we have our secrets. It's like it's us against the world and it hasn't been like that in forever. Like before she left to follow her dreams.

"Pinky promise."

She hugs me tight. "I'm so glad you're here." Her fingers run through my hair. "Let's get dressed so I can get married."

I pull my dress out, hold it to my body, and twirl. "I'm going to look so pretty."

My mom stands in front of me, holding her white satin spaghetti-strapped dress to her front. "We both will."

Once our dresses are on, we walk out of the dressing suite to find Cyrus waiting for us. He stares at me as he says, "Beautiful." I twirl for him and a wide smile spreads across his face before he looks at my mom. "He's waiting for you."

She nods, fiddling with her dress. "You guys go first."

I walk to Cyrus and he links our arms together as he hands me a basket full of flower petals. "Are you ready?"

I nod excitedly and the music starts. We slowly walk through the curtain, revealing a small room with four pews, Franklin, and the preacher. As I walk, I make sure to cover the ground with the petals evenly, guiding where mom will walk.

"It's almost like we're getting married, Scarlett."

I look up at Cyrus with a smile. "No, it's not, silly. I'm the flower girl." I hold out some petals in my hand to prove it.

He gives me a smirk and then blows the petals out of my hand. "Next time then." Not sure what he means, I shrug my shoulders and continue throwing the petals.

Chapter Three

Stella

Present

He's found me. The card falls from my fingers, slowly floating to the floor as an intense fear I haven't felt in five years washes over me. He can't be back, not after all this time. Not when I'm finally whole again. The second the card touches the ground, I move. Grabbing my phone, I call the person that saved me from Cyrus before. Riona. With the phone on speaker, I move to the safe and open it as her voicemail answers. The beep rings through the office as I pull out the manilla envelope Riona put together for me years ago. "He's back," are the only words I say before ending the call. She'll know who I'm talking about.

Knowing I can't wait around here any longer, I walk out of my office leaving everything behind but the envelope in my hand. Brent, one of our security guards, stands at the back door, ready to walk any of the girls to their cars and to make sure no unauthorized people come in. "Hey, Brent."

"What's up, Stella? Heading out for the night?" He gives me a charming smile.

I return his smile to hide my panic. "Yeah, I had an emergency come up. Do you mind if I borrow your car?"

"Sure." He pulls out his car keys from his front pocket. "Is something wrong with your car?"

"No. You can take it home tonight; the keys are upstairs. I just need a little anonymity." I take the keys from his outreached hand and he opens up the back door, letting me out first.

"Say no more." He steps outside after me, closing the door and making sure it locks before waving a hand towards the direction of his car. Like all the employees, his car isn't far from the backdoor and I hit the unlock as I look around the dark space, making sure no one is waiting for me.

Not seeing anyone, I move to the driver's door and open it. "Thanks again, Brent."

"No problem, Stella. See you tomorrow." He gives me a wave as I slide into the seat and start the car. I let out a long breath as a plan starts forming in my head.

I need to get out of the city tonight. As I drive, I'm constantly watching for any cars that seem to be following me and at every stoplight, I'm scanning the faces of all the pedestrians that are walking around at this late hour. Would I even recognize him if I saw him on the street? I always thought I'd be able to pick him out of a crowd even now with how much he has haunted my dreams, but tonight even when I felt something was off, I didn't see him in the club.

Making several random turns throughout the drive and not seeing anyone following me, I find the closest public parking deck and park between two large trucks. With the car turned off, I finally open up the envelope to see what Riona put in it. I also have one of these in my apartment just in case, but I've never opened them. For the first year after escaping him, I had carried that one with me everywhere, ready to run at any given second. I was constantly looking over my shoulder for him, but eventually, I looked back less and started leaving the envelope at home. I even forgot about it being in the back of my closet until tonight.

Dumping the contents into the passenger seat, I find a driver's license, passport, cash, a phone, subway card, prepaid visa, and a note. I grab the note and open it.

Call when you're safe.

-Riona

Picking up the license and passport, I see my picture with the name Sadie St. Cloud. Scarlett Cunningham ceased to exist the moment I left Las Vegas and now Stella Johnson will join her. But this time it's going to be harder to say goodbye. I have a family here. I have Colton and Tanner. Yes, nothing more than a few kisses and spending time with them has happened but their attention and presence over the last few months has awakened something in me that I thought I'd never feel again, let alone trust that feeling.

Looking at the phone, I'm tempted to turn it on and call them. Ask them to come with me, but I know I can't. For the same reason I'm running, I won't put them or any of my friends in danger.

Finding a hoodie in the backseat of Brent's car, I slip it over my head and stuff the contents of the envelope into my pants and hoodie pockets. The hoodie swallows me as I stand outside the car and lock the door with the keys inside.

Pulling the hood over my head, hiding my pink hair, I move towards the stairwell and make my way down the two flights. Before stepping out onto the sidewalk, I stop by the parking attendant and hand him Brent's phone number with a $100 bill asking him to call him to pick up his car. Once on the sidewalk, I tilt my head down so my face is hidden, but I make sure to watch every person that passes me.

The subway entrance is only half a block down the street and I take the stairs at a light jog. Once underground, I pull out the subway card and swipe it at the entrance to the terminal. As I turn down the tiled tunnel, I look back over my shoulder to check out the people following me. No one jumps out at me. Just a few couples, a group of guys, and a family of four. On the platform, I wait for the next train going south with my back against a pillar and my head on a swivel. I can't afford to be surprised right now or mugged. Luckily the train comes quickly and I get on it and take a seat in the corner.

The subway car is pretty empty and when the doors close with only myself, a young couple making out, a woman with a child, and a teenage boy looking at his phone. I only have to get through ten stops to get to the bus station.

After several stops with a few people coming in and out, mine arrives. Before the train even stops, I'm standing and heading to the door. As they slide open, I step out and head up the stairs to the street level of Port Authority Bus Station. Finding a departure list, I see that buses are leaving for Boston, DC, Philly, and Atlanta in the next couple of minutes. Perfect.

Atlanta gives me enough distance to think and find somewhere to start new. I make my way to the empty ticket line and use some of the cash to purchase my ticket. I feel like my heart is beating out of my chest as I move through the terminal. The last time I was in a bus station, I was grabbed before even getting on it. I'm not making that mistake again.

Finding my bus, I show the driver my ticket and climb on. The bus is mostly empty, so I find a seat with empty seats surrounding it and slide to the window. I watch each of the other passengers arrive and take a seat until the driver comes on and closes the door, but I don't take a deep breath until we start moving. And I don't relax until we're out of the state. I made it out.

Chapter Four

Tanner

"Would you hurry up?" I yell to Colton who's still getting ready for our surprise date with Stella. She never did respond to our in office date suggestion so we're going for it. I already ordered Indian food that we're picking up on the way.

"I'm coming. I don't roll out of bed looking this great." He smirks at me and I roll my eyes.

We're identical twins in every way except for one. My hair is lighter than his and he keeps his longer on the top. "You don't look any different than me and I was ready twenty minutes ago."

"You really should put in a little bit more effort for her. It's probably why I'm her favorite."

He gives me a little shove as he walks by, and I hook my arm around the front of his neck and hold him in a headlock as I mess up his styled hair. "You're delusional if you think that." I push him out of arm's reach so he can't retaliate quickly.

He huffs as he straightens himself and runs his fingers through his hair. Shaking his head, he looks at me getting ready to strike, but my phone ringing stops whatever he was about to do. "Is that Stella?"

I pull my phone from my pocket and shake my head no. Bringing it to my ear, I answer, "Hi Ri..."

Her frantic voice cuts me off. "Tanner, please tell me you're with Stella right now."

Worry runs through me as I go on alert and Colton tenses off my reaction. "No, she's at the club."

"Fuck."

Something isn't right. I grab my car keys off the counter and head for the door with Colton on my heels. "What's wrong, Ri?"

"I just got a voicemail from her. Her stepbrother is back."

"Fuck." I look back at Colton. "Cyrus is back."

Anger flashes in his eyes. "Where's Stella?"

Ri must hear him because she answers and I put her on speaker as we both climb into my car. "She's not answering her phone. All she said was he's back."

"We're going to the club now. We'll find her and him."

"He's not going to get away this time," Colton adds.

"Keep me updated," Riona says before hanging up and I pull out of our parking garage and floor it to the club.

It takes us twenty minutes to get to the club and I know if Cyrus got her, we're too late. I pull into the employee lot and park next to her car. We both have our doors open before I even have the car off. We reach the back door and I pound on it twice before entering in our code. Brent stands on the other side of the door and when he sees us, he smiles. "What's up, guys? You here for one of the girls tonight?"

Colton and I used to spend our free time here. The girls are beautiful and have no attachments, but ever since Stella showed up to help rescue Aisling from when she was taken, four months ago, no one else has had our attention. "We're looking for Stella."

He doesn't seem to be on alert, so I know the worst case scenario of Cyrus showing up with a bunch of men to take her hasn't happened. Whatever is going on, it was done quietly.

"Oh, you just missed her like fifteen minutes ago."

"She was by herself?" Colton asks.

"Yeah, but she did ask to take my car which I thought was weird." Smart girl. If he had truly found her, he could've placed a tracker on her car. "But you know when the boss asks you for something you say yes."

I look back over the parking lot, seeing a lot of dark spots for someone to hide. "Did you watch her leave?"

"Yeah, like always. I walked her to my car and watched her pull out."

"No one followed her?" From this angle, I can see the street easily, which means someone could've been waiting on the street for her.

He looks at me confused. "No. Is something going on?"

Colton and I look at each other and then back at Brent. We don't want there to be a panic, but the security needs to be on alert. "Stella's past is back to haunt her. We're just trying to keep her safe. You guys need to stay vigilant."

Brent nods, understanding how serious this is. He might not know Stella's story, but everyone here knows the danger if their pasts come back to light. "Definitely. I'll let the others know."

I give him an appreciative nod. "Great." He steps away and takes position back at the door.

Looking at Colton, I toss him my keys. "Go check out her apartment, maybe she headed there."

Colton heads back out, with the door closing behind him, and I climb up the stairs to her office. As always, her office is decluttered and neat, so it makes it pretty easy to see what's out of place. Stella's chair is pushed back, receipts still cover her desk, the safe is open, and there's a big bouquet of roses sitting in the middle of her desk. While things aren't normal, it doesn't look like there was a struggle. I walk around the desk and my foot slides on a piece of paper. Picking it up, I read the message.

You look beautiful tonight, Scar.
Always the leading Lady.
Your Lord is here to collect you.

The dick is taunting her. I grab my phone and call Riona and she answers immediately. "Tell me you found her."

"Can't. I'm at the club, Colton is heading to her place. Brent said she left fifteen minutes ago, probably right after she left the voicemail, and she took his car. There's a bouquet of roses here and a note from Cyrus. That's what spooked her." I crunch the note in my hand and throw it across the room.

"Okay. Is there still a manilla envelope in the safe?"

I bend down and look inside. "It was open when I got here but I don't see an envelope, just cash and deposits."

Riona lets out a sigh. "She's running. That envelope was her escape plan if he ever came for her."

Why wouldn't she call us? Colton and I would do anything to keep her safe. "She doesn't need to run anymore; we'll always protect her."

"Focus on finding Cyrus and how he found her. I'll make sure she gets somewhere safe." I can hear Dante, Matteo, and Enzo talking in the background and they have a much larger reach than the Murphys. If she won't let us protect her, hiding in Russo territory is second best.

However, that doesn't mean I don't want to talk to her. Knowing a phone was in that envelope, I say, "I want the number, Ri."

"Yeah, yeah, yeah. You're getting all possessive over your Blossom and Shortcake." I can almost see her eyes roll through the phone. "Tanner, you know you won't be able to go after her, right? If he's been watching her, he's been watching you guys." Her voice is serious and I understand what she's saying but I don't like it.

Our call ends and I'm about to call Colton when Brent appears in the doorway. "Umm. I just got a weird call saying a pink haired girl left my car in their parking deck."

"Where?"

He gives me the location and I curse. She's really leaving the city. I want to go after her but it's too late to stop her. "Thanks. Get one of the guards to drop you off after work. She's not going to need it anymore."

He nods. "Also Carter mentioned when I was telling them to be alert that Stella had said the same thing tonight. Which reminded me that she did tell us something felt off."

I look up at him quickly. "She said that?" I move around the desk and take a seat in the chair as I log onto the computer. "About what time?"

"During the second show, close to the beginning."

"Thanks, Brent." He leaves me alone as I pull up the security feed and call my brother.

He answers, getting straight to the point. "She's not here."

"She's running. Riona's going to help her. We need to find this asshole so she can come home. Get back to the club. I have a feeling he was here tonight."

"Already on my way."

Chapter Five

Scarlett

Past - Age 13

"Shh... We need to be quiet." Cyrus smiles back at me as he holds a finger to his lips. I feel my cheeks heating from his smile as I follow him down the stairs of the side house he lives in. We're supposed to be in bed since Franklin and my mom are at the main house working. I'm not sure what they do so late at night because I'm not allowed in the main house, but I know it's got to be exhausting. Mom always comes back looking tired and in a haze.

"Where are we going?"

"On an adventure. I want to show you something." He grabs my hand and warmth shoots up my arm. It's such a weird tingling feeling that I want to pull my hand away to look at it. Jogging to keep up with him, we slide out the backdoor. He doesn't let go of my hand when we get outside and I can't help my smile. Cyrus and I have gotten a lot closer over the last couple of summers but for some

38

reason this summer when he picked me up from the airport, I got butterflies in my stomach and they've continued to flutter every time he looks at me.

Looking away from him, I see we're walking toward the mansion. "We can't go in there." I pull on his hand, trying to get him to turn around. "We'll get in trouble."

He chuckles. "We won't be seen." His grip on my hand tightens, pulling me towards the mansion. "Don't you want to know what goes on in there?"

I do, but I don't want to get in trouble with Franklin. He really scares me when he yells. "Do you not trust me?" Cyrus looks hurt at my hesitation and tries to pull his hands away but I don't let go.

"No. I trust you." I grip his hand with both of mine, silently pleading for him not to leave me out here.

"Good." A smile breaks across his face. "I want to show you all my favorite places."

We sneak around the side of the mansion where jazz music filters out the walls, reminding me of the *Vampire Diaries* episode where you get flashbacks of when Klaus and Stefan were friends during the 1920s before Klaus and Rebekah ran because their father was chasing them. Maybe Franklin and Mom own a bar. I try to sneak a peek through one of the windows, but a curtain is blocking my view.

Cyrus leads me to the backdoor and he immediately pulls me into a dark closet. I whisper his name as my heart rate increases, not being able to see anything. My breath catches at the feeling of his body pressed against mine and I wish I could see him.

"Do I make you nervous, Scarlett?" I shake my head no, even though my heart is racing and my palms are sweating. "You don't need to be nervous around me." Fingers brush through my hair and I lean into his touch. "I can't wait to show you my world."

He links his fingers through mine, and I hesitantly allow him to pull me with small steps. The sound of something scraping across wood sounds out before a whooshing sound and then a faint light line appears. The line widens and I realize it's a door that's a piece of the wall in the pantry we're standing in. Cyrus smiles back at me. "I told you we wouldn't be seen."

Stepping past him, I release his hand and walk through the opening to find a narrow hallway with pink insulation on one side and exposed drywall on the other. "What is this?" I place my hand on the drywall, feeling the vibrations of the people on the other side.

He steps up to me and whispers in my ear, "A secret passageway to spy on everyone. Come on, let me show you."

He once again takes my hand and wonderful sparks run up my arm. Does he feel the same thing? Is that why he's always taking my hand?

I follow behind him along the length of the wall until it ends at a T-intersection. He pulls me to slide past him and points to the right where a small alcove is with light coming from what looks like a window. I look back at him confused, but he just waves me to go ahead. Slowly I step closer to where the window is, squeezing his hand because I'm sure something is going to jump out. This is some kind of prank to get me in trouble.

As I get closer, I realize it's not a window but shaded glass that looks into a large common room. "Can they see us?"

"No, it's a two-way mirror." Stepping up to the glass, I take in everything that's going on. The room is filled with at least twenty-five adults lounging on couches, armchairs, or at the bar that's opposite us.

The men are all dressed in suits with their jackets unbuttoned or off and the women are draped over them in exposing outfits. I spot my mom next to the bar on a small couch with two men. She sits across them as she strokes the chest of the guy's lap she's sitting on and allows them to grope her. They run their hands over her exposed legs, stomach, and breasts. What is she doing? Where's Franklin? Why is she cheating? "Where's your dad?"

Cyrus steps closer to my back. "He's probably in his office, watching your mom right now."

What is she thinking? He's going to be so mad. I can imagine his harsh yelling as he degrades my mom and the sounds of objects crashing into the walls. "Why would she do this?"

"She's working. She's his Madame. Our most desired woman. Those are probably new clients my dad is wanting to impress."

I'm so confused. How is she working? Client, for what? Madame? "I don't understand."

"Let me show you." He pulls me out of the alcove and down the hallway we haven't been to yet. It leads to stairs that take us up. I'm nervous about what he's going to show me because I know I'm not going to like it. Whatever this is, my mom shouldn't be a part of this.

My heart beats loudly as we walk down the hidden hallway on the second floor. I can see the first opening up ahead and I place a fake smile on my face as Cyrus looks over his shoulder at me. "Don't be scared, Scar. I can't wait to show you the thrill pleasure can give you."

That doesn't make me feel any better, but I try not to show it. Cyrus crowds me into the opening but before I can look to my right, he guides me to the viewpoint on my left.

I gasp, covering my mouth with my hand as I see a man standing naked with a bare woman kneeling in front of him with her mouth wrapped around his penis. I'm horrified but intrigued as I watch him guide her along his length by her hair with a groan, loving what she's doing.

Cyrus braces his hands on the seal on either side of me, but he doesn't touch me. I can feel his breath move across my neck and a warmth settles in my lower stomach. "Do you see his pleasure?" The man throws his head back as he groans and the sound lightly flows through the walls. "See how she's loving it?" The woman reaches around the man to his ass and holds him there as she takes more of him in her mouth.

I nod, too focused on what's happening in front of me, Cyrus' presence, and how my body is reacting to everything. "We don't do anything wrong here. We just allow people to escape their lives and enjoy their time with whoever they want."

Sounds of conjoined moans come from behind us and I look to find another couple on the bed in a separate room. I step to that window, watching the woman's face as the man thrusts into her from behind. Her eyes close as her mouth opens and she grips the sheets underneath her. She definitely looks like she's enjoying what he's doing to her.

Hands rest on my hips as Cyrus steps close behind me so I can feel all of him. "Do you blame our clients for wanting to enjoy themselves with beautiful women who know how to blow their minds?"

His hands slowly slide up and down my sides as we watch them have sex. My breath seems to shorten with each stroke of his hands and the tingling in my lower belly intensifies. I lean back into him, taking comfort in his hard body, and his hands slide across my stomach until he wraps his arms around me.

"You don't need to worry about your mom. She's doing as she's told. Making those man fall at her feet." He places a hand over my beating heart. "You feel it, don't you, Scar? The excitement. The need. The desire." His words whisper across my ear and my breath catches as my cheeks heat.

Before I can find words to respond, the sound of someone walking towards us breaks me from the spell I'm in as I look toward the hall with wide eyes, expecting to see Franklin standing there ready to yell at us. As his steps grow closer, fear starts to boil up inside me.

Cyrus pulls me back further into the alcove until my back hits a wall and we're surrounded by darkness. Cyrus stands in front of me, blocking my view of the hallway, but I can still hear Franklin's steps. I hold my breath when it sounds like he's right next to us and Cyrus tilts my chin up so I'm looking at him. My eyes connect to his brown ones and I let my breath go slowly as our connection makes the outside world disappear.

His eyes have a warmth to them that tells me that he feels all the same feelings that I have for the last few weeks. I reach up, touching his cheek and he quickly closes the distance between us, pressing his lips to mine. Not sure what I'm doing, I follow his lead and when I open my mouth to try and catch a breath, he pushes forward. Our tongues dance together and the intensity between us gets to be too much that I pull back. I'm breathing hard as I look up at him, wanting to see if he liked it as much as me. He smiles down at me as his fingers run through my hair. "You're so beautiful, Lady."

I beam up at him. "Lady?" Like my doll.

"Yes. My Lady." He leans forward and places a quick kiss on my lips. "Are you okay with that?" I nod happily, even though I don't know what that means, but if it means we get to kiss some more, I want it.

"Good. I'll be your Lord."

I test the words on my lips. "My Lord."

Darkness fills his eyes from the nickname as he takes my hand. "It's going to be so much fun making you mine." I'm in a blissful daze as he pulls me through the secret hallways, out of the mansion, and into the side house. He wants me to be his.

He stops us outside my bedroom, and I look up at him wanting another kiss. Raising on my toes, I press my lips to his and he frames my face with his hands, not letting me pull back until he's placed at least four quick kisses on my lips. "Goodnight, Scar."

"Goodnight, Cyrus."

He waits until I go into my room and I can't help my smile as I fall back on my bed. Cyrus likes me. I touch my lips, still feeling his kiss. He kissed me.

I'm not sure how long I'm laying on my bed smiling, but it must be for a while because I hear the front door open and light footsteps coming up the stairs. When they get closer to my door, I call out for my mom and the footsteps stop outside my door. I call out again and the doorknob turns. When the door opens, I'm shocked to see how messy she looks and her eyes have a hollowness to them. As she walks closer, I recognize the haze in her eyes.

"Mom?" I scoot over on the bed and pat the spot next to me. She comes over and the smell of strong cologne and sweat fills the air. "Are you okay?"

"Of course, honey." She tries to put a wide smile on, but it looks painful.

I grab her hand and hold it in both of mine. "Cyrus took me to the mansion tonight." Fear shines in her eyes. "Please tell me this is what you want and Franklin makes you happy."

The fear turns to anger and she pulls her hand from mine and stands. "None of that is your business, Scarlett. You aren't allowed in that house; do you hear me?" Shocked at this change, I nod.

"You don't question me or my marriage again. You just need to stay out of my life." She storms out of my room, and tears start rolling down my cheeks as I curl into a ball and cry from my mom's hurtful words. She doesn't want me here anymore.

Chapter Six

Sadie

Present

The bus ride was long and exhausting. There were half a dozen stops and I only dozed when we were moving. I can feel the exhaustion in my body so when we get to Charlotte, almost half a day since I got on, I decided to get off. I was never going all the way to Atlanta anyway just in case Cyrus found out what bus I got on.

With the bus station in downtown Charlotte, I was able to grab a hotel close by. I swipe the key card to my room and my eyes go directly to the king size bed and I just want to fall into it. The door closes behind me and I turn the deadbolt, flip the door guard, and push the chair under the handle. Once I know I'm secure, I relax and start pulling out all the items from my pockets and lay them next to the bag of clothes and snacks I bought at the gift shop. Needing a shower, I remove my clothes and head to the bathroom. Time to wash off the last twenty-four hours.

Once I'm clean, I walk out of the bathroom with the towel wrapped around me and climb into bed. As I lay there waiting for sleep to overtake me, I turn on the phone and connect it to the wifi. Immediately three messages pop up from three different numbers on a secure messaging app.

Unknown 1: Be safe Starlight. Head to New Orleans. Club Risqué. Ask for Jaxson Wright. He's a friend and you'll be safe there. M

Riona. She's using our online names from when we first met. New Orleans. This Jaxson guy has to be a part of the Russos. If Riona's boyfriends trust him, then I do too.

Starlight: I'm safe for now. I'll call once I get to New Orleans.

Her response is immediate with a thumbs up and I pull up the other messages that are in a group chat.

Unknown 2: If you didn't want to have dinner with us you just had to say it. You didn't need to run.

Tanner.

Unknown 3: Once this is over you owe us a real date. Dressed up. Dinner. Drinks. Us eating you for Dessert.

Colton.

My cheeks heat at his words because we've been skirting around our attraction to each other and I know it's my fault. They've allowed me to call the shots and take things at my own pace and what I really want from them now is to take what they want.

Me: How can I say no to that offer?

Colton: You don't. Say Yes.

Tanner: Are you safe?

Me: Yes

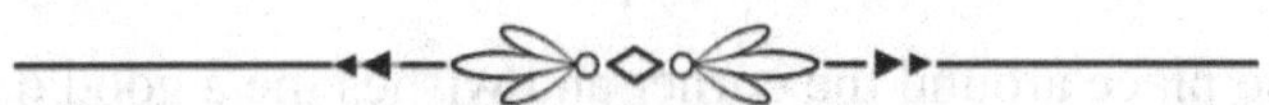

I stretch out on the bed, waking up as the sun rises the next morning. Today I need to keep moving but I need to get some clothes and change my look. He'll be looking for my pink hair, and as much as I hate to change my color, I need something less eye catching.

Climbing out of bed, I tighten the towel back around my body and head to the bathroom to get ready. Once dressed in my gift shop cotton pants and Charlotte sweater, I grab all my belongings and leave the hotel room. I won't be coming back. An older man sits behind the concierge desk as I walk into the lobby and he smiles brightly at me. "Hello, ma'am."

I lean my arms against his high counter with a smile. "Hello, I was hoping you could point me in the direction of a hair salon close by and a department store."

"Absolutely." He pulls out a downtown map. "There are shops all along these two streets." He points to the streets that run north of the hotel. "This here is a highly recommended salon." He leans forward and whispers, "My daughter is one of the stylists."

I chuckle and look down at where his finger is sitting, seeing it's just a few blocks away. "What's her name?"

49

"Shannon. She's very talented." A proud smile sits on his face.

"I'm sold. Hopefully, she'll have an opening. Now can you point out where the best breakfast place is?" He tells me about a diner style place around the corner and wishes me a good day while handing me the map. I thank him and go check out at the front desk.

After eating what seems like every item on the menu, I leave the restaurant and start shopping. I grab luggage, a purse, a phone charger, toiletries, and several outfits. With my arms full of bags, I head into the hair salon and a lady at the front desk greets me. "Welcome in. How can we help you?"

"Hi. I was hoping someone would be available to remove the pink from my hair and dye it a warm blonde? Preferably Shannon if she's available. Her father recommended her at the hotel."

"Of course." She looks down at her computer, checking the schedule. "She's just finishing up with a client. I'll let her know you're waiting."

"Thank you." I head over to the waiting area and start packing all my stuff in my new suitcase.

The front desk girl chuckles when she sees me. "Did the airport lose your luggage?"

I chuckle with her. "Something like that. I figured if I need to buy a new wardrobe, a hairstyle change is needed too."

"We'll definitely be able to help out with the new do."

Just as I'm zipping up my new suitcase with everything I bought in it, a stylist walks out from the back with a client. She says

goodbye to them and then she smiles at me, holding out her hand.
"Hi. I'm Shannon. I hear my dad sent you here."

I place my hand in hers, shaking it. "He did. He raved about you."

"He's so supportive. Come on back." I follow her back, wheeling my suitcase behind me.

She shows me to her station and I take a seat in her chair. "So, what are you wanting to do today?" she asks as she drapes the cape over me.

"I'm looking for a change. Get rid of the pink and go to golden blonde. I also want to take some inches off. Maybe this short." I bring my hand up and show her the length I want, just a couple of inches below my collarbone.

"Sounds good." Her fingers run through my hair. "I do love this pink. Is there a reason for the change?"

Yes, there is but I'm not burdening her with that. "I love it too but it's time for a change. Something less wild."

"Ahh. New job." I smile at her without answering. "I do specialize in vivids. What if the color is hidden?"

I beam at her. "That would be great. You have full power to do whatever."

"You're going to love it." Her excited smile is contagious.

Hours later, Shannon turns the chair and I see my hair is several inches shorter than the long hair I usually keep down to my lower back and my pink roots and ends are gone but now my hair is light blonde with muted rainbow pastels hidden underneath. It's perfect. Subtle but also unique. Now it's time to move on.

Chapter Seven
Scarlett
Past - Age 15

"You better run, Scar. When I catch you, you're mine." I giggle with excitement at Cyrus's voice echoing through the hidden halls of the mansion. His footsteps sound behind me as I run up the steps leading to the third floor. "You can't escape me." I squeal at the feeling of Cyrus's fingers brushing across my back as I reach the top step.

I smirk back over my shoulder at him and his heated grin has me turning down a hall that I know is a dead end. "My Lady wants me to catch her." Slowing to a stop, I turn, facing the only reason I enjoy coming to Vegas. He stands at the end of the hall with a dark shadow across his face.

"Come and get me." My body buzzes in anticipation as I walk backwards and Cyrus closes in on me. My back hits the wall and I grip the sides of my dress to stop myself from reaching out for him as my eyes drop to his lips.

Our makeout sessions are always so intense after he's chased me through this mansion. It gives me such a high, knowing I cause this reaction in him. My heart races and my breath shortens with each step Cyrus takes closer to me. I want his lips on mine. His arms wrapped around me, holding me against him.

Cyrus erases the last bit of space between us, standing so close that my breasts brush against his chest with each breath. Silence surrounds us as we stare at each other and I fight myself from reaching out for him to take what I need. He likes to be the one in control when we play his games. He wants to take what he wants.

"You play my game so beautifully, Scar." He reaches out, tangling his fingers in my hair and pulls me to him so our lips crash together. "But the game isn't over."

His arm wraps around my waist as he pushes on the wall next to us and it swings open, revealing a bedroom. A bedroom that looks identical to the ones on the floor below us. "It's all ours tonight."

I've never been in one of the mansion rooms and I'm not sure I want to. These rooms are for temporary lust, not for Cyrus and I. Cyrus sweeps me off my feet and a squeak escapes me in shock as I wrap my arms around his neck. He chuckles as he carries me to the bed and an unnerving feeling sits in my stomach as he sets me down on the edge. "Can we go back to the house? It doesn't feel right being in these rooms."

Cyrus towers over me, just staring at me for a few seconds, and I worry I've upset him. "No one is going to bother us." He bends down, placing a kiss on my lips. "I wanted to give you a special night." His lips press to mine again as he leans forward pushing me back on the bed. We move up the bed until his body covers mine and I can't look away from his eyes. "A night of just you and me."

That's what I want. Just him and me, it doesn't matter where we are. I reach up, touching his cheek, and his cocky smirk has me melting. Cyrus captures my lips in his in a wild kiss that has me arching into his body, gripping his hair, and pulling him closer to me.

"You're so needy for me." Cyrus' smile turns heated as his eyes roam over me, following the path his hands slide down my sides to my thighs. My dress rides up my legs, exposing my pink panties to him as he spreads them open. His thumb runs over the fabric, pressing the wetness against my lower lips and heat fills my cheeks in embarrassment. Is he grossed out? I never wanted him to see how damp my panties get during our makeout sessions.

I try to close my legs but Cyrus holds them open as he moves in between them. "Don't hide from me."

He leans over me and skims his lips over mine as his hands run up my inner thighs. "I want your panties drenched for me." Warm tingles settle at my core as he presses his lips to mine. I gasp as Cyrus grinds himself against my core, and he takes the chance to deepen the kiss. My hips move on their own, rocking against Cyrus' hardness as I lose myself in his kiss. He feels so good against me. The buzz is so much more intense than before and it keeps growing.

I grip his shirt, needing to hold on to him as the build gets to be too much and bliss explodes throughout my body. I'm breathless and dazed as the sparks die down and I smile up at Cyrus. "You're mine now, Scarlett."

Cyrus grabs my hand and brings it to his pants, pressing my palm against his hardness. "My turn now. Open my jeans, Scar. I need to feel your hand wrapped around my cock."

Nervousness has my hand shaking. I've never done anything like this. I don't know what to do. When I don't do as he asks, his grip on my hand tightens. I try to pull my hand away, but he won't let go. "Open my pants, Scarlett."

"Can't we continue what we were doing? That felt good."

He pushes back, shoving my hand away as he climbs off the bed. "I need more than just dry humping your thighs." Anger rolls off of him as I crawl to the edge of the bed. "Women beg for cock every day, Scarlet." His yells echo through the room, and tears fill my eyes. He's never yelled at me like this before. "And my own lady won't even touch me. Maybe I need to find a new one."

Cyrus glares down at me with disappointment and my heart breaks when he turns away from me. "No. I'm your lady." I stand from the bed and move so I'm standing in front of him.

"Are you?" I can't lose him. I have no one else here.

"Yes." Reaching forward, I grab the top of his jeans and open them, revealing his boxers.

"Go ahead, Scar. Push them down further. My cock is dying for you." Tentatively I press my hand to the front of his boxers and I'm shocked by the heat coming off of it. A deep groan comes from Cyrus as I run my hand along the heated length and curiosity fills me.

I push down his boxers and jeans just enough for his dick to pop out. His reddened tip and large veins look painful. Lightly wrapping my hand around him, I'm surprised at how smooth he is. "You're going to need to squeeze it harder than that."

Cyrus' hand covers mine, making me tighten my grip around his dick and forcing my hand up and down his hard length. Letting him guide my hand, I look up at him to make sure this is what he wants. His eyes look heated as he watches our hands slide along his dick and pride fills me. I'm his Lady. I can give him what he needs.

His eyes connect with mine and he smirks at me. "I need your mouth, Scarlett. Kneel for me."

He presses down on my shoulder, and I slowly let myself fall to my knees so he dick is right in front of my face. "Fuck, you look perfect on your knees for me." I beam up at him, excited that I'm want he wants. "Open those lips for me. I can't wait to feel them around my cock."

Pulling my hand away from him, he holds it to the back of my head as he guides his dick to my lips with his other. His salty tip presses through my lips, and I look up at him waiting for instruction. "Tighten those lips around." Doing as he says, I close my lips around his length, making sure not to bite.

"That's my Lady." He thrusts into my mouth, unexpectedly hitting the back of my throat, making me gag and I push against his thigh with my free hand, trying to get him to pull back. "There's no stopping this." He grabs my hand, holding it with my other, and starts thrusting into my mouth again. Tears burn in my eyes and roll down my cheeks each time he hits the back of my throat and presses his hips into my face. His hold keeps me from pulling away so I just stare up at him, hoping he can see I don't like this.

He doesn't seem to see me as he's watching his dick slide into my mouth. Not being able to look at him anymore, I close my eyes and wait for it to be over. Cyrus' grunt and groans quickly grow frantic as do his thrusts and his dick grows in my mouth before he pulls out. "Fuck, Scarlett." Hot liquid squirts onto my chest and I open my eyes to find Cyrus looking possessively at me. He reaches forward and I look down, watching him run his finger through his release, spelling his name. "Mine."

His covered finger comes to my lips and presses into my mouth. "Taste me." With my eyes connected to his, I suck his finger clean and swallow the salty taste.

"I knew you wouldn't disappoint me." He lets go of my hands and wipes the tears from my cheeks. "Go clean up. I'll take you back to your room."

He steps back from me as I stand and an uneasy feeling sets in my stomach as I head to the bathroom. I thought we were going to stay here tonight. Did I do something wrong? I know I didn't like it, but this was for him. I'll learn to like it. I'll learn to be better.

Chapter Eight

Colton

Present

Murphy Pub is dark inside as we drive in front of it but that's not unexpected. They're always closed on Sundays and Mondays and Killian uses that for our clan meetings. Tanner pulls around back and parks in the empty parking lot. As Killian's Chiefs, it's our job to arrive first and greet the other families. In the Murphy clan, there are seven families. The Murphy family is at the top with Killian as Captain and his sister, Riona, as his Reaper. Then there are the Flynns, O'Briens, Burkes, Walsh, Fitzgeralds, and Quinns.

Tanner and I have represented the Flynn family since we were eighteen when we let our drunk of a father drown in his whiskey. You could say we helped him out with it. It's what he deserved for beating our mom and us every time he was in a drunken rage, which happened almost nightly. Our mother was so blindly in love with him that she killed herself weeks later.

59

Ever since we took over, we've been on the move, traveling all over the world, creating contacts and deals in the weapons world. At least until about three months ago. We like to say it's because Killian took Captain from Lorcan for his betrayals and needed his Chiefs here but really it was a pink haired beauty that finally had us wanting to stay in one place.

We walk into the back of the pub and go through the kitchen to the private room in the back. Since Killian took over, he's been holding these meetings monthly, so I'm not surprised when I turn on the lights in the back room to see the pub staff have it ready for us. Crystal glasses sit at each seat, an empty water pitcher sits in the center of the table, and a small bar cart sits in the corner. Tanner takes the empty pitcher to fill it as I pour us two bourbons.

He returns with a full pitcher as the sound of the backdoor opens. I reach for my gun as I move from the room to figure out who's here. We're at peace within the clan and other crime syndicates now that Lorcan is gone, but it can be broken at any moment. Keith Burke strides through the kitchen and I give him a nod as I release my grip on my gun. "Colton."

"Keith." A man of few words. Keith is the oldest head of the seven families, but he was the least resistant to the change in leadership compared to the other two who still have the oldies in charge. Hopefully, they'll let their heirs take over soon. It'll make the changes Killian wants to make in the future easier. Leaning up against the metal workstation, I take a sip of my bourbon, waiting for everyone else. Henry Walsh and Patrick Fitzgerald arrive a couple of minutes later and just like Keith, they greet me with my name as they move to the back room.

I shake my head at their backs and send a text to Killian, letting him know everyone is here. A couple of minutes later, Aisling and Riona walk through the backdoor, their arms linked, looking the complete opposite of each other. Aisling has her blonde hair up in a ponytail and she's in a hunter green suit, where Riona's red hair is down and she's in black leggings and a crop top with a puffy jacket. Killian is close behind his fiancé and sister, looking like the boss he is in a black suit tailored to him.

"Colton," Aisling greets me, gleefully, as both women head to me. Aisling rises on her toes and kisses me on the cheek. Now that's the kind of greeting I wanted.

"Hello, my beautiful Queen." She rolls her eyes and waves off the nickname. "How's the wedding planning coming?" Killian and Aisling are getting married at the end of the month on New Year's Eve.

"All good. Everything is set. I'd like Stella to be there." She gives me a pointed look and that's something I want too.

"Me too."

Riona steps up to kiss my cheek as well. "Have you heard anything?"

She shakes her head. "Nothing yet but she should be there soon. Jaxson has orders to let Dante know when she arrives."

I shake Killian's hand in greeting and Riona hooks her arm in mine, allowing me to escort her. "What have you found on Cyrus?"

"Nothing. He's not on any of the cameras at the club or surrounding areas. If he was here, it was as a ghost." We head to the bar and I pour Riona a vodka tonic.

"I don't want him to find her. We need to use everything we have to find him first." She takes the drink as she looks up at me worried. Riona has recently been through hell and I know she doesn't want Stella living through another nightmare.

Tanner joins us as we step away from the cart. "We're running facial recognition now to see if we can catch him in the city. There was someone there that night that spooked her; once we figure out which customer that was, hopefully he'll be a connection."

"The flowers?"

"Already tracked down. They were paid for in cash. The store didn't get a name," Tanner answers.

"I'll dig into the dark web to see if I can find any trace of him. No one should know she's left the city. I have already talked to the club security, telling them to keep it quiet. If someone asks, say she's sick or we have her working with Mrs. Claus. I want him to think she's still in the city."

We nod in agreement as Killian calls out, "Alright let's get started. Hopefully, this will be quick."

Killian sits at the head of the rectangular table, with Aisling to his right for the Quinn and O'Brien family, Riona next to her, and we sit across from them. The remaining three take the last of the seats, Fitzgerald next to Riona, and Walsh and Burke next to us. No one takes the other end of the table.

Aisling leans forward in her seat with a loving smile. "Just some quick announcements first. Our wedding is at the end of the month and you're all required to be there. Please make sure I have your RSVP before you leave tonight." She narrows her eyes at Burke and he gives her a single nod.

Aisling smiles down at her best friend. "Our alliance with the Russos, while not shaky, will now be set in stone with marriage. Let's congratulate Riona on her new engagement."

"Woot. Woot. Way to go girl," I holler out with a chuckle as she glares at me. We knew Dante, Matteo, and Enzo were going to propose this weekend.

Tanner shakes his head next to me as he chuckles. "Congratulations, Ri."

She smiles at him and everyone else as they verbalize their congrats. "We wish you a happy marriage, Ri. You might be marrying into the Russos, but you will always be a Murphy." Killian raises his drink in the air and everyone follows.

"Slainte." The cheers ring through the room followed by an echoing thump of us tapping our glasses to the table once and then taking a drink.

"Alright, let's get down to business. Burke, how's everything going in your region?"

Chapter Nine

Scarlett

Past - Age 16

"It's going to be a fun two weeks. I have so much planned for us." Cyrus hooks his arm around the back of my neck as we head to the front porch of the side house. This house looks less exciting every year after my mom flipped out at me when I was thirteen. We haven't really spoken since that night. Cyrus is the only reason I've come back every summer.

Franklin and my mom are walking out of the house when we step onto the front porch and I seek out Michelle. Maybe this summer it'll go back to how it used to be. Her eyes are empty as she scans over me and I hold my breath, waiting for any kind of acknowledgment, but she doesn't give it to me. Instead, she pulls on Franklin's arm. "We're going to be late."

She walks past me like I'm not even there. My eyes follow her as she heads to the car, just hoping she looks back. With each step she takes, my heart cracks open further.

"Hey." Cyrus squeezes his arm around me tighter and pulls me from Michelle. "You're going to barely see her while you're here. My dad said they'll stay in the mansion if you want."

I shake my head. "No, I don't want to upset her even more by kicking her out of her home."

"It's your home too."

"Temporary home." We walk into the house.

"Until next summer. You're going to spend the whole summer with me before you go off to college, right?" He drops my bag by the stairs and we head into the kitchen.

"We talked about this. My grandparents have the whole summer planned." I look back at him as I grab water from the refrigerator.

"Maybe I just need to convince you to tell your grandparents to fuck off." He presses his body against mine, trapping me between him and the counter. "I won't be spending my summer alone."

I wrap my arms around the back of his neck and melt into him. "I want this trip too. I want to see the world."

"I'm your world." His hands slide over my hips and the heated buzz I've become familiar with from his touch settles low and I clench my thighs together. He lowers his lips to mine and I welcome his kiss, pulling him closer.

I let out a surprised squeal as Cyrus grips the back of my thighs and lifts me onto the counter. "You're my Lady, right?"

"Yes, I'm yours."

His hands skim up my thighs and under my dress. I let out a breathy moan as his thumb runs along my core over my panties. "Open for me." I spread my legs wide so he can step in between them and I rock my hips forward against his finger. Last summer Cyrus taught me how to enjoy his touch and ever since, I've craved it, wanting the euphoric feeling.

When we would talk over the phone while I was at school, he'd tell me to imagine my fingers were his and he would tell me all the things he wanted to do with me. But nothing I did ever compared to what his touch does to me. "Please, Cyrus."

He smiles down at me with a dark look in his eyes as he pushes my panties to the side and runs his fingers through my wetness. "Every part of you belongs to me."

He pushes his finger inside of me as his thumb rubs circles over my clit and my back arches, wanting more. I want the feeling only he can give me. The feeling that it's just the two of us in this world. He thrusts his fingers in and out of me as he rubs quick circles over the wonderful bundle of nerves. "Oh yes. Don't stop."

I grip onto his shirt and the edge of the counter as I let my head fall back with a moan. "You glow so beautifully for me, Lady. It's my favorite view of you." Our eyes connect as I feel myself building to the edge of an epic climax. "Give yourself to me. Trusting me."

"Yes." I ride his hand trying to push myself over the edge, but he won't give me what I want. "Cyrus." I groan in frustration as my pleasure keeps building.

A cocky grin forms on his face. "Tell me you love me."

"I love you..." Cyrus hooks his fingers, running them across my upper wall, and I squeeze around them as I fall over the edge. He rubs rough circles on my clit, sparking something powerful inside me and I scream out his name, letting the feeling wash over me. His fingers continue to move inside me slowly as my body relaxes, and I open my eyes, finding him smiling down at me.

With his other hand, he runs his fingers through my hair. "I'm so lucky you're mine." He leans forward and kisses me. "I want all of you, Scarlett." Another kiss to my lips before pulling back and I lean forward wanting more. "Let me have all of you."

The heat in my lower belly starts to flutter again as he moves his fingers faster inside me and he pushes his thumb on my sensitive clit. "Let me have all your firsts." He kisses along my neck and my breath shortens at the blissful feeling that's slowly building again.

"You have all of me." The energy between us is so intense right now I want to give him anything.

"Then show me. Give me what I want." I'm panting as I rock my hips, knowing I'm close again.

I moan and Cyrus groans as he steps forward and rubs himself against me. I can feel his hard length through his pants and my mind freezes. I want everything with him, but I'm not ready for that. I don't want to be like my mom, so willing to give myself to anyone. I love Cyrus but this house is not where I want to end up.

"I'm not ready." I place my hand flat on his chest, letting him know to stop. His grip on my hair tightens and it's almost painful for just a second until he releases me so fast, I fall back slightly. He turns his back to me and I quickly close my legs and slide off the counter. I don't take a step toward him as I watch his body coil tight and his hands fist. "Cyrus?"

He quickly turns back to me with a soft smile on his face, but it doesn't meet his eyes. "It's okay, Scar. We'll go at your pace." He reaches out his hand for me to take. "Come, let's bring your stuff up to your room and I can tell you all the plans I have for us while you're here."

I take his hand and smile up at him, hoping to get his eyes to brighten. "But your birthday is a surprise."

I chuckle as we walk upstairs. "A surprise? Must be something special." We walk into my room and he sets my bag down.

"You only turn seventeen once." He pulls me to him and kisses my forehead. "I'll give you a day you won't forget."

Chapter Ten

Scarlett

17th Birthday

"Happy Birthday, Scarlett." Cyrus' soft whisper pulls me from my sleep and I melt into his chest as he holds me from behind.

I hum as I wiggle my ass back against his hard length. "Good morning." Since I arrived a couple of days ago, Cyrus has slept with me every night holding me just like this. Every morning I wake up with his length pressed up against my ass and knowing what's about to come has me already wet even as I wake up.

Cyrus grips my hips as he pulls my ass back against his hips and he positions his erection in between my thighs. "You know what to do babe, ride me. Let me feel your gorgeous thighs tighten around my cock." I moan at his dirty words as I rock against him, feeling him slide against my panty covered sex. "You're so good for me, Lady. Always giving me what I want."

His hips start to thrust against my ass as he chases his need and I whimper wanting my own pleasure. "You want me to make you come?"

"Yes, please." I grind down on him as my clit pulses, wanting to be touched. "Touch me."

His hand slides from my hip, across my stomach, and into my panties. My hips buck forward at just the slightest touch to my clit and he chuckles behind me. "So eager for me. Take off your panties. Let me have better access to your wanting heat."

"Cyrus," I say his name with warning.

"I know, Scar. I won't cross the line. I just want to feel your warmth on my cock." He starts pushing down my panties and I lift my hips, allowing him to get them over my hips. When they reach mid-thigh, he leaves them, running his fingers back up my leg.

One hand goes back to my center where he cups me, rubbing the palm of his hand on my clit as he slides two fingers inside me. His other hand slides over my ass and his finger runs along my crack. "I'm going to use this amazing ass to get myself off. Would you like that?"

As he asks, he presses down on my clit and brushes his fingers over my top wall. "Yes." I moan from the amazing feeling.

"Come for me, Scar. Get my fingers wet with your come so I can get my dick wet."

My body hums with pleasure as the pressure builds and Cyrus continues to play my body perfectly. I grip the sheets in front of me as my moans grow louder and I grind down on his fingers.

"Why are you holding out on me?" He pinches my clit as he presses up on my inner wall and I scream out my release.

"That's it, Scar. Come all over my hand. Make it glisten." He strokes my hair as I come down. "Such a good girl." I moan as he pulls his fingers out of me. "You're going to make my dick all wet."

Looking back at him, I watch him wrap his hand around his erection and he slowly starts to pump himself. "Your juices feel so good on my cock. I can't wait until I'm buried deep inside you, feeling all your warmth." He leans over and places a kiss on my lips. "Roll on your stomach for me. Let me use your round ass to hug my dick."

He pushes slightly so I roll forward until I'm on my stomach. "That's it. Now get on your knees, lifting your ass in the air." I follow his instructions as his hands roam over my skin pushing my shirt up my body, exposing my back.

"So beautiful." He moves behind me, pressing his body to mine and I feel his erection slide in between my ass cheeks. It's such a strange feeling having him rub there. I whimper, trying to find pleasure in it. "Shh. Touch yourself. I want you to come again. Come with me. They say if a man and a woman come together, their souls are linked forever. You want that, don't you, Lady? Forever."

I melt into Cyrus' hold from his words as he grips my hips and thrusts against my ass. I reach underneath me, circling my clit, trying to find that buzz as his thrusts start to pick up. Quickly the weird feeling turns to beautiful pleasure and my body vibrates as I build close to the edge.

Cyrus' fingers join mine and I let out a moan. "I'm close, Scar. I need you to come." Once again, he pinches my clit and I detonate in a wave of euphoria. Cyrus' groans mix with my moans as I feel his seed spill onto my back and down my ass.

We both crash to the bed, breathless, with him next to me. Looking over his face, I give him a lazy smile. "Mornings are starting to be my favorite." I reach out and run my fingers along the edge of his jaw.

He grabs my hand and places a kiss on it before leaning over and kissing my lips. His kisses don't stop there as he rises, kissing my shoulder and then my ass. "You're perfect for me."

I sit up so my ass is resting on my heels. "Maybe you're perfect for me." I lean towards him and he meets me so our lips are barely touching.

"If only that were true." He presses forward but only for a quick kiss. "Now go shower so we can start your surprise day. You'll need to pack for overnight and wear something comfortable you can move in. We're going on an adventure."

"Where are you taking me?" He climbs out of bed and I watch him walk across my room naked.

"You'll have to hurry up to find out." I climb out of bed and hurry to the bathroom, excited to see what he has planned.

When I step out of the bathroom after showering, I find a small camping backpack waiting for me. I love camping in the desert. You can see every star shining brightly in the sky. Excited, I quickly get dressed and pack what I need. I leave my room with my blonde hair pulled into a ponytail, my face void of makeup, with a pink tank top, tan shorts, and tennis shoes on, and the backpack over my shoulders. I bounce down the steps, swing around the banister at the bottom, and head toward the kitchen.

As I approve my steps slow as I hear Cyrus and Franklin. "You need to get it done."

"I am," Cyrus responds to his dad.

"You're taking too long." What are they talking about? "Don't make me send someone else to get it done. You want it, take it. Don't take no for an answer."

Cyrus' voice strains in anger. "Don't threaten me with what's mine. It'll be done today. I even send you..."

I move into the kitchen to hopefully defuse the argument because I don't want Cyrus to be in a bad mood today. "Hey! Are you ready?" I smile at Cyrus as both he and Franklin look at me.

He returns my smile and I relax when his smile reaches his eyes. "Yeah. Let's get out of here." He walks toward me and hooks his arm around my shoulders. As we walk out, he looks back at Franklin. "We won't be back until tomorrow. I have a special day planned for Scarlett."

I look up at him, but my eyebrows crunch together at the darkness in his eyes as he looks at his dad. I rub my hand up his back, and his face brightens when his eyes connect with mine. We head out of the house and Cyrus takes my bag when we get to his car and opens my door. "My Lady." I giggle at his joke and I climb in.

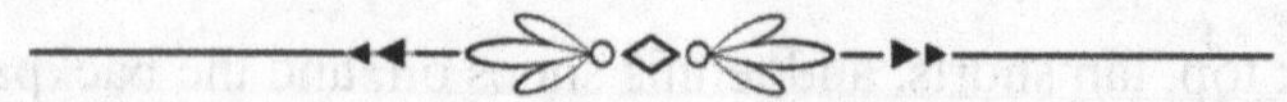

I snuggle into Cyrus' chest as we swing in the hammock outside our tent where we're staying tonight and stare up at the beautiful night sky. Today has been amazing. We hiked all day and then Cyrus surprised me with this beautiful and romantic campsite with a fully equipped dome tent. He even grilled us some steaks and potatoes for dinner. He's made me feel so special today. "Thank you for today." I look up at him. "It's been the best birthday."

He runs his fingers through my hair as he leans forward and places a kiss on my lips. "You deserve a special day. A day all about you. My special Lady." He kisses me again but this time deeper, pulling me to him. I shift slowly so I don't flip us until I'm laying on top of him and he grips my ass, holding me against him.

As our kiss gets more desperate, I grind my core down on his growing erection. "You're killing me, Lady." He swats my ass playfully. "You better get this gorgeous ass inside that tent." I giggle as I throw the blanket off us, climb out of the hammock, and jog to the tent with Cyrus close behind me. I turn to Cyrus as I stand in the middle of the tent and his eyes burn with desire as he closes the cloth door behind him. "Take off your clothes, Scarlett."

My body buzzes, wanting to follow his command, but my hands shake as I move them to the band of my lounge shorts. I haven't been completely naked in front of him yet. Any piece of clothing was a good barrier to stop us before things got too far.

"I want to worship you tonight. Kiss every inch of your skin." He tracks my shorts to the ground as he sets his phone on the stand on top of the dresser and my insides flutter as his eyes track up my bare thighs to my apex where he finds me bare there as well. "Please, Scar." The need in his voice has me reaching for my hoodie and pulling it over my head, leaving me with nothing on. I fight myself to keep my arms at my side and not fold them across my chest as Cyrus takes in my body. "You're beautiful," he whispers as he moves toward me, removing his clothes as well. "And all mine."

When he reaches me, his hands go on either side of my face and I look up at him, wanting him to break this intenseness between us. He leans forward and kisses my lips then my nose, forehead, and cheeks. "Lay down on the bed, Lady. Let me kiss the rest of you." I walk backwards, keeping my eyes on his and he matches my steps until my calves touch the edge of the bed. Sitting back, I climb onto the middle of the bed and lay out flat. Cyrus breaks our connection to scan over me as he grips his hard erection and pumps himself. My core heats up at the image, and I rub my thighs together to try to release some of the pressure.

He catches my movement and a smirk pulls on his lips. "You like what you see?" I nod, gripping the sheets so I don't reach for him. "Me too, babe. I could watch you like this all day." He leans forward, resting his hands on either side of my legs and kisses the top of my right foot. I squirm underneath him as his kisses grow closer to where I need him. He kisses my hip and I suck in a breath as he moves over my wet core, but instead of kissing my mound, he moves to my left ankle, and I whimper.

Cyrus kisses up my left leg, making me even more desperate. I try to scoot down the bed so he will move faster but he grips my hips, holding me still. When he reaches my apex again, I raise my hips, trying to show him where I want him but once again, he ignores my whimpers and kisses my belly. "I'm going to kiss every inch of your body before I give you what you want. I want you so turned on, so desperate that one touch to your clit will have you screaming your release."

I moan, closing my eyes, and sinking into the bed, wanting what he said. He takes my left wrist and kisses the inside of it, working his way up my arm. His body hovers over mine as he kisses my shoulder and collarbone, and when his face is above mine, he smiles down at me. "Do you feel you worshiped, Scarlett?"

"Yes." My voice is breathless and soft. His smile grows at my answer as he lowers his mouth to the right of my face and kisses my collarbone, shoulder, and down my arm. I suck in a breath as his lips move to my stomach and up to my breasts. His hands slide up my inner thighs as he presses a kiss on the top of each breast and I bring my knees up, spreading them wider for him.

"You look so beautiful spread up for me. Your pussy is so wet, needing me."

"Yes, I need you. Please touch me. I need to come."

"I love you begging. I'm going to need to hear more of it." He lowers again to my breasts as he sucks a nipple in his mouth and flicks the hardened tip with his tongue, causing me to arch up into his mouth.

A whimper leaves my lips as his fingers graze over my lower lips but not giving me what I want. "Please, Cyrus." I squirm underneath him, trying to get some kind of release from the buildup I have sitting in my low stomach. "I need you." He switches breasts, flicking his tongue against my nipple while circling his finger around my clit but not touching it. "I can't take it. Please make me come."

He lays his tongue flat against my nipple and slowly licks up my chest and neck. "Please, Cyrus. Touch me."

"How bad do you want it?" he whispers next to my ear.

"So bad, please," I pant.

"Would you give me anything?" His finger moves down my slit, and he circles my hole that's dripping with need.

I nod uncontrollably as I rock my hips, trying to get him to move. "Say it, Scar. Let me hear you say it."

"Yes. I'll give you anything." Goosebumps break across my skin as the words leave my lips but they're true if it gets him to give me what I want.

A winning grin pulls across his face. "Are you ready to scream for me?" He doesn't wait for my answer as he plunges his fingers inside of me as his thumb presses into my clit with rough circles, and I feel like I leave my body as I scream out from the rush of pleasure that courses through me.

His fingers continue to give me pleasure as I ride out my release and quickly, I feel myself building again. "Oh god. Cyrus. It's too much."

"You're glowing, Scarlett. So beautiful. You're going to come again for me. Soak my fingers." His other hand goes to my breast where he kneads it until his fingers roll around my nipple and I moan out. He adds another finger inside me and grazes my upper wall and I grind myself down on his hand, fighting through the stretch.

"You're doing so good, Lady, stretching around my fingers, getting ready for my cock. Such a good girl." My body buzzes from his dirty words and I moan as I grow close to falling again. Cyrus masterfully works my body quickly into another orgasm and I bite down my low lip to stop the scream that spills up my throat.

"That's my Lady." I feel him shift closer to me as I lay dazed from the two amazing orgasms. "You're all ready for me now."

Before I can even take in his words, I feel his erection at my entrance and he quickly thrusts into me, pulling a scream of pain from me. I grab onto his shoulders with my nails, digging into his skin as I look up at him with tears in my eyes. I didn't agree to this. I wasn't ready.

"Cyrus," I whimper.

"Shh, Scarlett. You're okay. I promise I'll make it feel better." He pulls out and pushes back in and I tense from the pain. "You need to relax, Scar."

"I don't want this." Why is he doing this?

He continues to move and I scratch across his shoulders. "You promised me whatever I wanted. You knew I wanted you." He leans forward to kiss me, but I turn my head. "I'm done waiting for what's mine. You want me to be happy, don't you?" He kisses my temple as tears roll down my cheeks.

He's my everything and all I want is to make him happy, but how could he do this? He knew I didn't want to have sex yet and he took it anyways. "I want to be special to you, Cyrus. Not another girl from the mansion."

"You are special. You're my lady. No one else can say that." He continues to thrust into me slowly and with each thrust, the pain starts to ease.

"Promise me we'll leave this city and start somewhere new." His thumb moves to my clit, sparking a little bit of pleasure, and I rock into that feeling.

"Anything you want." He leans forward and this time I don't turn away from his kiss but welcome it as I wrap my arms around his neck and pull comfort from him. His thrusts pick up as the pain disappears and I find myself rocking into him with each thrust, drawing the little pleasure I can.

"You feel so great wrapped around me, Scar. So warm and slick. Better than anyone else. An absolute dream." He groans out the last words and his thrusts go erratic until he stills on top of me, coming inside of me.

His fingers brush my hair from my face as he places a kiss on my lips. "I want everything from you. Your mind, body, soul, and heart."

"You have it all, Cyrus. I love you so much." His smile has me smiling back, but I wince as he pulls out of me. We both look in between us, and I blush with embarrassment at the blood on his dick. He growls at the sight, and I'm worried that he's mad until his eyes connect with mine again and I see possession in them. He slams his lips to mine and I melt into him.

He kisses my forehead before climbing off the bed, and I turn on my side, curling into a ball, hoping to relieve some of the pain. Cyrus comes out of the bathroom a couple of minutes later with his phone in hand and curls around me, kissing my shoulder. His hand slides around my waist and rests on my stomach. "We could've made a baby tonight, making you mine forever."

I chuckle. "Not tonight or in the near future. I'm on birth control."

"That's okay. I want you all mine for as long as possible."

"I love you, Cyrus."

My eyes fall shut as sleep pulls me into the darkness. But as I slip into a dream, I hear Cyrus whisper, "Now he can never take you away from me."

Chapter Eleven

Sadie

Present

It's well into the night when my train pulls into New Orleans. The dinner crowd has long gone home and the party crowd has come out. But even with the loud music and drunk tourists, the holiday decorations draw my attention. Green and red lights shine up the brick walls and every pole and balcony has garland or lights wrapped around them. I can't believe I forgot Christmas is only a few weeks away. I haven't celebrated it in years. The last time was with my grandparents, and I guess I won't be celebrating it this year either.

Looking for Club Risqué, I weave through the crowd, pulling my bag behind me. I'm glad I decided to change into my new black ripped skinny jeans and lacy bodysuit. I need to be blending in right now and I'd stick out like a sore thumb in the Charlotte sweats I was wearing.

Taking the next street, I see the sign for Club Risqué and a line of people waiting outside it. Not wanting to wait, I walk right up to the bouncer. "The line is back there," he says without looking at me.

That's rude. "I'm here to see Jaxson Wright."

His eyes shift to me with a smirk as he looks me over. "We're not hiring any dancers right now."

"Good thing I'm not looking for a job." I try the only other thing I could think of. "The Russos sent me."

The bouncer stands taller as I say the name of the family that runs the Italian mafia here and I hold his stare as he speaks into his headset. "Jaxson, there's a..." He pauses, looking at me for my name.

"St...adie. Sadie." Hopefully that's the name Ri gave him.

"Sadie here asking for you." He's quiet for a few seconds, listening to what Jaxson is saying.

"Yes, sir." He unclips the red rope blocking me from entering and waves me in. "Jaxson will be waiting for you at the end of the hall."

"Thank you." I give him a grin and walk past him and into the club. The entrance is a long black hallway barely lit and the music vibrates off the walls. A broad towering shadow fills the end of the hall and I slow my steps. I can't see who it is. Could it be Cyrus? Has he somehow found me?

"Sadie." A voice I don't recognize calls out my name and I pick up my pace to reach him.

"Jaxson?" I stop in front of the man who stands a head taller than me in a nice tailored black suit with his brown hair half tied back and his golden brown eyes looking back at me.

His face is expressionless behind his beard as his eyes burn into mine like he's trying to read my thoughts before they skim over my body. I feel myself gravitating towards him as he assesses me, but before I act on that pull, he breaks whatever connection that was there and turns away. "Follow me."

I find myself walking a step behind him before I even realize it. What was that? How does he have such a hold on me? I'm so focused on him that I don't even check out the club I just walked through. He opens a door and steps to the side, revealing an office. I look behind me as I step inside and see a few women dancing on individual stages, around poles, with barely any clothes on. Risqué for sure. A smile pulls on my face as I understand why Ri sent me here. It's like almost being back home just in a sexier city and club.

The door closes behind Jaxson and it acts as a sound barrier, leaving us in silence. My eyes track him across the room as he heads to his desk. He nods to the seat across from him as he lowers himself in his. Taking that as an invitation to sit, I leave my suitcase by the door and take the empty chair. Jaxson leans back in his chair with his arms crossed and his eyes locked on mine. "Dante and Riona gave me a brief overview of your situation, and I just have to know, are you going to bring trouble to my front door?"

His eyes are stern as he watches me, and now that we're in a lighted room, I can see the creases in the corner of his eyes and the slight age in his skin. He's got to be at least in his mid-thirties. "I promise I don't want to bring you any trouble and I don't want my ex to find me. If he does, I'll leave. I don't want anyone hurt because of me."

"Okay. Dante said your name was Stella, but you'll be going by a different name. Do you want me to call you Stella or Sadie?"

My body feels like it's waiting for his next command as he looks at me. "Sadie is probably for the best." Why is my voice all breathy? "If I'm going to be working here, everyone will need to call me that."

"Work here?" I don't know what the plan is with Ri sending me here, but it has to be working. This place is a dream. She knows my love of pole dancing.

"Yeah. I managed Ri's burlesque club in New York, even danced in its early days." I can feel myself getting more and more excited at what I can do here. "I can be a bartender, waiter, dancer…"

"Not a dancer," Jaxson blurts out.

"Okay." I try not to sound disappointed at his abrupt dismissal. "I can do choreography, the books, really anything."

"The girls do their own dances." He must see my deflation because he tries to lighten the mood by suggesting, "How about you start behind the bar and we can go from there?"

Works for me, I'll get to watch the dances that way. "Sounds great. Let me find a hotel and I'll be back."

He sits up abruptly, stopping me from standing. "You're here for protection. You can't be in a hotel with me here. My apartment is upstairs. You'll be staying with me."

What? That seems excessive. "Oh no, you don't need to house me. I can find a place close by."

He shakes his head no, not even considering it. "How about this? Give it a week upstairs and then you can decide if you want to live somewhere else."

Not wanting to disrupt the plan that Ri and Dante have for my protection, I smirk at Jaxson with a nod. "I can work with that. Should I get to work?" I point behind me to the door.

He looks down at his watch. "We're only open until midnight so it'll only be a couple of hours. If you'd rather rest a little, I can leave you alone in here."

I stand from my chair. "I slept on the train. I'd prefer to work, dip my toes in the water and all."

He chuckles and I freeze in shock at the sound. I like it, maybe even more than his stern stare. "Alright, I'll introduce you." He reaches for the door and his woodsy scent surrounds me. Slowly I raise my eyes to his face as he remains unmoving, and I find him looking back at me. I suck in a shaky breath with how close we are, but I don't step back. His lips part as he sucks in the air between us and my eyes drop to them, wondering what they'd feel like against mine. Would he kiss me softly or take what he wants and demand everything from me? God, I want to find out.

Surprised at myself for thinking that, I pull away from Jaxson, breaking the moment. I shouldn't be thinking about kissing a stranger when I have Tanner and Colton. They're fighting to eliminate the one person that haunts me so I can come back to them. Dropping my eyes to the floor in embarrassment, I ask, "Are there any rules I need to know about for the club or Russo business?"

He steps back from me too and closes his eyes for a second. "Club rules are probably the same as your old place. Be respectful of the employees. No free drinks or dances. No one touches the dancers or staff. If someone is high ranking within the Russos, they will be in the VIP area and they do get free drinks. If you serve there, you hear nothing."

That's all standard and expected. "Okay, works for me."

"If anyone gives you trouble, let me or one of the security guys know. I'll introduce you to everyone after we close." I give him a nod and he opens the door for me to go out first. His hand rests on my mid back as he leads me through the club to the back wall where the bar is and a spark runs down my back. I find myself slowing my gate so his hand presses into me more because it's like I can feel his touch everywhere. What is going on with me? It's like I'm in heat or something. I never react to men like this, well other men. Tanner and Colton are the only ones that make me feel alive with just a touch or even a smirk.

We reach the opening to the bar and I quickly duck under the fold up door since drinks are waiting to be picked up on it. Plus I need to put some distance between Jaxson and me. I smile back at him when I stand on the other side and I think I see a smirk for just a second before it falls. Someone behind me has me looking back, and I find a young guy standing close to me. Whoa. I step away from him, pressing my back to the folding door.

"Hey." This guy steps closer to me, eliminating the little space between us, and I flinch away as he reaches out.

Heat fills my cheeks in embarrassment when I realize he's just setting a drink on the tray to be collected. "Hi."

He chuckles at my embarrassment. "Sorry for crowding you. I'm Jake." His free hand is held out in front of him and I slide mine into his. I wait for the tingling feeling I get from Jaxson, thinking my body is desperate for some pleasure since it's been years and I was ready to go there with Colton and Tanner, but nothing happens.

Jaxson introduces us since I was standing there too long waiting. "This is Sadie. She'll be working the bar with you. Can you show her around tonight?"

"Absolutely." Jake uses our joint hands to pull me into his side. "It would be my pleasure." I look back at Jaxson as Jake pulls me away and I'm shocked at the hardness in his eyes. What's that about?

Chapter Twelve

Jaxson

What the fuck? When Dante called saying a friend of his needed protection, I was expecting a girl to show up distressed with fear in her eyes. I didn't expect the gorgeous woman with long legs, rainbow hair, and a smile that took my breath away. A smile that had me screwing up all the plans. I was supposed to take her to a safe house but that's not what came out of my mouth. Now I have to figure out how she's going to sleep in my apartment. Both bedrooms are taken, but maybe she can take Phoenix's room tomorrow. She can have my room tonight.

She laughs at something Jake says and I glare in frustration. They're supposed to be working, not laughing. I'm supposed to be working, not sitting here, staring, but I can't seem to move from the spot at the bar I took as soon as she stepped away. I keep telling myself it's to make sure no one bothers her. Not that she's noticed I'm sitting here.

A loud group of men enter the club, drawing my attention. Those are the kind of men that could try their chance at getting with a beautiful woman. A chance that none of them have. Some men can accept that while others don't. It's the latter I want to keep away from her. She's definitely going to attract attention, especially from the regulars.

The guys take some seats around the right stage and I turn back to the bar to find her standing in front of me with a glass of brown liquor sitting in between us. "Thought you could use this if you're going to hang around."

I reach for the drink and intentionally brush my fingers over hers. "I just want to make sure no one gives you any trouble."

Her smile is wide as she holds her arm up and pokes her small bicep. "I'll be alright. I'm tougher than I look." I chuckle before I stop myself.

"Well. Well. Well. Looks like we have some fresh meat."

I close my eyes and wipe the smile from my face before turning to Manuel, one of the Russo underbosses and a pain in my ass. He and I used to be childhood best friends until money became more important than friendship. "Don't talk about my staff like that."

"Oh, come on. You know I mean no harm." He looks at Sadie with a cocky grin as he holds out his hand, making sure to shake his wrist slightly to emphasize his Rolex. "I'm Manuel. You can come join me in the VIP area anytime."

She looks at his hand but doesn't reach for it. "Sadie. Since I'll be working, I don't think that will happen." She gives him a weak smile before looking at me. "I should get back to helping Jake."

She moves away from us and I'm relieved she didn't fall for Manuel's flashy style. I've lost several waitresses and dancers to his cheeky grin and expensive gifts. Those women never see what he's hiding and I'm not talking about his involvement with the Russos because I used to be in his shoes. I'm talking about whatever shady stuff he's involved with on the side.

His eyes track her as she helps Jake with an order and I don't like his attention on her. An evil grin pulls across his face as he catches me glaring at him. "Ice cold Jax has an eye for the new girl. How interesting."

I look away from him to her with a fake uninterested look. "I don't know what you're talking about, *Mannie*. I was just getting a drink."

I stand from my seat and turn my back to him, heading to the office. I'm going to need to keep an eye on him and keep my distance from her. He's too interested and that's not good.

Chapter Thirteen

Scarlett

Past - Age 18

"Congratulations Class of 2016. We wish you all the luck at your respective universities and careers." My friends, classmates, and I all throw our caps into the air as we cheer. High school is over. Summer's here. Then it's NYU for me. Or should I say me and Cyrus. We'll finally get to start the future I wanted and he promised, away from our parents and that mansion.

Grabbing my cap off the ground, I look around for him. He told me he would come to cheer for me. I haven't seen him since last summer and this summer my grandparents have the whole summer planned. They're sending me off with some friends to travel around Europe. I've been waiting for this trip to finally get out of the places I've grown up and to see how other people live. Today will be the only time I'll see Cyrus this summer until I meet him in New York.

Family and friends of my classmates start to swarm onto the stage to hug and kiss their graduates, but I don't see him.

My grandparents fill my eyeline with smiling faces as they gather me in their arms, sandwiching me in a hug. "We're so proud of you, Scarlett." My grandma kisses the side of my head.

"You worked so hard to get what you wanted for your future. It's been such a privilege to watch you grow into this amazing student and woman." My grandfather squeezes me tighter, and I beam at both of them.

I know they didn't plan on being the ones that raised me, but every day they loved me like a daughter and granddaughter and I've always wanted to make them proud. To show them that they didn't need to worry about me like they worry about my mom.

"I love you guys so much." I kiss both their cheeks. "Thank you for giving me everything." I give them one final squeeze before we separate.

As I pull away from them, I'm hoping to see Cyrus standing behind them but instead, I see one of my best friends, Hannah, as she pushes through them and surrounds me in a hug. She sways us back and forth in excitement. "We did it! Woohoo! I can't believe it! Europe, here we come."

Before I can say anything, she's letting me go and running towards another one of our friends. I chuckle as I watch her, happy to spend the summer with her and Katie, traveling. Our last hoorah before we separate across the US to different universities.

My grandmother hooks her arm with mine and starts moving us off the stage and I look around one last time for him. Disappointment washes over me when I don't see him waiting for me. I can't believe he didn't come. He promised. I plaster a fake smile on my face as the two people who have always loved me talk excitedly about our dinner reservation at my favorite restaurant.

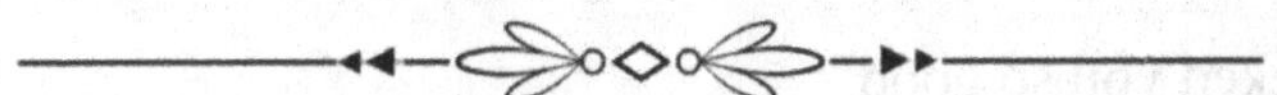

We arrived in Athens, Greece a few days ago and I've been trying to ignore the fact that I haven't heard from Cyrus once. Not even one I'm sorry. And I know he's alive because I checked in with Michelle. Now he's ruining my trip because I can't get how upset I am out of my head. I guess that was his plan. Piss me off enough to not enjoy the trip I have been planning a year for because he didn't want me gone all summer.

I shake him from my head as Katie comes out of the dressing room in a beautiful white sundress with pink flowers on it. She's beaming at us as she twirls. "I love it. Do you love it?"

"Hell yeah, I do. That dress was made for you." Katie's smile brightens at Hannah's words.

"That dress looks amazing on you," I add. She'd be ridiculous not to get it.

She jumps up and down, clapping. "Great. I'm getting it. Okay Hannah, your turn." She pulls Hannah up off the couch and takes her seat.

Hannah disappears behind the curtain and Katie bumps my shoulder with hers. "Stop thinking about him. He doesn't deserve the headspace you're giving him."

"Yeah," Hannah yells from the dressing room. "This summer is about you and us. You can think about him as you hook up with another guy tonight." She steps out from behind the curtain wearing a green patterned crop top and a long boho skirt. "Screaming Cyrus never fucked you so good."

I chuckle at her bluntness as she checks herself out in the mirror. "I'm not going to do that."

"Well, you don't have to scream it." Katie gives me a wide smile.

"I'm not hooking up with anyone tonight." I roll my eyes with a smile on my face.

"You can say that now but wait until you have the European men all over you with the outfit we chose." Hannah wiggles her eyebrows at me.

"What outfit?" We each chose our own things to try on.

"Something sexier than what you chose." Hannah tilts her head towards the dressing room telling me to get in there. Intrigued by what they have picked, I stand from the couch and step behind the curtain. The only items left hanging in the dressing room are a white jean miniskirt and a blue top that has a lot of straps.

Okay, this is definitely not what I normally wear. Wanting to pacify them, I undress, slide the skirt up my legs, and wrangle myself into the shirt, tying all the straps around my waist.

"This shirt is way too hard to get into." I step out of the dressing room and look up at my friends to find shock on their faces. "What?" I look down at myself as I turn towards the full-length mirror. "Did I put the shirt on wrong?"

Looking up at myself in the mirror, I'm shocked at how much skin I'm showing. "You look hot, Scar," Hannah says.

"You need to show off this body more," Katie adds.

I wrap my arms around my waist, trying to cover up. I don't show off skin like this. My mom dresses like this. I don't want the attention she gets. I start backing up to the dressing room, but Hannah calling out to me stops me. "Scar, what's wrong?"

She has gotten up from the couch and is walking to me with concern in her eyes. They don't know about Franklin's business or my mom's involvement. "I'm just not comfortable in this. I feel naked." I flatten my palms over my stomach, trying to cover more.

Katie shoots up from the couch and quickly grabs another shirt. "How about this instead?" She holds up a spaghetti strap lavender top that is flowy and the straps cross over the back.

Relief washes over me as I nod and take it from her. I quickly remove the revealing top and pull the lavender one on. Feeling myself again, I step out of the dressing room and look in the mirror. A smile pulls on my face as I look at myself. This is perfect.

"You look great. So beautiful." Katie comes up behind me and rests her chin on my shoulder.

"You'll have everyone double taking tonight." Hannah puts her chin on my other shoulder and I beam at both of them in the mirror.

"We're all going to have eyes on us tonight."

"Yes!" Hannah cheers.

"We're going to have so much fun!" Katie adds.

A few people also shopping look over at us and I quickly push them into the dressing room. "Let's get out of here." We all change and head back to the hotel with our new outfits to get ready.

"I can't believe this is our last night in Athens. I feel like we just got here." Katie hugs my left arm as we ride down the elevator after spending hours drinking and getting ready.

"Yeah, but we're going to Rome next." Hannah applies her lipstick in the reflection of the elevator door.

"Yes, we all know you're ready to drool over all the Italian boys." I bump her hip as she closes her lipstick.

"No, you got it wrong. They'll be drooling over me." She winks as the doors open and walks out. We follow behind her, quietly chuckling at her confidence.

As we walk through the lobby to head to dinner, someone calling my name has us all stopping. I recognize his voice immediately which has me frozen, facing away from him while my friends turn to the man they have only seen photos of.

"Oh shit, is that?" Hannah looks between me and where Cyrus must be standing.

"Scarlett." I finally turn to see him standing there in jeans and a gray shirt with a smirk on his face and a suitcase sitting next to him. We don't say anything as we just stare at each other. Seeing him has all the confusion and disappointment turning into anger. How can he just show up here when he hasn't tried to reach me in days?

"Aww. He flew across the world to apologize." Hannah swoons.

"Do you want us to give you some space?" Katie whispers. I nod, not wanting to have this conversation with them hovering nearby. She squeezes my arm before unlinking it with hers. "We'll wait for you at the hotel bar."

Hannah and Katie leave us and I cross my arms over my chest. "You're not going to say hi." Cyrus steps towards me and I fight myself not to step away.

"I'm not the one who needs to talk."

"I know you're mad that I didn't come to your graduation, but I didn't want it to turn into a big thing with your grandparents. You know they hate me." He tilts his head to the side with a pout.

That isn't going to soften me. "You promised."

"I know and I shouldn't have." He steps in front of me and wraps his arms around my waist. "But I've planned a trip for us to make up to you." Bringing his hand up, he pushes my hair behind my ear. "A week of just you and me in Santorini." His lips press to my forehead. "A week of love before we start the rest of our lives together."

I melt into him, unlinking my arms and wrapping them around his neck. "That sounds perfect, but we leave for Rome tomorrow."

"Skip Rome and come with me." His hands slide down my back and grip my ass. "Don't you want to spend time with me?"

I lean back not letting him sink me in and forget I'm upset. "I wanted to spend my graduation day with you."

"And now you can get a week in a beautiful city."

I open my mouth to argue because Rome is a city I've always wanted to see, but he leans forward and kisses me. "Let me show you how sorry I am that I didn't go to your graduation."

He kisses me again before I can say anything. "You're still my Lady, right?" I nod looking up at him and his eyes darken with desire. "Good because I'm never letting you go."

Chapter Fourteen

Scarlett

Age 18

Coming to Santorini has helped me forgive Cyrus. How could I stay mad at him when he's shown me around the city and planned dates at the most romantic spots on the island? Every day, I fall more in love with him.

My favorite part though is sitting out on our balcony at sunrise, watching the city wake up with the sun. Santorini is beautiful. I bring my coffee to my lips as I watch a boat come in, probably filled with fish. Arms wrap around my waist and I lean back into Cyrus with a sigh as he kisses my neck. "Good morning, Lady."

"Good morning, my Lord." I turn my head, looking back at him, and he presses his lips to mine.

"Come back to bed. It's too early to be awake." He nuzzles into my neck.

"Look how beautiful this is. You miss it every morning."

"You are the beautiful thing I want to look at. Naked and laid out on the bed looking up at me like I'm the only man for you." His hands slide underneath my shirt and I melt into him while pulling his hands from my shirt.

"Be in this moment with me, Cyrus. Watch this beautiful city with me."

He sighs and steps away from me. "Anything for you." A sharpness in his voice has me looking back at him. "I'll order us breakfast but later you're all mine. I've got something special planned." His eyes scan over me right before he turns to go back inside and my core heats with anticipation of what his dirty plans could be.

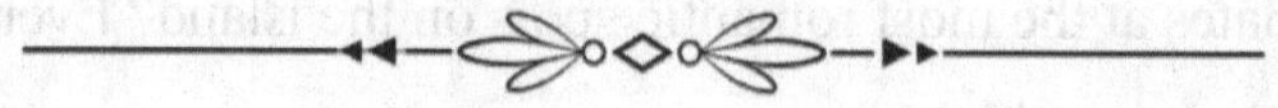

"Are you ready for your surprise?" I turn towards Cyrus from the little jewelry stand I'm looking at to find him smiling while holding a bundle of white, purple, and blue flowers.

Beaming at him, I step into his body and he wraps his arm around my waist while holding the flowers for me with his other. "For you, my Lady."

"Thank you, my Lord." I lean up as I take the flowers and kiss him. "They're beautiful." I bring the bouquet to my nose and smell the vibrant flowers.

"And they're just a part of the surprise. Come on." His arm hooks around my neck and leads me away from the street shops.

"Can I get a hint to the surprise?" I smile up at him, and he smirks.

"It's just something to show everyone you're mine."

What could that mean? Did he buy me jewelry? Is he getting a tattoo? Oh, that could be cool. Maybe he'll let me design it. My name with flowers like the ones I'm holding woven in. I might get one for him too. Butterflies flutter in my stomach with excitement for something permanent linking us forever and nervousness about how much it'll hurt. Needles aren't my favorite.

We don't go far before Cyrus stops us on the edge of a cliff that looks over the city, and it's beautiful seeing the winding stone paths that run through the white buildings with blue roofs leading to the coast. This view is what makes this city so breathtaking, but I'm confused about why this is my surprise. I look out over this city every morning from our balcony.

Looking around, I try to find a tattoo shop but all that's here is a small white stone church that looks like it has a lot of history. Cyrus runs hands across my shoulders as he removes his arm, drawing my attention from our surroundings and my breath catches as I see Cyrus' smile as he drops to his knee in front of me and takes my hand. "Scarlett, since the moment I saw you, I knew you would be mine, and when I met you, your beauty shined. That day I told you we would walk down the aisle together again and I want that to be today. My Lady, please make me the happiest man and marry me today. Be mine now and forever?"

My heart sores as I nod yes because forever with him is what I've always wanted. Cyrus picks me up into his arms as he stands and slams his lips to mine. "Finally."

"I love you so much, Cyrus," I whisper against his lips and I feel his smile widen.

"Mine." He starts moving and I wrap my legs around his waist as he heads towards the church.

I run my fingers through his hair and giggle. "What are you doing?"

"Making it official." A dark possession fills his eyes.

My eyes widen in panic. "We can't have sex in a church."

He stops and gives me a heated smile. "My dirty girl, I'll have you wherever I want…" He adjusts me in his arms so his erection runs across my core. "And I will have you after I make you mine, give you my name, and slide a ring on your finger."

His feet start moving again and I squirm out of his hold and stand in front of him. "We can't get married today. Our family isn't here. I don't have a wedding dress."

He wraps his arms around my waist and pulls me so our bodies are against each other. "Scar, we don't need anyone here. All you need is me. Don't make me wait. I want to take you back to our hotel tonight as my wife." He leans forward and skims his lips across my neck. "You look beautiful in anything and a wedding dress won't make this day any more special. All it will be doing is laying on the floor once you have that ring on your finger just like these shorts and top will."

He raises his head from my neck until our eyes connect and his lips brush over mine. "Marry me today, Scar. Give me your love and celebrate with me."

I let out a soft moan as a smile pulls across my lips and Cyrus' smile grows with mine as he picks me back up and continues to the church. "That's my Lady, making me happy." He carries me into the church and doesn't put me down until the door closes behind us and even as my feet touch the ground, his hold keeps me close to him.

"Mr. Cunningham, I see she said yes." An older gentleman dressed in a priest robe with a strong Greek accent steps out from behind a podium and starts walking the short distance to us.

"I didn't expect her to say no." Cyrus smiles at the priest and gives me a wink.

"You must be the beautiful Scarlett." The older man reaches his hand out as he gets close and I place mine in his to shake with a smile.

"Yes, I am."

The priest shakes Cyrus' hand. "Young love is so pure and sacred. I'm happy to join you both in love, health, and happiness."

I smile up at Cyrus with so much excitement that we're actually doing this. This is the future I wanted. Us together married, being a family, and growing our family. It just might be sooner than expected but that's okay. Now when we move to New York, we can truly start our lives together.

"I see that you already have your bouquet." I look down at the flowers and smile at how much Cyrus planned this. "Would you like a few minutes to freshen up before you walk down the aisle?"

Cyrus looks down at me with the priest's question and kisses me. "Go."

I step away from Cyrus and head to the door that's to the left of the church entrance. Entering the bathroom, I head directly for the vanity and look at myself in the mirror. I'm actually about to get married; I almost feel like I'm looking at someone else.

Not wanting to make Cyrus wait too long, I quickly run my fingers through my hair to detangle it and flip it forward and back to give it some volume. I don't have any makeup with me but luckily the sun has my cheeks a perfect pink and my mascara still looks perfect from this morning.

Happy with how I look, I pull out my phone and take a quick picture of myself holding the flowers in front of me and send it to Hannah and Katie.

Scarlett: I'm getting married!!!

I don't wait for their response as I push my phone back into my pocket and head out of the bathroom. I can hear the instrumental music as soon as I open the door, but I don't see Cyrus or the priest. Moving closer to where I left them, I finally see them standing at the other end of the aisle, waiting for me. Cyrus is facing away from me, but the priest sees me and smiles. "Please stand."

I'm confused for a second because we are standing but then I notice the two people from the first row pew. Realizing this is it, I bring the flowers to my front, hold them with both hands, and start walking down the aisle. The two strangers turn to look at me as I walk and I start to feel uncomfortable and nervous, but when Cyrus turns and our eyes lock, I completely relax. When I'm within reach, Cyrus holds out his hand and I happily slide mine into his.

Standing next to Cyrus, the priest takes one step up so he's slightly taller than us and nods to the two strangers. "You may be seated." I don't look back to watch them sit as I take a breath readying myself. "We're here today to join Cyrus Cunningham and Scarlett O'Hare in holy matrimony. Their love is strong and growing and while they're young, they know they're ready to make these vows, linking themselves to each other before God." The priest pauses and signals for us to face each other.

I beam up at Cyrus as we both turn, and he takes my hands in his. "Scarlett, please repeat after me." Cyrus' smile turns possessive as I repeat my vows, promising to love, cherish, and obey Cyrus for the rest of my life.

As Cyrus promises to care, provide, and honor me, he slides a ring onto my finger. I feel like I'm vibrating with excitement, knowing Cyrus will always be with me and will always love me. "I'm happy to pronounce you Mr. & Mrs. Cunningham. Cyrus, you may now kiss your bride."

A desired darkness flashes across Cyrus' eyes as the priest says those words and he pulls me to him, slamming his lips to mine in a fiercely passionate kiss. "I'm never letting you go."

Just what I want to hear. "Good."

Cyrus pulls the flowers from my hand, drops them on the floor, and picks me up. "I need to make you mine."

He carries me towards the bathroom as he kisses down my neck and tries to pull the strap of my top down. "We can't have sex here. They'll hear."

"Exactly. You like watching, I bet you love having someone hear you scream as I fuck you." I'm not going to lie because the thought has me grinding against him. "Fuck, Lady, you do love that."

"Not here." I bring my lips to his ear and whisper, "I want you to fuck me on our balcony so everyone below can hear us."

He looks irritated that I won't let him fuck me here and I'm confused. I thought my suggestion would turn him on more. "Fine, but we're going back now. We don't have much time."

"Then what are we waiting for?"

Cyrus carries me out of the church and flags down a taxi. He holds me in his lap, kissing my lips or neck continuously as the taxi driver takes us to the hotel. As we pull up to the front of the hotel, our door opens before the car stops, and Cyrus is throwing cash at the driver while he gets out with me in his arms. I giggle at his eagerness and loop my arms around his neck.

The elevator doors open as we approach them, letting a family out. In one swift moment, Cyrus puts me down, pushing our floor button, and presses me against the wall with his body as he looks down at me. "When we get to the room, I want you naked and laid out on the lounge with your..." My phone starts vibrating in my back pocket which pulls me from his intense stare. I look down to grab my phone and he grabs my chin, turning my face back to him. "I wasn't done. I want your legs spread so I can see all of what's mine."

My breath catches at the look in his eyes and I'm not sure whether to melt into him or pull away. "You're going to do as I say, right Scar? Give me everything I want." I nod, speechless and he slides his hand down to my neck and then over my shoulder.

"I can't wait to mark you as mine." He leans forward, skims his lips down my neck, and nips the curve of my neck. The elevator doors open as Cyrus' phone starts ringing and the growl that comes out of him has me clenching my thighs together.

My body leans with his as he pulls back to grab his phone. "What?" I'm not sure who's on the phone, but Cyrus isn't happy about the interruption. "Can't it wait?" He grabs my hand and pulls me from the elevator to our hotel room as he listens to whoever is on the phone. "I understand." Cyrus looks at me with an unreadable expression as he hangs up the phone. He swipes our room key over the lock, and I push the door open, getting nervous.

"Who was..."

"Scarlett, that was my father. Your mother has been trying to reach you."

What? That doesn't make sense. What does she want? A sinking feeling settles in my stomach and I pull away from Cyrus, hoping it will stop whatever he's about to say but it doesn't. "Your grandparents are dead."

Chapter Fifteen

Sadie

Present

"I know I've only been here a few hours and I might be overstepping. If so, feel free to tell me to mind my own business because it's your club and I'm sure it's..."

"Sadie." Thank God he interrupted me because that was getting embarrassing. Why am I so nervous about telling him my idea? It's just us in the club as he finishes up closing. Everyone left half an hour ago and they were all very welcoming, but what if he doesn't like my idea?

Jaxson focuses his attention on me and I can see the hint of a smile pulling on his face, and I know he's internally laughing at my rambling. My heart beats faster with him looking at me and I look away so I don't start talking again without saying what my idea is. Why am I so nervous about what he'll think?

"The dancers are amazing here. Have you ever thought about doing choreographed numbers at shift change? I think it could really entice your clients and open their pockets. Instead of them having to look at three different stages, they can watch the dancer in front of them. It'll also help the less experienced girls. I could work with the girls to teach them some dances when the place is closed."

"You strip?" His eyes roam over me and an expression I can read has me clenching my thighs together.

"I don't strip but I can pole dance. The girls and I back in New York used to take classes thinking of adding them to the show, but I was the only one that really got into it. I can show you if you want."

I go to stand but his abrupt "No," stops me. "We should be heading upstairs. Let's talk about this tomorrow."

I smile at him as we both stand. "That wasn't a no."

He gives me an amused look as he grabs my suitcase. "I guess it wasn't."

With his hand on my back, he leads me to the back of the club, past the dressing rooms to a door next to the exit. Just like Mystique. A warm smile pulls on my face because I miss my friends.

He unlocks the door and waves me through, and I start up the stairs at the sound of the door locking behind us. "You can take my room tonight and I'll get Phoenix's room ready for you tomorrow."

Jaxson passes me on the stairs to open the door for me. "Oh no, I don't want to take anyone's room. I'm really okay with getting a hotel room."

I take a step back as he looks down at me, holding the knob. "Not an option."

I'm not going to put anyone out. "Then I'll take the couch. At least I'm guessing you have one of those." I give him a cheeky grin and he looks away to hide his smile as he opens the door.

"Yes, I have a couch and it's a pull out."

"Even better." I walk past him as the door swings open and into a small open space with a couch, TV, a small two seater table, and the kitchen. It's quaint and homey. Heading to the couch, I fall on it and let out a sigh. It's soft and cozy and I could easily sleep on it like this.

Jaxson looks down at me as he places my suitcase at the end. "I'm not going to convince you to take my room, am I?" I shake my head no and lean my head back on the cushion.

"Fine. I'll get the couch ready if you want to use the restroom." He points to the door that's right inside the hallway.

"Thank you." Standing from the couch, I grab my suitcase and head to the bathroom.

After changing into my pajamas and going through my nighttime routine, I step out of the bathroom to find the door in the corner opened and Jaxson sitting at the end of his bed in only a pair of basketball shorts. Oh my god. Why couldn't he have a dad bod?

Of course not. He has to be all muscle with strong shoulders, a large chest, muscular arms, and defined abs. He looks up from his phone, pushing his shoulder length hair away from his face like he can sense me drooling over him and I quickly look away and head to the pulled out couch. "Goodnight, Sadie," Jaxson says to my retreating back and I let out a soft "Goodnight" as I internally berate myself.

Making sure to keep my back to the hallway, I climb into bed and bring up the messaging app.

Starlight: I made it safe.

M: I know. Enjoy the bayou.

I close out the message thread with Ri and open the one with the men I should be ogling at.

Me: Hey! You guys would love it here.

Colton: What kind of sinful trouble have you gotten into?

Tanner: Anywhere you are we'd love.

I smile at their words.

Me: No trouble yet. Video call in the morning?

Colton: I'd never say no to seeing your beautiful face.

Tanner: Call whenever.

Me: Goodnight

Tanner: Sweet dreams Blossom.

Colton: Dream of me Shortcake.

I set my phone on the side table next to me with a smile hoping they do fill my dreams.

The sound of a soft crunch pulls me from my sleep and I turn towards the sounds to find a little boy with blonde hair in dinosaur pajamas sitting next to me on the bed, chewing on an Eggo waffle.

"Hi." He smiles down at me as he moves closer to me.

"Hi." I greet him confused. Why is there a kid here? I look at Jaxson's room to find the door closed.

"Would you like a waffle?" The little boy holds out an uneaten plain waffle.

Not wanting to upset him, I take it. "Thank you. What's your name?"

"I'm Phoenix." Phoenix, as in Jaxson's roommate? Well, I guess he never said he was a roommate, but he definitely didn't say he had a son. "What's your name?"

"Sadie." I sit up on the bed and lean against the back of the couch. Phoenix moves to sit next to me, mimicking me. I hold my waffle up and pop it against his. "Cheers." He giggles as I take a bit of mine and he does the same.

"Your hair is really pretty." He reaches up and touches the ends of the colored part. "So many colors. How did you get them?"

"I had them colored."

He looks eager as a plan forms in his head. "With a marker?"

"No, hair dye."

"Can I do that to mine?"

"You're not old enough yet, but I'll make you a deal, okay?" He nods excitedly. "If your parents say it's okay, I can use Kool-Aid." Where is his mom? Does she know I'm staying here? Does she live here as well? Oh my god! Did I drool over a married man last night? Where is Jaxson? I have so many questions.

"Really!? That will be so cool! Dad. Dad. Dad!"

Jaxson's door swings open and he appears buttoning up his shirt. "Nix, I told you…" He stops when he sees me sitting next to Phoenix and us both eating waffles. "Not to wake her." The side of his lips turn up as he shakes his head. "Morning."

"Morning."

"I didn't wake her up," Phoenix whines. "I was very quiet."

"He's telling the truth." I smile at Jaxson, not telling him that his son was watching me sleep.

"Dad…please…please…please, say yes." The kid vibrates with excited energy and I can't help but chuckle while looking down at him.

Jaxson ties his hair back into a bun as he stands at the end of the mattress. "Say yes to what?"

"Kool-Aid hair."

Confusion covers his face. "I'm sorry what?"

"He said he wanted hair like mine." I grab a section and wave the end at him.

"Sadie said she could do it if you said it was okay. Pleeease Daaaad." Phoenix gets on his knees next to me and gives his dad a puppy dog pout.

Jaxson closes his eyes for a second as he takes a breath. Maybe I shouldn't have said anything until I spoke to him. When his eyes open, connecting with mine, I see he's not angry. "Making another mark," he whispers before looking at his son. "We'll talk about it later. You need to go get dressed or we'll be late for school."

Phoenix hands me his unfinished waffle, jumps off the couch, and runs to his room. "I'll be fast."

"Nix, she isn't your trashcan." Jaxson shakes his head as he walks around the bed and takes the waffle from my hand. "Sorry."

He stands over me and I tilt my head back so I'm looking at his face. "You have a son. I'm definitely not taking his room from him."

"We'll talk about it later," he says in the same tone he said it to Phoenix. Stern but gentle and it does something to me. Luckily, he walks away to help Phoenix before I embarrass myself.

What is wrong with me? I never react this quickly to a man. Even with Colton and Tanner, it was a delayed attraction but that was mostly from the shit I was healing from. It took years and a lot of therapy to trust a man again and Tanner and Colton were one of the first, but they weren't around a lot. When they were around, they were with Riona or fooling around with Bianca. The little attention I'd get from them, I'd soak it in wishing I wasn't so broken. But when Aisling was taken several months ago and Ri needed me to help get her back, even in the small role, it made me feel alive and not just surviving.

After that, I started making flirty comments back to Colton and returning Tanner's suggestive smiles, and while I could've jumped into bed with them from the beginning, they respected that I wanted to take it slow. Having them dote on me, wanting to take me on dates, stealing kisses, holding hands, and just wanting to spend any spare time with me was a huge turn on.

It was something I never really had, at least not for real. But all the feelings and desires that have been building up are ready to overflow and instead of showing them how much they mean to me, I'm in New Orleans drooling over the man that's assigned to protect me. A man that is probably married or has a life partner that he had a son with.

I need to burn some of this energy before I jump Jaxson or tell Tanner or Colton to forget about finding Cyrus and come get me. Maybe Jaxson will let me use the stage downstairs to work on some dances to show the girls. I get out of bed and grab some workout clothes. "Hey, Jaxson."

I run right into his chest as I turn to head to the bathroom and he grabs my upper arms to stabilize me. "You okay?"

I'm frozen for a second as I look up at him with our bodies pressed against each other. His question finally registers and I snap out of the trance he seems to always put me in when we're close and step back. "Sorry." Once there is a good couple of feet between us, I ask, "Can I use the club stage to put some dances together to show the girls?"

"I haven't said yes yet." He smirks at me and I move past him to the bathroom and stop at the doorway, looking back at him.

"But you will and it's a good workout." His eyes run over me and my breath catches, hoping he's picturing me on that stage. That's definitely not helping this feeling I have towards him. Stop wanting him.

Phoenix runs out of his room in khaki pants and a polo drawing my attention away from his father. "I'm ready. Let's go, Dad. Bye, Sadie." He grabs his dad's hand and pulls him to the door while waving at me.

"Have fun at school, Phoenix." I wave to him and look up at Jaxson waiting for his answer.

"There are spare keys in the drawer there." He points to the drawer next to the refrigerator. "Just be done before noon. There's going to be some business happening before we open and I don't want you anywhere near it."

I nod. "Thanks."

"I should be back before then after dropping him off and running some errands." I give him a nod in acknowledgment before slipping into the bathroom and closing the door. The front door closes a few seconds later and I lean against the door. Yep, I'm in trouble.

Chapter Sixteen

Scarlett

Past – Age 18

Everything has been a blur since Cyrus uttered the words that shattered my world. Weeks of my heart feeling like it's been ripped out of my chest. They were murdered in our home. I can't seem to stop crying, knowing I'm never going to be able to see the two people who have always loved me and raised me again. Cyrus has been my rock through it all, taking care of everything since I can't find the energy to get out of bed. The meds he's been giving me aren't helping with that since they keep me pretty tired, but they do keep me numb. It still feels so raw.

I lost my shit about a week after we returned when he wouldn't let me go to their funerals. I haven't even been back to Texas. Cyrus insisted we come to Las Vegas first when we left Greece. I haven't been able to say goodbye to them yet.

I only seem to be awake now when I need to sign something for the estate because my grandparents left me everything or if Cyrus needs me. I'm his wife so I need to be able to be present when he needs his release. Cyrus left me a little while ago to go to work at the mansion and I can feel the drowsiness of the pill he gave me before he left set in. My eyes get heavy as I sink into a darkness where everything is okay.

The bed dips, pulling me out of my escape and my eyes fly open. My mom sits on the edge of the bed looking down at me with red eyes and dark bags under them. "Honey, I need you to sit up and take this. It'll counteract the pills Cyrus gave you."

"No, I don't want that. It doesn't hurt when I'm asleep." I shake my head and try to bury it back into the pillow.

"I need you awake, Scar. You're in danger here." She leans forward and brushes her fingers over my cheek. "I wanted you away from here. Franklin isn't a nice man and Cyrus is following in his footsteps."

I try to push away her hand, but the meds are making me sluggish. "Cyrus isn't like him. He loves me."

She grabs my face, forcing me to look at her. "He killed Granny and Papa. This has been a con the whole time. They only wanted us for our money."

I pull away from her. "No, you're wrong. He was with me."

She wipes a tear from my cheek that I didn't realize I had shed. "They had been dead for almost a week before they were found. He wasn't with you." My head is spinning as doubt filters in. "Please Scar, take this. You need to leave now."

Not paying attention as I try to put together everything she said with what I know, I take the pill she gave me. "How do you know he killed them?"

"I overheard the two of them talking about it in the kitchen. Franklin was congratulating Cyrus for taking them out and locking you down." She holds up her hand and points to her wedding ring and I look down at mine. Was it not real? Does he not love me?

"You need to leave tonight." She pulls the sheets back and pulls me towards the edge of the bed. "Get dressed. I have everything you need in here." She puts a backpack on the bed.

I can feel whatever she gave me working as energy courses through me. It's like I've had a pound of sugar and now I'm on a jittery sugar rush. Her desperation has me getting out of bed and quickly getting dressed. Once I'm ready she pulls me from my room and out the front door to her car.

"You need to go straight to the bus station and buy a ticket anywhere." She opens the driver's door and pushes me in as she throws the bag in the backseat.

"Aren't you coming? You can't stay here." Panic fills me at doing this alone and leaving her.

"I have to stay to give you a chance."

She bends down and places her hands on my cheeks. "I love you, Scarlett. I'm so sorry I brought you to their attention. I tried to keep you away. You were never supposed to have this life." She kisses my forehead. "Now go. GO."

She stands, closing the door and I reach forward, turning on the car. I look back at her before shifting into drive and then slowly pull away. I follow her directions and head straight to the bus station. The next bus going out was heading to Phoenix, so I buy a ticket. The closer I can get to Texas the better.

I have thirty minutes before the bus leaves, so I move to the far corner of the station as far away as possible from people. As soon as my butt hits the seat, I feel the adrenaline from everything drain from my body. I lean my head back against the wall and take a deep breath. Should I have left? What if she wasn't telling me the truth?

I just left my husband who has been my rock based on the words of my mom who hasn't cared about me in years. Did I just screw everything up? But what if it's true? I married a man that killed my grandparents. The man I love took the only other two people I love for what? Money? My heart hurts at the loss and the thought that Cyrus has been lying to me, that he doesn't love me. I try to think back to every time he's told me he loved me, but I can't think of any. I've told him hundreds of times, but I can't think of once he has. He loved calling me his.

I'm so focused on how my life is blowing up that I jump at the sound of my name. Looking from the ceiling, I see two men standing in front of me too close. I stand ready to move away from them and they both lunge forward, grabbing me.

"No." I try to fight them kicking and screaming, but it's useless as they drag me out of the station. Screaming louder, I hope to get someone's attention, but my stomach sinks when I notice the few people here intentionally looking away. They're just letting this happen.

I'm thrown into the trunk of a car and one man grabs my hands and binds them together. "He's going to make you wish you never ran." That's all the second man says before they close the trunk, surrounding me in darkness.

Chapter Seventeen

Cyrus

Age 23

"What the fuck did you tell her?" My father backhands Michelle across the face and she falls into the kitchen island.

"I didn't tell her anything." She glares at him.

He grabs her hair pulling her head back. "You're lying. Do you think we don't have cameras in this house? We watched you help that girl escape." He turns her towards me and pushes her down on her knees. "You took something that's his."

Her glare would kill if she had any power. "I told her to run from you. You're a monster. I know what you did and she knows too. I hope she gets away and never sees your face again."

I step up to Michelle with a wicked smile. "Oh, she's going to see my face again. It's yours she'll never see again. She's mine and I never lose what belongs to me." Pulling out my phone, I show her the photo my guys sent me twenty minutes ago of Scarlett sitting at the bus station.

"No. No. No." She fights against my father's hold on her hair, but I just chuckle as I raise the gun in my other hand to her forehead. I'm tired of looking at this used up whore.

"Michelle, you've played your part well…" The sound of the front door opening has an exciting buzz running through me. I guess Scarlett will see her mother's face one more time. "But your time is up." My father lets go of her and I pull the trigger.

A scream overtakes the sound of the gunshot as Michelle's body falls to the floor and I look over my shoulder to my Lady. She's screaming for her mom as she tries to fight against Keith and Vince's hold on her. I walk over to what's mine and grab her chin between my thumb and pointer finger. "You can't leave me, Scarlett."

Tears stream down her cheeks as she stares past me at her dead mother. "Why?"

"Because you're mine and no one is going to take you from me. I've worked too hard to get this." I look at my two men who are still holding her arms and nod toward the stairs. "I'll show you what being mine will be like now." She could've stood by my side and had everyone admire her, but she ran. I'll show her what her new life will truly be like.

They start pulling her away and she fights against them. "Please let me go. I don't want this. I don't want you."

I storm towards her and pull her blonde hair until her head is bent back as she cries out. "What did you say?"

Tears make her blue eyes sparkle as she looks at me hurt. "You aren't the man I loved."

"No, I'm the man that owns you. It seems you need to be reminded of that." With my hold on her hair, I pull her from my guys and lead her up the stairs to her new room.

The bedroom door closes as I push Scarlett face down on the bed, knowing my guys followed me. They're here to collect their payment for bringing her back to me, but they'll have to wait. I need to show her who she belongs to. She fights against my hold as I keep her face down on the bed and I tear her shorts and underwear down her legs.

"Get off of me," she screams as her arm swings back, trying to get me off her but I grab her wrists, letting go of her hair and hold them at her lower back. I unbutton my pants and push down my pants to release my growing erection. Having her fight and scream has me so hard. "Please don't do this. I don't want this."

I lean over her so my body pushes her further into the bed as I hold my erection at her opening. "I don't care what you want. You're here to serve me in whatever way I want. You're only good for this."

I slam into her as she screams out "No." Tears stream down her cheeks as I thrust into her over and over, taking my pleasure from her body. "Please help me," Scarlett pleads to my guys and I chuckle because she has no idea. Wanting to see her face as I break the news to her, I pull out of her, quickly flip her over, and thrust back in. She tries to scratch my face, but I grab her wrists again and hold them over her hand.

"They aren't going to save you, Scar." I use my body to hold her down and continue fucking her, taking what's mine. "They brought you back to me." Fear shines in her eyes as she continues to plead for me to stop, but I don't hear any of it. I can feel my release tingle down my spine so I pick up my pace and thrust into her harder. I can see the pain in her eyes and I remember the similar pain she had when I forcibly took her virginity because she wouldn't give it to me. And just like then, it has me ready to explode.

"You're their reward for bringing you back to me." Pure terror reflects on her face and that's all I needed before I come, releasing myself deep inside her. As I come down from that amazing high, I feel my guys move to either side of me and I look down at Scarlett with a wicked smile as I pull out of her and stand. "Don't worry, it's just for tonight, but be good to them. It's something you need to get used to."

Realization settles in and Scarlett starts to move away, but they grab her and pull her up the bed to the headboard. She screams as they handcuff her to the bars and starts kicking out at them. Keith grabs her legs as he gets in between them and I turn to leave them. "You're so beautiful, Scarlett, I can't wait to see all of you."

I hear the sound of her shirt tearing as I step out of the room and as I close the door behind me Scarlett's terrified scream has me wanting to watch the fun. "Don't touch *me*."

Chapter Eighteen

Scarlett

Age 18

My body jolts as the door clicks behind Cyrus' two goons and I stay curled in the fetal position. The moment they unlocked the cuffs, I curled in on myself and buried my face into the pillow. I couldn't look at the men who violated me and took something I wasn't willing to give. Disgust makes my stomach roll and I rush to the connected bathroom and fall to my knees in front of the toilet. I heave over the open seat, but nothing comes up and a sob rips out of me.

I just want this feeling to go away. The dirty feeling from their touch, mouth, and release. Using the toilet, I push myself off the ground and get into the small stall shower. Ice cold water falls over my skin, but I don't flinch away. I'll take anything to wash the filth away. The water eventually turns hot but that isn't what has my

127

skin red, it's the loofah that I'm using to remove them from my body but I can still feel them. Will their touch ever go away?

A shiver runs through me as Cyrus' last words before leaving the room comes back to me. "It's something you'll need to get used to."

Cyrus isn't the man I thought he was. The man I knew would never have been so violent, never would've... No, I won't think about it. I need to get away from him. I can't stay here.

Stepping away from the water even though I can still feel their touch like spiders crawling over my skin, I turn off the shower and wrap a towel around my body. As I step out of the bathroom, my stomach rolls at the sight of the soiled sheets and my torn clothes on the floor. Don't look at it.

"If you don't see it, it's not real. Just like grandma told you when you thought you had a monster in your closet when you were a kid," I whisper to myself as I look straight ahead and move around the bed to the dresser, hoping there are clothes in it.

Pulling open the drawers, I find lace bras, panties, silk nighties and pajamas, and crazy leather straps that hide nothing I've only seen in porn. I run my fingers over the leather and fear washes over me. This isn't for making love. It's for holding you down. The buckles have a tear run down my cheek as I think of the cuffs the goons used. I slam that drawer closed and quickly grab a bra, panties, and the longest pajamas I could from the other drawers.

As soon as I'm covered in the tank top and shorts, I head directly for the door. It has to be in the early morning by now so hopefully everyone is asleep. The handle turns as I slowly press down on it and I let out a breath that it isn't locked. Once I push the handle all the way down, I try to pull the door in, but nothing happens. I push down on the handle harder, thinking the latch hasn't fully retreated, but when the door still does move, I let the attempt of a quiet escape go.

I frantically yank hard on the handle using my whole body, pushing and pulling, hoping for my escape. Frustration and desperation take over as I let out a scream. When that doesn't work, I bang on the door, trying to get anyone to open it. My banging quickly turns soft as I feel my energy drain and I sink to the floor. They locked me in.

Anger courses through me because they, no he, has taken something else from me. He took my choice and now my freedom. I push up from the floor and as I stand my eyes connect with the large mirror above the dresser and my reflection. The hidden hallways.

Cyrus has shown me through all the hidden hallways, having our fun playing hide and seek and more recently getting each other off while watching what happens in the rooms. Oh my god, could the girls be held here too? Is this really a brothel or something much darker?

Reaching out for the closest thing I can pick up, a ceramic jar, I throw it at the mirror. The bowl shatters against it but there isn't so much of a crack on the mirror. I scream out as I grab another item and throw it, hoping Cyrus is there watching. I want him to feel the hate. "I wish I never met you."

"I hate you."

"You're a monster."

"A murderer."

"A rapist." With each spew of hate, I throw whatever little object I can find.

"I'll never be yours again." I grab the lamp from the nightstand and yank it from the wall and when I turn back to the mirror Cyrus is standing there, next to the dresser, as a hidden door closes.

"You'll always be mine. I own you, Scarlett." Cyrus moves towards me fast and I throw the lamp at him as I try to get as far away from him as possible, but he easily hits it away and grabs me around my neck, pushing me against the wall.

"No." I try to pull his hand away, but he just tightens his grip. "Don't touch me."

"I can do whatever I want. You have no one to save you." He leans forward so his lips skim my ear. "I've killed everyone that loved you and I will kill you if you don't learn to behave."

He pulls back and his evil smile causes a shiver to run through me, knowing he'd do it. "You're a monster."

"Yes, I am and you belong to this monster." With his free hand, he runs the back of his fingers across the side of my face and tucks my hair behind my ear. "You're going to bow to my needs in every way. You'll be the Lady of the mansion. Someone everyone will want a piece of, but it'll only be me who will decide who can have you. You'll make me very rich." He slams his lips to mine and

I fight to get him off of me. He laughs against my closed lips before pulling back with excitement in his eyes.

"You disgust me." I sneer at him.

"Don't worry I'll break that out of you." He releases his hold on me and steps back. "You have until tonight to come to terms with this or you're going to wish you were lying next to your mother in the unmarked hole in the middle of the desert." I glare at him and he smirks like he loves my hate. "Rest up, wife. Tomorrow will be fun."

The ring I was happy to have on my finger not even a day ago burns now when he calls me his wife and I quickly pull it off and throw it at his retreating back. He freezes mid step when it hits him and I hold my breath, waiting to see what he's going to do.

Slowly he turns, looking down at the ground, and when he lifts his head, fury is burning in his eyes. I sink back against the wall as he slowly stalks towards me. Fear washes over me, knowing I messed up and I'm about to witness his evil monster again. Cyrus moves like lightning, backhanding me across the face as soon as he's close enough, and I fall to the ground, hitting my head on the corner of the nightstand. My cheek burns and my head throbs as I try to crawl away from him, knowing he isn't done.

He grabs my hair and yanks me to my knees with my head back. "Pick it up." He pushes me back down and I catch myself so I'm on my hands and knees and right in front of me is the gold band. "You don't want me to have to ask again," Cyrus hisses.

I quickly grab it and slide it back on my finger, scared of what he's going to do. "You will never take that off again. If you do,

I will lock a collar around your beautiful neck." A sickening feeling settles in my stomach as I stare down at the ring, listening to him leave.

Chapter Nineteen

Colton

Present

We changed all our plans for this morning the moment Stella asked to video call last night. I've gotten used to seeing her almost daily so not seeing her beautiful face, expressive eyes, and bright smile for three days has had me waiting by my phone since the moment I woke up and Tanner is the same way. I've never seen him so attached to his phone.

My phone starts to ring on the coffee table and I lunge for it, seeing a picture of Stella smiling. I cropped a picture of her, Ri, and Ash together so it's only her.

"Told you she'd call me." I give Tanner a cheeky grin as he joins me on the couch.

"Your name was probably first on her contact list." He returns my grin, knowing he's bursting my bubble.

133

I give him a quick glare before smiling at my phone as I hit accept. Stella's sweaty face and reddened cheeks fill the screen and her smile grows as Tanner and I fill the camera lens. "Hi!"

"Hi, Blossom," Tanner greets.

"Hi, Shortcake." I smile back at her taking in every inch I can see. She looks okay. Not a scratch on her but I have noticed one thing missing. "No more pink hair."

"I figured it would be smart to change it, but I haven't conformed completely." She turns around and lifts her ponytail showing the underside of her hair that is now multi-colored. It suits her just as much as the pink did.

"I guess I can't call you Shortcake anymore."

She chuckles. "You'll have to think of something else. I didn't really like Shortcake anyway. I was more of a Rugrats kid."

I gasp in fake shock. "What?" She chuckles. "Why didn't you tell me?"

"Because I liked you giving me a nickname." She blushes.

"I can always call you Dove, like I used to." The first time I saw her she looked so pure and innocent, needing to be saved. Dove was the first thing that came to mind. I only stopped when she changed her name to Stella.

"I'd like that." Her smile brightens.

"Did you secretly dislike Blossom too?" Tanner asks.

She shakes her head. "I like being your Blossom."

"What are we to you, Dove?" I raise my eyebrows suggestively.

Her cheeks redden as she bites her lower lip. "You're my guys."

"No special nicknames," I egg her on.

She leans forward and whispers, "It's your names I want to be calling out."

Well damn. I'd love to hear her calling my name as I make her come. I bet my name would never sound better. "You better be screaming our names."

She chuckles at my comment but doesn't continue our tempting banter. "I've been working on some new dances to show the girls here. Do you want to see?"

"Hell yeah," I answer.

"Is it a burlesque club as well?" Tanner asks. Stella moves back from her phone and I see the pole behind her. Not a burlesque club. "Are you going to strip for us, Blossom?" Tanner leans closer to the screen and I push his face away to get a closer look.

"Not that you have many clothes to remove." She's only in a sports bra and small spandex shorts.

"I'm not taking off my clothes. Do you want to watch or not?" She points at me like she's telling me to behave but she knows I won't. Not with her.

"Wait, I want to see this on the big screen." I give the phone to Tanner and pull out a cord to connect it to the TV.

"Are you liking where you are?" Tanner talks to her while I set up for our viewing pleasure.

"Yeah, I do. I almost feel like I'm home in this club except for all the boobs." She chuckles. "I like Jaxson too; he seems to be a good guy. We're still trying to figure out where I'll be sleeping since he won't let me get a hotel. He wants me to take his son's room and I told him I was fine on the couch."

I look back at Tanner confused. She's supposed to be staying in a safe house. "You're staying with him?"

"Yeah, in the apartment above the club. The people that work here are nice too. But there was one guy last night that gave me the creeps. He was trying to flirt but it came off gross. Nowhere close to your flirting." Her face appears on the TV as she smirks and I know it's for me.

"You know it, babe." Heading back to the couch, I sit down next to Tanner. "We're all ready for you. Show us your moves." Tanner hands me my phone and I quickly set the call to record as she finds her music. I have a feeling I'm going to be watching this dance later and alone.

Tanner bumps my shoulder. "I want a copy." Something I already knew. Pushing him away, I prop the phone on the coffee table and get comfortable.

The music starts and my eyes track to Stella's ass as it sways to the beat of the intro on her way to the pole. As the first verse starts her hand wraps around the pole and she struts in a circle. When she's back to where she started, her hands go over her head and she grips the pole as she slides down it until her knees are bent. She gives us quick peeks of her covered sex as she spreads her knees open and rotates her hips from one side to the other.

Then as the chorus starts to build, she spins and straightens her legs so she's bent over with her ass out. Fuck me, she walks her hands up the pole and seamlessly spins around it with her knees bent and feet hovering off the ground until she fans her legs out and slides to her knees. Her hands roam to her breasts but movement behind her draws my attention. A man walks from the left side of the room and stands next to the stage, transfixed by her. Looking at Tanner, I notice he sees him too and I'm about to call out to her, but she turns looking right at him. A smile pulls on her lips as she continues to move into the chorus again and I try to focus on her instead of this unknown guy. He better be Jaxson.

The tricks and sexual intention behind the dance intensify as the song continues. For her final trick, she flips upside down and spreads her legs so they're parallel to the stage, then spirals them until she's touching the ground, facing us. The song ends as she leans against the pole, sliding down it, and roaming her hands over her beautiful curves with a desperate need in her eyes.

I'm so fucking turned on as Stella stares at us breathing hard. If I was there right now, I'd already have her laid out on the floor, ripping off her shorts and burying my face between her legs.

"You're breathtaking, Blossom. So beautiful."

I hook my finger at her. "Come a little closer, Dove, let me tell you what I wish I could do to you right now."

She chuckles. "You'll have to whisper them to me later. A nice little bedtime story." She stands from the floor and looks down at the man. "Guys, this is Jaxson."

Stella grabs her phone, moves over to him, and sits on the edge of the stage. "Jaxson, this is Colton and Tanner." His eyes move between us and her and he seems to be having a hard time finding the right words. I know the feeling because all I can think about are the dirty things I want to do to her.

"Nice to meet you, man." Tanner of course is in full control. "Stella, can we talk with Jaxson for a second?"

She turns the phone back to herself and smiles at us. "Okay. I'm going to go shower, but I expect you to tell me what you're going to talk about later." I chuckle at her. She's not fighting about being asked to leave even though she knows we're going to talk about Cyrus. She's fine with the updates.

"This isn't the last you're going to hear from me. I have a bedtime story to tell you." I give her a sexy smirk.

"Promises. Promises." She pauses for a second and blows us a kiss. "I miss you guys."

"Miss you too, Blossom."

"Can't wait to get you home, Dove."

She gives us a wave and hands her phone to Jaxson. He watches her walk away and I wish the camera was facing that way so I don't have to watch him drool over our girl.

We hear a door shut and Jaxson looks down at us. "So you're her boyfriends?"

Tanner answers, "Something like that."

While I say, "Yes."

"I didn't mean to walk in while she was dancing. I figured she was done since she had been doing it for hours." He runs his fingers through his hair, looking uncomfortable.

"If she didn't want you watching she would have stopped." He can worry about us being pissed at seeing our girl like that, but she was okay with it and she has all the power in doing what she wants. He looks confused that we aren't threatening him. Oh, there will be threats but not over something she's okay with.

"Look, we just wanted to talk to you about her safety and give you an update on Cyrus." Tanner leans towards the phone on the coffee table and I match his movements.

"And learn about this guy that creeped her out last night," I added.

"I'm keeping an eye on Manuel." Good, he already knows about it. "I'll keep her safe. He nor anyone else will get to her."

Oh, I'm going to be asking Dante if he knows this Manuel guy. "Good because we haven't been able to locate Cyrus, her ex. He was definitely watching her, but it was through someone. We haven't found a trace of him in New York."

"What's the story there? This feels like more than escaping domestic abuse." Jaxson sits down knowing something dark is in her past.

"Stella was Scarlett before we met her. She was basically groomed by her stepbrother since she was a little girl and when she graduated high school he killed her grandparents, tricked her into marrying him, killed her mom, and then forced her into sex slavery. She lived that life for years and fought to escape. We helped her do that and sheltered her from Cyrus' reach until a couple of days ago. He was the only one that got away from us when we saved her and a dozen other girls."

He's silent for a few long seconds before asking, "You have no idea where he is?"

I shake my head no. "We've had a hit out on him for his head or location for years and nothing has come up."

"He's either underground or hiding behind someone." Jaxson comes to the same conclusion we've assumed for years.

"We're trying to track down who was here watching her," Tanner says. I wish this could be simple so she can come home. Instead, we're picking at breadcrumbs trying to find a ghost.

"Just keep an eye on her and let us know if something happens." He nods. "Also don't let her run again if he reaches out. There's no go bag this time and I can't have her vanishing on us. We won't be able to keep her safe if she does."

The seriousness in his eyes tells me he'll protect her. "Will do."

"We also saw how you were looking at her. If you hurt her, we'll have to kill you and that'll probably upset her, and I try to only make her smile. Got it?" I give him a 'you get me look' and he chuckles with a nod.

"Nothing is going on."

"Yeah, you keep telling yourself that." I shake my head at his lie. Do I want to share her with anyone else? No. But I wasn't lying when I said I only want to make her smile. So if she's feeling something towards him and he's making her happy, I'm good.

"She's easy to love," Tanner speaks the truth that we both found out quickly.

Chapter Twenty
Sadie

Dancing for the last few hours and putting together a few dances has been so much fun. It's been a couple of years since I've danced or choreographed numbers for Mystique and I've missed it. When I called Tanner and Colton, I was excited to show them, but the moment the song's opening beat filtered through the speakers, my heart started to beat faster and it had nothing to do with the thrill of dancing. It had everything to do with their eyes on my body.

With a little more sway in my hips, I teased them with my pole work and made sure they saw my desire for them in my expressions. Then Jaxson showed up and I was thinking about actually stripping and showing them how much their attention has me wet and ready for them. I know if Tanner and Colton were here right now, I wouldn't have made it upstairs. The club cameras would be getting a fantastic show. Jaxson is here but that isn't something I can act on, at least not for real.

My hands roam over my naked skin as the shower rains down on me. Gripping my breasts and pinching my nipples, I close my eyes and imagine they're Jaxson's hands as he presses up behind me and starts kissing down my neck. "I can't resist you." I let out a soft moan as I throw my head back and move one of my hands down my stomach to my aching clit.

With the first touch, I buck against my hand, wanting Colton kneeling in front of me. "You like his touch, don't you, Dove? Let me see how much." I lift one of my legs to the edge of the tub and push a finger inside my warm core. "You're loving it."

The last of my men appears in my mind standing in front of me, stroking himself. "Fuck," I whisper as I fall into the fantasy of having all three of them with me in this shower. Riding my hand, I pump my fingers inside of me and rub my palm against my sensitive clit. I'm building so quickly I lean back against the tiled wall as my knees shake. Instead of the cold tile, I imagine Jaxson's warm body and he wraps his arms around me, holding me up.

"I got you. Fall for us, Sadie." I grip my breast as I pull my wet fingers out and rub my clit in tight circles, just how I like, and come calling out for the three of them in my head. My knees start to give out and I reach out for the shower curtain and grip it tight as I ride the high out.

"Fuck me that was hot," I whisper out loud as I open my eyes and look around the bathroom that I can see since I pulled the curtain open a little bit. Oh god! Did I actually call out their names? Did Jaxson hear? I try to listen for any sounds that would indicate that Jaxson has come upstairs but all I hear is the shower. Hopefully, he's still downstairs. A smile pulls across my face as I start washing up. I might have a bedtime story for Colton tonight too.

Jaxson is sitting on the folded up couch when I walk out of the bathroom in some lounge clothes with my hair braided in pigtails. Don't act weird. It doesn't matter that he saw you dancing and then you had an imaginary foursome that had you coming and screaming out his name. I'm sure he'll be thinking of me on my knees for him after some of those moves when he wraps his hand around his length later. I look at his crotch, wondering how big he is.

What's wrong with me? I avert my eyes and keep them focused on the ground so hopefully he can't read my dirty thoughts. "Hey."

"Hey. I got us some lunch." He doesn't sound like he heard me pleasuring myself in the shower or caught me staring in between his spread legs as he leans forward on the couch to eat his sandwich.

"Thank you." I grab the wrapped sandwich and sit on the opposite end of the couch.

"I just got you what I got. I hope a hot club sub is okay." He smiles at me and I smile back, feeling myself loosening up.

The smell of the heated bread, meat, and cheese has my stomach growling. "It's perfect. I can eat anything."

"Good to know. I also picked up some groceries so we don't need to go out."

I smirk at him. "Are you locking me in your tower?"

"Not locking, it's just that the fewer eyes on you the better."

Fewer eyes? Really it's just two eyes. "They haven't been able to find him, have they?"

He shakes his head no. "Just give me a few days to work on a plan and then if you want to go out and explore, we can talk about it. Until then, if you want to go outside just use the roof patio."

I look up at the ceiling, not realizing there could be something above us. "Roof patio?"

"Yeah. Just go up the fire escape." He points to the window.

"Show me?" I stand from the couch, excited, and grab my sandwich still in the wrapper, and his other half that isn't in his hand. He stays on the couch and stares at me. I hold out my hand that has his other half on it for him to place the half in his hand down. "Well, come on."

He chuckles, standing from the couch, places his sandwich in my hand, and goes to grab the wrap but I pull away. "You can get the drinks."

"Whatever you say, Sunshine." I smile at the name as a giddy feeling buzzes through me.

He grabs our two water bottles and heads to the window where the fire escape is. The window opens with ease and he climbs through with no problems. Me on the other hand, I look at the window like it's a calculus problem because I'm going to need to use at least one hand to prop myself up. I must have a look on my face because Jaxson chuckles as he's bent down looking at me.

"Just hand them over." He has the bottles tucked under his arm and he's reaching out for the sandwiches. I hand him his and he quickly reaches out and grabs mine with the other hand.

"Hey."

"Well, come on." He smiles at me mimicking my tone from a few minutes ago. Leaning on the window seal, I swing one leg through and set my hand on the top of the window so I don't dump my head and slide through. Standing in front of Jaxson, I try to grab the sandwiches back but he moves away. "Up the stairs."

I glare at him with no heat behind it before turning and climbing up the steps. At the top I pause, shocked by the view of Bourbon Street. It's beautiful. On the other side of the roof, a few chairs are set around a square table and two lounge chairs are next to it. Jaxson walks past me and heads to the lounge chairs. "This is great. I could come up here every day."

"Just be careful of the edge. The railing is old."

I nod as I run my hands along the rusted metal railing. It's beautiful with the spiral design. I take the open chair and smile over at Jaxson. "Can I ask you something?"

He nods as he starts eating again. "I'm sure you have a lot of questions. Go for it."

"How did you end up with this place?" I unwrap my sandwich and my mouth waters.

"It's not mine. The Russos own it, but Dante gave us the apartment when Phoenix was born."

"Where's Phoenix's mother?" I look at his ring finger to make sure I haven't missed it.

He looks away from me and down at the ground. "She passed away when he was two."

"I'm sorry. Were you married?"

He shakes his head. "But I loved her very much."

My heart hurts for him. I know how it feels to lose someone you love. "Will you tell me your story?"

"We grew up here in New Orleans as neighbors. We were childhood sweethearts. I would've done anything for her. After we graduated high school, I got into business with the Russos, and Vicki went to college. We were doing good until she started partying a lot. She started doing drugs only at parties and then got addicted to cocaine where she couldn't go a day without doing a line or two. I didn't notice because I was caught up in the life, enjoying all the benefits but I was never as bad with the drugs as her.

"I got a wakeup call when she had a miscarriage. I finally saw the problem that she had. So, I cleaned up the business I did for the Russos, got her away from the partying, and helped her get sober because we wanted a family more than anything. When she got pregnant with Phoenix, she was so happy. I was so happy because we were finally getting the life we used to stay up as teenagers talking about. She stayed sober through pregnancy and the first year after Phoenix was born, but then Manuel ruined it."

Wait? Manuel? "The guy from last night?"

"Yeah, he was our best friend growing up and was dealing at the time for the Russos. It was date night and my mom had Nix. Manuel invited us to a party and she really wanted to go. We got separated at the party, talking to different groups, and when I found her, Manuel was making lines on the table and she had a rolled up bill at her nose as she snorted one. I lost my shit and left telling her not to come home unless she was sober." He pauses and his voice sobers as he continues, "She ended up overdosing a few months later."

Such a tragic story. "She never came back?"

He nods. "She did but she was always high and looking for money."

"I'm so sorry. That's awful for you and Phoenix."

"We did have a few good years and I make sure to only share those stories when Nix asks about her." He explains like he doesn't want me to focus on her bad habits.

I reach out and squeeze his forearm. "You're a great dad."

He gives me a weak smile and we're quiet for a second. "I need you to stay away from Manuel not just because of the issues I have with him. I believe he's into some shady stuff."

He doesn't need to worry about that. I don't want anywhere near him. "I don't want anything to do with him."

"Just be careful." I smile at him, liking that he cares for my safety, more than just protection from Cyrus.

Knowing the mood needs to be lifted, I switch to another subject. "Are you going to tell me what you thought of the dance?" I'm eager to hear his opinion.

Jaxson runs his eyes over me before a smile pulls on his face. "You definitely know how to dance and draw men in but you're not dancing for the clients. I can't be getting assault charges."

I chuckle. "Not what I meant. Do you think it's a good idea to do choreographed numbers?"

"How about this? You take Phoenix's room and you can teach the dancers." He smirks at me, giving me a deal that we both want but I'm not backing down on my side.

"No. I'm not taking his room. The couch is fine."

"Fine, my room and you can teach the dancers and Kool-Aid dye Nix's hair."

He's already a yes to both. "What happened to whatever I say?"

He narrows his eyes at me, but I don't break our connection. "Fine but you'll have to get used to Nix waking you up every morning."

I'm okay with that. "I liked our waffle date this morning."

He shakes his head at me, smiling. Hanging with him today shows me he's not the stern man I met last night. That was just a facade. "I'm not going to convince you to change your mind, am I?"

Victory feels good. "Nope. I don't want to put either of you out."

"You aren't. I just want you to feel safe and welcome."

I lean back on the lounge and smile up at the sun. Sleeping on the couch or in a bed won't make this apartment, the club, or the father and son that live here feel any safer and more welcoming than it already is. It feels like home.

Chapter Twenty-One
Scarlett
Past - Age 18

I've been locked in this room for four days with no escape from him. That's not without trying though. My first day after Cyrus started my "training" and left me a crying mess on the floor, I found the lever to open the hidden door but I only got to the kitchen before I ran right into one of Cyrus' friend, Vince. My punishment was being slapped across the face so hard it left a bruise and busted my lip and then Cyrus forced me on my knees and held my head, letting Vince use my mouth as his prize for catching me. Next time I'd make sure not to get caught.

The next day I tried the lever again, promising myself I'd be smarter about it, but when I opened the door I found his other friend, Keith, waiting for me. Knowing nothing good was coming at seeing him, I tried to slam the door in his face, but he stopped the door with his foot. He pushed the door open, knocking me back and I tripped, falling to the floor. Before I could try to get back up, he was on me with his hand on my throat and his other tearing off my bottoms. As he thrusted into me and squeezed around my throat, he laughed at my screams or my attempts. Right before I passed out, he told me, "Keep playing the games, Scarlett. I love winning."

Today, I was playing to win. I was complacent when Cyrus came in for my morning "training" allowing him to use my body in whatever way and acting like I wanted it, just so he could finish and leave. Because when he leaves, my breakfast is delivered. The last two days I've been tracking when my bedroom door is opened and every morning about ten minutes after Cyrus leaves, a guard comes and delivers my breakfast while I shower, lunch is delivered around noon, and dinner about an hour before the mansion opens its doors to its clients. Cyrus always has dinner with me; he calls it my business lesson because he tells me all about how the mansion works and what he's planning to do now that he's in charge.

Instead of getting in the shower when Cyrus leaves, I turn it on and close the door so the guard thinks I'm in there. Pulling on some pajamas because they're still my closest option to real clothes, I hide in the corner where the door will open against me.

Right on schedule, the guard opens the door and walks in carrying a tray. He doesn't even look for me with the sound of the shower running. Slipping out from my corner, I sneak up behind him and shove him as he approaches the dresser to set down the tray. I hear his grunt as he crashes into the dresser, but I don't look back as I race out of the bedroom.

With the handle in my hand, I pull the door behind me and as I turn just before it closes, I see the guard starting to right himself, covered in food. In panic, I slide the lock on the outside of the door and step back just as the door starts to shake but I can't hear a sound coming from him. A chill runs through me realizing that nobody could hear my screams.

Knowing I don't have a lot of time, I look around the open floor I am on, eyeing the three other closed doors at each corner. I slide along the wall and head for the stairs that are open in the middle of the mansion. There are no hiding spots so I need to move quickly and quietly in order to get out of here. I chose to do this at breakfast instead of lunch because I'm hoping the women are still asleep from last night and the guards aren't patrolling as often.

Leaning over the railing, I look down the flight of stairs to the next floor and listen for any sounds. I have to get past this floor and then the next set of stairs lead straight to the front door. When I don't hear anything, I move on my bare feet down the stairs one at a time, in a crouched position, until I can see the entire floor. Seeing it's clear, I sprint down the rest of the stairs and swing around the banister to the next flight.

The front door comes into view and I don't stop to make sure it's clear. I race down the steps and close the space across the foyer. My body slams into the door as my feet slide across the wooden floors. Voices start getting louder and I frantically claw at the doorknob until I hear the click of the door unlatching.

Several footsteps sound behind me as I pull the door open ready to run but I come face to face with Cyrus and his two friends waiting for me with their arms crossed over their chests and excited smiles across their faces. I step back from them ready to run in the opposite direction but the feeling of being crowded from behind stops me. Cyrus looks over my shoulder confirming that the other guards have surrounded me. "We got this. Go back to your duties."

Retreating footsteps have me wanting to look back to make sure they're gone but I can't risk taking my eyes off the three monsters in front of me. Cyrus steps forward and I take a step back. "Don't move."

I freeze, stopping myself from shifting back. He closes the distance between us and reaches out, tucking my hair behind my ear and I fight myself not to flinch away. "It seems you enjoy the games you're creating for us by continuing to try to escape. Just like old times." I stay silent as he moves around to my back. "So, we're going to spice it up a bit." He pauses and I can feel his eyes boring into the back of my head. "We're going to play a little hide and seek. You get a five minute head start to make your escape but your punishment when we catch you will be severe. What do you say? Should we play?"

I don't turn to look at him, just glare at his friends in the doorway. "What choice do I have?"

His breath brushes across my hair and I shiver in fear at his closeness. "If you don't, you'll get your punishment now."

I step away from him and turn so the door frame is at my back. "I'll play." I'd rather have the chance to escape, even though we're in the desert, than to just give up.

"Good. Your five minutes start now." I take off running towards the back of the house as Cyrus calls after me, "I'll always find you, Scar."

God, I hope not. Knowing I won't make it far on foot running through the desert with the heat, brush, and animals, I head for the only place I know that has car keys. Running through the kitchen, I don't even acknowledge the guards eating as I bust through the back door and race to the house I used to look forward to seeing every summer. I don't think I've ever run this fast as my feet dig into the course ground, allowing me to reach the house in seconds. I don't slow down as I crash through the backdoor and head straight to the front where I know a bowl of keys sits. Slowing down enough not to crash into the table by the front door, I grab a familiar keychain that I gave Cyrus years ago and move to the front door.

Expecting to see Cyrus again smiling at me, I slowly open it but when I see no one is there, I fling the door open and head straight to his car, not caring if the door closes behind me. Luckily Cyrus never locks his car so I'm able to get in without trouble but putting the key in the ignition is another story. My hands are shaking so much from the adrenaline that it takes a few times to get the key in.

As I turn the key, I look around, making sure Cyrus and his friends aren't closing in on me since I'm not sure how much time I have left. Not seeing anyone I shift the car into drive and slam the accelerator to the ground. The tires kick up rocks before the car jerks forward.

Gripping the steering wheel tight to steady the car, I fly down the driveway. The last time I did this, I was running too but this time I'm not stopping. As I reach the edge of their property I turn left instead of right towards the city. This time I'm heading to California.

Trying not to draw attention, I drive down the two way highway going the speed limit because the last thing I need is to be pulled over without my license and in pajamas. I start to relax after about fifteen minutes on the highway without any cars chasing after me and I realize that Cyrus never gave me time for when I win.

It doesn't matter how far I get from him; he'll always try to pull me back. My heart sinks at the thought of always running. I'll never get the life I wanted. I won't be able to go to college, be in a real relationship, have long lasting friends, build a career, or have a family. Nothing that will ever tie me down or hold me in one place. Even though that seems like a lonely life, it's better than the life Cyrus is forcing me into.

A bump from behind throws me forward and brings me out of my head just in time to see an SUV ram into the back of my car again through the rearview mirror. I can see Cyrus in the driver's seat with a wickedly happy grin on his face and my blood runs ice cold. No, I'm not going back.

I hit the accelerator to the floor, jerking the car forward, trying to put some distance between us but he's still there riding the bumper. I fight to keep the car on the road while praying for it to go faster. When I look back again in the rearview, Cyrus is gone. Where did he go? I look to my right and fear has my whole body locking as I see Cyrus driving in the opposite lane, taking advantage of the open road. I'm never going to outrun him.

I watch as he jerks the steering wheel to the right and I scream as he clips the back corner of the car causing me to lose control. The car just spins in circles until I hear another bump and instead of spinning, I'm now tumbling as the car rolls. My head hits the window and stars form in my eyes. The car finally stops moving with me upside down and my eyes start to droop as I lose consciousness but before I completely blackout, I see Cyrus' shoes and hear him say, "You can never escape me." Everything goes dark, knowing he's right.

Chapter Twenty-Two

Scarlett

Age 18

My head is screaming and my whole body feels like it's been trampled by a stampede. I groan from the pain as I try to move but I'm restrained. Panic overtakes the pain as I open my eyes to find myself bound and bent over a leather bench. Frantically I pull at the leather cuffs on my wrists and ankles and my panic only gets worse when I notice I'm not alone. Multiple males laughing has me snapping my head up to find Cyrus, who is right in front of me, and the three other monsters, who stand a couple feet behind him, surrounding me in a semicircle in the middle of the lounge room.

Cyrus smiles down at me, looking excited at whatever he has planned. "My beautiful Scarlett, you played well but you'll never beat me." He raises his hand and I see the paddle he's holding as he taps the edge of it in his other hand to avoid the metal studs. "But the time for your games is over."

Terror fills me as he moves behind me, running the wooden paddle down my bare spine, and tears burn in my eyes as I look at Franklin and Cyrus' friends, knowing that they're looking over my naked body. I fight on the restraints again, wanting to get away from their prying eyes. Eyes that look like they want to eat me alive until there's nothing left.

Sickness rolls in my stomach as Franklin steps closer and his eyes burn down my skin taking the same path as the paddle. A violent smack lands on my ass cheek and I scream out in pain.

"You will never try to run from me again," Cyrus says as he lands another hit with the paddle. "It's time you take your place as Lady, standing next to your Lord." Another hit and I bite down on my lip as tears run down my cheeks. I feel degraded and ashamed with each hit, knowing he's enjoying hurting me. Disgusted that the others are watching and getting off on it.

With each hit, Cyrus tells me what he wants but I'm not listening because the pain is the only thing I can think about. When it gets to be too much, I yell out, "Stop. Please, stop." I sob out as another hit comes. "I'll stop running. I'll listen. I promise. Please stop."

I hear the paddle drop to the floor and relief rolls through me until Cyrus grips my hair and pulls my head back until I'm straining against the cuffs and my back is arched painfully. I look up at him, wanting to beg, but he looks down at me with a devilish smile and dark eyes. "This is nowhere close to being over. I want you shattered on the floor at my feet." He throws my head down and I slam back into the bench with my chin taking most of the impact, making me bite my tongue.

Blood fills my mouth and I cry out, "You don't have to do this."

"But I want to." He grips my ass cheeks in each hand and squeezes hard like he's squishing some fruit in his fist. "Your ass looks perfect with your blood covering your skin and running down between your cheeks." He loosens his grip and rubs his hands over the tender skin and I hiss at the pain. "Your body is begging for me to finally take you back here."

His thumb pushes against my back hole and I instantly fight against the pressure. "No. No. No." Chuckles surround me as I try to move away, yelling my protest.

A loud snap rings through the room as searing pain burns across my back. I wail out as I contort my body, trying to move away from the pain, but it only makes it worse. "Stop fighting my son. He owns you. He can take whatever he wants. The only words out of your mouth should be, 'Yes, my Lord' or 'Please, my Lord'."

I turn my head to look at Franklin, seeing a small whip in his hand, and I glare at him wanting him to drop dead. "I hate YOU!" I scream out the last word as Cyrus thrusts into my ass.

Pain. That's the only thing I feel, see, and hear. I'm being torn up on the inside by Cyrus as he violently fucks my ass with animalistic grunts and being cut open on the outside as the whip slices up my back with each harsh snap. I'm locked in this dark tunnel as I scream, just wanting a second of relief, but it doesn't come. The pain continues for what feels like hours and I'm not sure there will be anything left of me once it stops.

The first thing I noticed, bringing me out of the dazed state I was in, was the whipping sound had stopped. The next thing was pain radiating not only from my back and ass but also from my core all the way down my thighs. Then I realized I could move. The restraints were gone. Looking up, I don't move my body as I once again see the four men in front of me in a semicircle.

"Stand up," Cyrus orders and my eyes move to his as my body reacts before my brain, pushing against the bench until I'm able to get my legs under me. My body screams from the movement but I continue until I stand completely naked in front of them, knowing I look untouched from the front and bloody from the back.

"Turn for me." Once again, I move as soon as the order is given, turning in a slow circle. I hear their sounds of desire, want, and being pleased when I face away from them, but I feel nothing. When I face Cyrus again, I stand there waiting for my next order.

Cyrus steps forward as I watch him but also look past him. He reaches up and moves hair from my face. "You did so good, Lady. Broke so beautifully." I continue to stand there without moving or speaking, letting him run his fingers over my face. "Look at me." My eyes shift to connect with his and I feel hollow. "Go back to your room and clean up. I'll give you a week to heal and then my Lady will be presented to all our guests."

I move to go upstairs but Cyrus grabs my arm, pinching the skin in his fingers but that pain doesn't register. "Answer me."

"Yes, my Lord." My voice comes out as a harsh whisper from all the screaming I did.

Chapter Twenty-Three

Sadie

Present

"Hey Sadie, can you do me a favor?" Sherry calls from the bar entrance as I set four glasses of bourbon on her tray. She's one of the eight dancers/waitresses. It's actually a great system. Every hour the girls switch around. If they aren't on stage, they're waitressing. It gives a seductive but also a personal touch.

"Sure, what's up?"

"Can you deliver these to Manuel and the guys he's with?" She looks back to the VIP area, fidgeting with her hands. "I have got to go to the restroom and he hates waiting."

I look over at the VIP section to see four men laughing but Manuel's face is the only one I can see. "Yeah absolutely." I duck under the counter as she runs off and I call out to Jake letting him know I'll be back. Lifting the tray from the counter, I rest it on my forearm and move through the club.

Manuel smiles at me when I step into the VIP area like he was expecting me. I look behind me to find Sherry standing at the opposite end of the bar and she mouths, "I'm sorry."

"Sadie, so great you could join us."

Looking back at Manuel, I put a fake smile on my face. "Hello, Manuel. I'm just dropping off your drinks."

"Gentlemen, this is the new bartender I was telling you about." The two men on either side of Manuel turn toward me and undress me with their eyes.

"She's as beautiful as you said. Definitely a desired one," the man on the right says.

"Will you be dancing for us tonight?" the man on his left asks like he can't wait to see me without my clothes.

"I'm not a dancer." Staying as far as I can away from them, I place their drinks on the table. A sinking feeling sits in my stomach that I need to get out of here. With the last drink on the table, I move to step back, but the man sitting across from Manuel grabs my wrist and I look down at him. He's looking up at me and my whole body runs ice cold. I know him. He was one of Cyrus' special clients. Venom. "Join us. We'd love to get to know you."

I try to pull away from him but his grip only tightens. My whole body starts to shake in fear. Does he recognize me? Is he still in contact with Cyrus? Oh my god, what if he tells him where I am? I try pulling again and a sadistic smirk pulls across his lips.

"Oh my god, thank you so much for covering for me," Sherry's voice sounds behind me and Venom lets go. "How are you liking your drinks?" I don't wait for their answer as I get the hell out of there.

Instead of going back behind the bar, I head straight to Jaxson's office. He came down a little while ago after having dinner with Phoenix and getting him ready for bed. His babysitter is with him now. Entering his office without knocking, Jaxson looks up shocked but when he sees me, he instantly stands. "What's wrong?"

"He... he... I..."

"Sunshine, breathe. Did something happen?" He rubs his hands up and down my arms. I nod frantically, still panicking from seeing Venom again.

"Sherry... Manuel... Venom... me."

"Okay, breathe with me." He takes my hand and places it on his chest.

"Breathe." He sucks in a big breath and I try to do the same.

It takes me a few tries but I'm able to get a few deep breaths in. "Venom is here. Manuel got Sherry to get me to deliver their drinks. They creeped me out talking about how I was just as beautiful as he'd described."

"I'm going to kill him." Jaxson tries to move past me, but I grab onto his shirt.

"No, don't go." It's me that needs to go. I let go of his shirt and step back from him. "I can't stay."

I turn to leave but Jaxson hooks an arm around me and pulls me against his chest. "You're not going anywhere." His arms wrap around me and I crumble in his hold.

"Venom saw me. He's going to tell Cyrus where I am. He'll come for me." I grip his shirt in my fist and sob. "Why can't he let me go? I just want to be free." He holds me as I break until there are no tears left to shed.

With a deep breath, I loosen my grip on his shirt and wrap my arms around his waist, enjoying his comfort. His hands slide up and down my back. "I'm not letting you leave. You're safe here, I promise."

I'm not safe anywhere and neither are they. "He'll hurt you and Phoenix. I won't let anyone else I care about die."

I try to pull away again, but he holds me close to him with his hands framing the sides of my face, making me look up at him. "He doesn't know you're here."

Shaking my head in his hold, I plead, "Let me go. I can't risk the two of you. Venom will recognize me and tell him."

His thumbs run over my cheeks, wiping away the leftover tears. "It's been years. Maybe he doesn't even remember. Did he seem to question who you were?"

"No. He was just enjoying my fear. Just like he used to."

"Then you're safe tonight. Hang out here, at least until they leave." He nods to the black leather couch sitting against the same wall as the door. I nod, pulling away from his hold and his hands run over my waist and down my arms, not dropping his touch until I'm out of reach.

He runs his hand over his beard as he turns back to his desk. "How about you give Colton and Tanner a call? They'll want to know what happened and to hear your voice."

They're going to lose their shit, but I know they need to know. As I lay down, I look over at Jaxson, wondering if staying is the safest thing. Not for me because I know he'll protect me. But for him.

Chapter Twenty-Four
Scarlett
Past - Age 21

It's been three years since the day Cyrus broke me. Three years of having to allow clients' hands roam my body. Three years of looking at Cyrus like I love him, like I want him. Three years of slowly putting myself back together. And three years of planning how to destroy Cyrus and burn this place to the ground.

This place is hell and not just for me. When Cyrus took over the mansion, he brought in a new clientele that wanted things darker and more painful. Things the other woman didn't want to do.

Things that were forced on me. At least until Cyrus got tired of sharing me. Then he did the unthinkable. He started taking girls and women off the street, females who came to Vegas for vacation or were going home from a night working. They were never seen again unless they came here. Cyrus' new clientele really enjoyed those new women. That was when the first piece was put back into place for me.

Over time, I was able to make Cyrus think he should let me into the business and that's when I learned that when the clientele got bored of the women, he would sell them to a black market sex trafficking ring and then take new women. I knew I needed to find a way to save these women and hopefully myself. With me being his perfect lady, he started giving me more freedom to roam the mansion without a guard and leaving me alone in the office to work on the books when he had something else to do.

Being left alone, with the web at my fingertips, was where a plan was formed and where I found them. They call themselves M. We met through a messenger board trying to figure out where girls were being sold. I was trying to find the girls Cyrus sold to hopefully find a way to save them and they were inquiring about when the auctions were. There was just something about their questions that felt different than the rest.

We privately started talking, testing each other to make sure our motives were pure and trustworthy. Last week they proved themselves by busting one of the sex trafficking rings some of the girls were sold to. It was all over the news and Cyrus was losing his mind. He walked around yelling at everyone until he came to me to relieve the rest of his anger and anxiety. Now it's time to prove myself.

Last night a sixteen year old girl went missing on her family vacation when she snuck out to go clubbing. I know the girl is here because Cyrus is leaving to sell another girl tonight and he only gets rid of a girl when he has already taken a new one.

The mansion being quiet at night is a rare thing, but with one of the rings being busted, Cyrus took extra precautions when he left. He took Keith, Vince, Franklin, and some of the guards with him, leaving no one here to run the place tonight. He even locked us in our rooms so we wouldn't get into trouble. Which is perfect because while he'll suspect what I'm about to do was me and want to punish me, he won't be able to prove it since I never opened my bedroom door.

I learned a long time ago that cameras surround the house. One outside every bedroom, several throughout the whole first floor, and a camera covering each entry to the mansion. Over the last year, I've memorized every camera angle and practiced moving around the house without being caught. It became a game I'd play with myself whenever I had to roam around checking on the clients and making sure they were happy. Then when Cyrus would leave me alone at his computer, I'd try to track myself through the footage. Now I'm only on camera when I want to be.

I wait until it's after midnight, knowing the few guards left are drunk enough from the bar that they're already passed out or about to succumb to their drowsiness. I slip out of my bed dressed in a light blue nightie and grab my robe from the armchair. Slipping it on, I walk over to the mirror and slide it to the right and the hidden door pops open. Another thing Cyrus let his guard down about. He stopped locking it a couple of months ago after leaving my bed.

With swift moves, I slide through the opening that's just big enough for me to fit through because any further the hinges creak.

Once in the secret hallway, I slide the door close and use my fingers along the wall to find my way. I didn't want to chance someone seeing a light if I used one. The girls he takes never make it to the bedrooms. Only the girls he employs for the normal clientele have those rooms. Instead, he holds them in the basement in these weird glass boxes where they can be watched sleeping, showering, going to the bathroom, and being chosen for whatever sick pleasure the client wants. It also makes it so they have to see all the horrible things that are being done to the other girls.

I make it all the way down to the first floor but since the finished basement is only a few years old, these halls don't go any lower. This is one of the parts I need to be careful about. I need to get out of the pantry and move across the kitchen to the door that leads down to the basement without a guard catching me and not showing up on the cameras.

I take a deep breath and slowly let it out to relax but I can feel myself getting worked up from the nervous anxiety. The last time I used this exit was three years ago and it ended with me running into Vince and being forced to take him in my mouth as my punishment. Once I've calmed down, I slowly lift the lever unlocking the door and push out quietly just enough to make sure I'm alone. I'm met with complete darkness, so I slip out into the pantry and push the shelving back until I hear the latch click. One room clear, one more to go.

Twisting the knob on the pantry door, I open it only an inch so I can look out and listen for any noises. From this vantage point, I can see the entire kitchen except for the corner right on the other side of the door and the back entrance to the mansion. No one is in the kitchen, but I don't step out for a few minutes, listening for any sounds from the guards. It's hard to hear if any of them are still awake because of the music they're listening to but when I don't hear any talking or laughing, I cross my fingers and push the door open more but just enough to slip through, so it doesn't appear on the camera watching the backdoor.

Once out, I stick to the wall sliding toward the front of the house to avoid the camera that sits in the corner above the backdoor angled toward the large island in the middle of the kitchen. There's also another camera in the opposite corner that watches that side of the kitchen, leaving just about a foot from the walls that aren't surveilled.

Moving slowly, my back glides across the wall until I reach the first hall opening that I have to cross. I look down the hall to make sure I'm clear before tiptoeing across it and pressing against the middle wall. Once again, I shuffle down the wall and tiptoe across the second walkway until I'm in the corner right by the basement door. Now this is the part I really need to be careful of because I can't open this door more than six inches or you'll be able to see it in the camera.

I take a few quick breaths before sucking in a large one and opening the door. I don't let the breath go until I'm on the other side with the door closed behind me. Not knowing if I was caught on camera or not, I shake out my nervousness and move down the last set of stairs. When I come to the bottom, I freeze at the horror of seeing this place for real. I've only heard about it from Cyrus and occasional glimpses of the security feed from the one camera. This was the only feed Cyrus keeps locked away for his eyes only and I only saw it because I'd looked over his shoulder. He likes to store the recordings of the clients for blackmail.

There are four glass cells down here, one in each corner, and in the center there's a large holding contraption in the shape of an X, a leather bench I'm very familiar with, a four poster bed, and something that hangs from the ceiling that has hooks attached to it. Geez, it's a living nightmare. A chill runs through me so I look away from the contraptions and look at the four women that are looking back at me in shock. They look beaten, weak, thin, and terrified. I bring my finger to my lips signaling for them to stay quiet and then point up to the camera. They all nod and I reach out for the key fob they keep right next to the stairs.

Now this is where I can't step out into the room. I need to get the fob to this first girl so she can unlock her door and the others. The glass cells are about ten feet tall, but the tops are open. I have only one chance to throw this and get it in without being seen because if I miss, I'll be forced to step out into view of the camera. Holding up the fob, to show the girl in front of me, I make a throwing motion so she understands.

She steps back until her back is on the far wall. Please. Please. Please, let this work. With a steadying breath, I throw the fob underhanded and watch as it soars through the air. It hits the top edge of the glass and my heart sinks thinking it's going to fall back towards me, but it doesn't. By some miracle, it falls into the cell and the girl lunges for it.

She and the other girls free themselves within seconds and I wave them towards me and start up the stairs. When we're halfway, I stop and turn to them. "When I open this door, you're going to run directly for the backdoor that'll be diagonal from us." I signal in the direction it will be. "You're to go in the direction of the house back there but don't go in. Follow the driveway down to the main road and help will be waiting for you. You'll need to move quickly because I don't know how long Cyrus and his men will be gone. Do you understand?"

They all nod and we continue up the stairs. I crack the door open just to make sure the kitchen is still clear and then push it open signaling for the girls to go. Three of them run past me but the fourth, the girl who was taken yesterday, hugs me, and whispers, "Thank you," before running after the other girls.

I don't wait to make sure they make it to the driveway as I move back along the wall to the pantry and into my room. As I lay in bed trying to fall asleep, I can't get the smile off my face. I saved those girls. I might not have been able to save myself, but I saved them. Maybe one day I'll be free too. Free of this life. Free of this city. Free of this mansion. Free of Cyrus. That will only happen one way. His death.

Chapter Twenty-Five

Jaxson

Present

Colton and Tanner took what happened as well as I did but they were able to vocalize it. Even with the call not on speaker, I could hear every one of their threats towards Manuel and Venom and I want to lock her in this office and act out each one. Seeing her fear when she came in here, watching her cry, and hearing her tell them how well she knew Venom has me wanting to wipe them both from the earth so she never has to worry about them again.

Venom is an evil I've never experienced before and I'd love to force the torture he has caused onto him, but I'm not sure he's a threat for the reason Sadie does. Vile men like him don't remember their victims' faces. They just feed off the fear they inflict and move on to the next. He's a problem for the same reason Manuel is. They have for some reason locked in on her and her talking about how they assessed her and had given their approval feels bad. She's in more danger than we thought and Cyrus, wherever he is, isn't the bigger threat.

I've been watching them through the security cameras and one of them has had an eye on my office door like they're waiting for her. I look over to her and smile seeing her curled up on the couch, sleeping. She fell asleep listening to Colton and Tanner rambling on about some story when she asked them to distract her and the smile on her sleeping face when I laid a blanket over her tells me that they did.

My phone vibrates on my desk and I look away from her to see a text from Tanner.

Tanner: Here's what we've found on Venom. He's bad news and Riona is ready to take him out. Don't be surprised if he shows up dead soon.

A file attachment pops up, but before I can click on it another text comes through.

Tanner: Keep her safe.

Knowing he's done, I pull up the file he sent over.

Vernon Kingston aka Venom

Heir of Kingston Media, a multi-billion dollar media company based in California.

CEO Victor Kingston, brother.

Arrest record (2006-2008):

13 counts of rape

5 assaults

2 murders

Pictures after pictures of teenage girls with bruises and bite marks covering their bodies, fear in their eyes, and blood dried on their skin fill my screen until I get to the end where there are pictures of women lying on the dirty ground with their clothes torn open and their dead eyes open in terror. He got his nickname, Venom, because he likes to bite.

Jesus Christ. I flip through the case files detailing all the awful things he did to them and every case was dropped because vital evidence went missing or his attorney had his dental records and DNA thrown out.

This makes me sick that people let a monster like this walk free just because he has money. And these were from over a decade ago. Imagine what he's doing now, knowing he can get away with anything.

Movement on the screen has me looking up from the file and I watch Manuel and his three friends stand from the table. While Venom and the two others walk out, Manuel moves across the club heading here. Reaching into the top drawer on my desk, I pull out the gun I keep there and stand from my chair. Before he reaches the door, I'm walking out, turning the lock behind me, and closing the door. "Oh, Manuel." I give him a shocked look like I had no idea he was here. "What do you need? I'm just about to make my rounds."

"I just wanted to say goodbye to Sadie and ask her if she can serve us at the meeting tomorrow." Manuel and another underboss have a meeting here before we open with a new supplier.

"Sorry, she went home early. She wasn't feeling good. As for tomorrow, when hired she was very specific that she couldn't work before 4 p.m. since she's taking classes at the university. Mila is already on the schedule for you."

He looks at me with suspicion and at the closed door behind me. A fake innocent smile pulls across his face as he pats my shoulder. "Alright man. Can't blame a guy for wanting the prettiest girl serving me. Tell her I'll see her around."

"We do have the best of the best." I signal for him to step out of the small alcove we're in and make sure to stay behind him as we walk across the club. While keeping an eye on him, I scan the club making sure his friends are gone because I don't like leaving her unprotected in a room with a flimsy lock. When we reach the end of the bar, I turn like I'm going to go behind it but keep an eye on him as he walks down the hallway towards the exit.

Jake appears on the other side of the bar. "Is Sadie okay? I almost jumped the bar when I saw him grab her."

"Yeah, she's fine. Shaken up but fine," I say, keeping my eyes on the hallway to make sure he's not coming back.

"She quit, didn't she? That's too bad. I liked her, she fit in well."

I chuckle at him. "She didn't quit. Just sent her home for the night. Do me a favor though, let me know if you see any of the guys Manuel was with hanging around."

"Yeah, I'll keep an eye out."

I give him a nod and make my way back to my office. Typically I like to be out here as another hand or security, but tonight the woman in my office needs my attention. Unlocking the door, I step inside and my eyes go directly to her. She's in the same position I left her in but her phone that sits next to her chest on the couch is lit up with a notification. Moving over to her, I look down at the phone to see a text from an unsaved number.

Knowing she's only using a secure app to talk with Tanner and Colton, I pick up the phone and silently curse when I read the text.

Unknown: You escaped them, Scar. I knew you just needed to know I was looking. Your Lord is ready for his Lady to come home.

What the fuck? I take a screenshot of the text and send it and the contact to my phone before deleting the text and turning off the phone. He didn't sign his name, but I have no doubt that it came from her ex. Definitely not something I want her to worry about now.

Chapter Twenty-Six

Colton

Past - Age 21

Our driver pulls around the circular drive and stops at the front of the massive house. "Damn, this place looks cool as hell. Are you thinking what I'm thinking?" I look back at my brother, my twin.

"Of course, I know what you're thinking. Elite sex club. You've been throwing the idea around constantly. I worry that's all you think about." Tanner smirks at me. "But we're not here to acquire a new business on the other side of the country. Ri wants us to scope out the place and find her informant."

"I know but it's giving me ideas for that new property she bought." I smile at him as I thrust the air and he just rolls his eyes.

There's a knock on my darkened window and my smile slips from my face. Game time. We were with Aisling and Riona last night when those four girls appeared in the darkness looking beaten, violated, and terrified. Hearing their stories has me wishing I could

181

tear apart this Cyrus guy. Unfortunately, I can't lay a hand on him tonight as he schmoozes us, trying to get our membership of $50,000 each. He sells this place as a sex club for all kinks but it's really a brothel and a front for the sex slavery that's also going on.

We give each other a nod before stepping out of the town car. Just like our looks, our moves are identical. We button our suit jackets when we're fully standing and I wait for Tanner to round the car before we both move up the three steps to where a burly man in a classic security black suit and white button up waits.

"Mr. Stanton." The man nods at me and then Tanner. "Mr. Stanton. I'm Vince and I'll be showing you around before you'll join Mr. Cunningham in the lounge." Tonight, Tanner and I are Jeff and Jordan Stanton, businessmen who recently acquired the Stardust on the strip. This isn't just a membership Cyrus is hoping to get but a partnership to grab girls.

"We were hoping this tour would be with Cyrus," Tanner speaks up as we follow Vince into the mansion. The foyer doesn't match the sandstone desert look the outside has. Instead, it has a colonial look with wooden floors, white walls, and a massive staircase leading upstairs, front and center.

Before Vince can respond, a boisterous voice has us looking up. "Gentleman."

The tall slender man smiles down at us but it's not from happiness; it's like he's imagining the possibilities. He'll be rudely awakened when I show him all the possibilities I have imagined. Something moving behind him catches my eye and I feel like all the breath in my body is sucked out at the beautiful blonde with blue eyes in a white silk slip that shows off her unbound breasts, small waist, and the curve of her hips. Who is she?

"I'm sorry I'm going to miss the tour, but I have some business to attend to with my Lady." He looks back over his shoulder at the dove and she steps forward only looking at him. But it's not want in her eyes. It's almost like she's waiting for something. As she gets closer, I see the bruises on her upper arms from being grabbed and some are peeking out from underneath her collar from being choked. What business does he have with her?

I want to reach out to her and take her out of this house, forgetting our plan, but Tanner's voice stops me. "Will she be joining us later as well?" Pulling my eyes away from the beauty to look at him, he puts a heated smile on his face and slowly looks her over.

A grumble in the back of Cyrus' throat answers that question but his words only solidify it. "She won't be joining us." He grabs onto her arm and pulls her down the hall to the right and I chuckle drawing her attention.

"I guess he doesn't like to share." I wink at her. "Next time, Dove."

Redness fills her cheeks right before Cyrus pulls her hard, making her stumble, and he angrily whispers something to her as they move out of sight. Looking at my brother, I see him staring after them with the same look I have. When he looks at me, we both give a slight nod silently agreeing we're saving her.

Vince showed us around the first floor where the two lounge rooms are, the bar, and a display room for the men that like a good show. I'm not going to lie, I'd love to see the Lady of the house on display for me, reacting to my brother's touch. He and I have been sharing girls since high school. The first time happened when I walked in on Tanner fucking Lacy, the head cheerleader, in the men's locker room, and instead of screaming and covering up, Lacy beckoned me in with a finger and a needy moan. After that, her gossip spread throughout the school about how great we were and the twin kink took off. Never regretted it for a second.

We stop back in front of the large staircase and Vince smiles proud of himself. "How about a drink, gentleman? Then you can enjoy the perks of the place." His eyes follow a brunette who walks past us, leading a guy upstairs.

"This place is impressive," I say as I watch the couple disappear on the second floor. "But a little tame. We..." I look at my brother for just a second before plastering a wicked smile on my face, "like things more..." I pause, acting like I'm thinking of the right word, "disturbed."

Tanner adds, "Savage."

Vince chuckles and nods like he wants to swap stories, but he doesn't. "We definitely have something for your tastes. Those activities happen in the basement."

"Can we see what you have to offer?" Tanner steps close with an eager smile.

Vince turns partially towards the hallway Cyrus and his Lady walked down earlier and nods. "It's a beautiful setup. One I've used multiple times. There's something for all pleasures." He looks back at us. "But you'll have to wait to have your fun down there. Tonight, it's being cleaned since we're in between merchandise. In a couple of days, we'll have everything for you."

We nod with a smirk in understanding. Vince thinks we're eager to have some fresh meat but really, he just confirmed for us that we have a couple of days to kill these assholes before they take, abuse, and assault innocent women. But we can't wait too long because we have at least one woman already in this house that needs saving.

Chapter Twenty-Seven
Scarlett
Age 21

Cyrus is pissed about the girls. He stormed into my room when he got back, yelling and threatening my life. I thought he was going to kill me as he had his hands around my throat. I actually welcomed my death because it meant I'd finally escape him, but of course he wouldn't give me that freedom.

Right when I was slipping into the darkness, he let go and my body acted on its own, fighting death by sucking in air. He left me on the ground of my bedroom after throwing a silk slip at me with a matching collar telling me, "Your punishment is just beginning. You save those girls, but it'll be you who'll be taking their place."

I didn't say a word as he accused me because I knew it wouldn't matter. I was ready to take the punishment. At least I was at the time. Now that I've been down in this basement for who knows how long, I wish I would've run with them. Cyrus, Franklin, Vince, and Keith have all been down here inflicting their nastiest kinks on me. I don't think there's a spot below my chin that isn't covered in bruises or blood but it's hard to tell since I'm tied to the large wooden X, spread eagle and I still have the silk slip on, but it's now torn and bloody.

Franklin and Vince are the worst. They only get off on the pain and my screams, but Vince is the only one of the two who releases his pleasure in me. Luckily Franklin goes somewhere else for his release whenever he's inflicted enough pain to blow. I truly don't know how my mom survived for so long. She had to deal with him daily and I only have to deal with him when I'm deemed in need of a punishment.

Keith likes the fight but it's something I figured out years ago so I never fight him. He gets frustrated but he still uses me. Cyrus just likes to tie me up or hold me down. He wants to claim his ownership over me after he lets his father and friends use me. Cyrus left me tied to this contraption hours ago. At least I think hours since I can no longer feel my arms and my legs are shaking from standing wide for so long.

I just hope this doesn't last too much longer. I let my head fall forward and close my eyes hoping the exhaustion will pull me asleep. It's the only way I can pass time down here. The door slamming and thunderous footsteps has me snapping out of my light daze. Cyrus, Vince, and Keith run down the stairs with a deadly look in their eyes and I brace myself for whatever beating they're about to inflict.

"Get her unhooked," Cyrus commands as he stands in front of me. He grips my chin hard, lifting it so I'm looking directly into his eyes and he looks like he has an evil plan forming. "They can't save you, Scarlett."

The buckles around my ankles unlatch and my knees give out, causing me to fall forward and pull against my wrist restraints. I let out a scream in pain and Cyrus wraps his arms around my center, holding me up as the others unhook my wrists. I grimace in pain as my arms fall to my sides and my shoulders burn from moving back to normal.

"They can take everything here. I will restart somewhere else, but they can't have you." He tucks my hair behind my ear. "You're my Lady."

I want to pull away from him, but I can't feel my limbs. Cyrus lets go of me and I claw at his arms, whimpering as I start to fall to the ground. Keith and Vince grab me under my arms, holding me up.

"Let's get out of here." Cyrus pushes my hold off of him and turns his back to us. Keith and Vince follow after him, dragging me with them as I try to get my feet underneath.

"Wait." I scramble to climb the steps to prevent more bruises but they're moving too fast. "Stop. Please." They ignore me and just lift me higher.

Tires screeching and gunshots from the front have the girls screaming and Cyrus picks up his pace. "Shit." He looks back at us. "Move it."

They rush through the kitchen to the backdoor as the front door bursts open and I scream out, "What's going on?"

"Just your betrayal coming to light." Right outside the backdoor, a black SUV sits and Cyrus runs around to the driver's side. "Get her in the back."

Realization of what's going on finally sets in. M is here. This is my escape.

I start to fight against Vince and Keith's hold and scream out. "Help. Please help."

Cyrus yells, "Shut her up." Keith and Vince try to push me towards the open backdoor on the passenger side.

Getting my body to move, I kick forward, bracing my feet on the door opening and lock my legs, stopping them from pushing me in. They start hitting my legs, trying to get me to buckle but I hold out, even when they pull back and try to throw me in. I need to keep fighting because if they get me in that car, I'll never be able to escape Cyrus and I can't live with that.

I bend my knees and push off the SUV, hoping to send myself and both of them to the ground. I let out a yell as I push just as two gunshots ring out. Hitting the ground hurt more than I thought it would and I groan out, stunned by the pain. "Oh shit."

I roll onto my side and curl in on myself as I hear Cyrus yell out, "I'll always find you, Scar."

The SUV lurches forward as gunshots pepper the side of it. Please hit him. End this. I watch until I can't see the SUV anymore in the darkness, even with the commotion around me, and as someone kneels in front of me. "Shit, Dove. What did they do to you?"

Something wraps around me from behind and I look down to see a cream blanket over my shoulders. I grab the edges and tighten it around me as I notice a motionless Keith lying to my right. I don't need to look to my other side to know Vince is dead too.

"Can you look at me, Dove?"

I lift my eyes to the voice I recognize from before I went down to the basement and they're met with his hazel ones. A weird sense of calm washes over me and I feel myself take a large breath. "I'm Colton. It's nice to finally meet you, Dove." He holds his hand out palm up and I hesitantly slide mine into his. He lightly grips it to shake it, and I can't take my eyes off his.

My head tilts back as he stands and helps me to my feet. Someone calls out his name and I look behind me to see a beautiful redhead standing in the doorway. Her smile widens when she sees me. "Starlight? Oh, thank God. I was worried we were too late." She steps outside so she's within arm's reach of me but doesn't try to touch me. "I'm M but you can call me Riona."

Turning to face her, I let out a sob and throw myself at her, hugging her. "Thank you."

Chapter Twenty-Eight

Sadie

Present

It's been a week since I last saw Venom and I've been on high alert, expecting Cyrus to show up at any second, but he hasn't. Not that he'd be able to get to me. Jaxson has been my shadow. Never leaving my side when we're out of the apartment. He's made me feel safe even when I'm scared. However, he's not really sleeping. I've caught him a few times, when I wake up in the middle of the night from nightmares, sitting in the armchair in the corner of the living room, watching the front door. Every time I tell him to go to bed, he always says he won't leave me out here alone. I've got to find a way to get him to sleep.

One of the greatest things about keeping myself locked up is spending time with Phoenix. That little man is stealing a piece of my heart every time he wakes me up with a waffle and comes home from school telling us about his day. This weekend as I was dying the top of his hair blue and purple, he asked me to chaperone his field trip to the Farmer's market in a couple of weeks with his holiday day camp. I'm so excited to go with him but I could see the stress on Jaxson's face when I agreed, but how could I tell him no?

I was able to talk Jaxson into going back to his regular routine tonight where he has dinner with Phoenix and gets him ready for bed before coming down. Phoenix has been missing his time with him and I don't want him to think he's not the priority. The smile Phoenix gave Jaxson when he asked him what book he wanted him to read tonight had my eyes tearing up. As much as I love spending time with him and Jaxson, me needing protection is hurting him.

Jaxson saw his son's excitement too which made it easier to tell him not to hover at the bar when he finally came down. Plus, the fact that Manuel hasn't been in for the last two days. But I'm not stupid thinking Jaxson's not watching my every move through the cameras.

"Hey, Sadie!" Mila and Zara lean against the bar in front of me as I make a few drinks.

"Hey!"

"We want to do the dance you've been teaching us at the shift change." Mila gives me an excited smile.

We've been working on the dance for the last few days before opening. "That's great!"

They look at each other, smiling like there's something else. "We want you to do it with us."

I shake my head. "I can't do that. Penny is dancing with you."

"She's not as comfortable with the dance yet and doesn't want to mess up on center stage," Zara quietly responds.

"Then one of you should take center stage."

They shake their heads and Mila points at me. "You perform it the best. If we're going to do it and get the reaction we want, it needs to be you."

I look over to the office before looking back at the girls. "I'm not a dancer here."

"Well, you should be. You love doing it. I saw how happy you were when you were showing us," Zara tries to convince me.

I do love it, but I know Jaxson would lose his shit if he caught me. "Please, just the one dance. You'll be back behind the bar after a couple of minutes." Mila smiles like it's simple and planned.

I really want to do this, but I know I shouldn't. "I can't dance in this." I look down at my black leather crop top and black skirt.

"I have something you can borrow." Mila beams at me, knowing I'm about to give in.

Damn, these girls are good. Not thinking of any other reason to say no, I say, "Fine." Looking at Jake, I point at him. "Keep your mouth shut."

He chuckles and acts like he's zipping his lips. "You're delusional if you think he won't notice."

I look at the office door again before ducking under the counter. "Not delusional, wishful thinking." He just shakes his head at me as we rush through the club to the dressing rooms and a gleeful excitement washes over me.

"People are going to go crazy over this," Zara squeals as she pulls me into the dressing room and to their lockers.

Mila reaches into hers and pulls out a gold sequin bra with corset baring that will stop just above my waist and matching panty bottoms. "We have similar ones in black."

They start undressing and I step to the side and follow suit. Once I have the outfit on, I look at myself in the mirror and my jaw drops. Damn, I look hot. I pull out my phone, take a picture of myself, and send it to Tanner and Colton.

Me: Shhh... don't tell Jaxson.

"Wow, you look great." I turn to see Penny standing next to me.

"Thank you, but you'd look just as great in it. Next time, you're doing the dance because I'm pretty sure Jaxson is going to kill me."

She scoffs. "Kill you, no. Fuck you, yes."

My cheeks heat at the thought. "What?"

"Oh, girlie, we all see how you two look at each other." My eyes widen because if she can see how I look at him, then he must be able to.

The three girls that were on stage walk into the dressing room and Mila and Zara each grab a hand, pulling me to the stage entrance. "Do you want heels?"

Looking down at their feet, I see them both in sky high heels. "No, I'm good barefoot."

We step out onto a dark stage and I take my spot in the center and they stand a couple feet away on either side of me. I take a deep breath just as the music starts and the spotlights turn on. We step forward at the same time and the rush of performing has my body buzzing. We move in unison to the slow seductive beat and when we do our first pole twirl and leg fan, the men sitting around the stages are zeroed in on us. Catcalls start as we slide down to our knees and I'm shocked at the rowdiness. When I suggested this, I thought it'd keep the client's attention and have them tip more, not cause a scene.

Security starts to move close as one of the guys sitting near me stands. Turning my back to them, I work my way back to my feet and climb the pole. As I twirl doing the final trick, I see Jaxson standing at the edge of the stage looking like a sexy bull about to charge and the man that was standing is back in his chair holding his nose.

The song ends with me squatting, knees apart, leaning against the pole with my hands gripping it above my head. The next song starts up and I see that Mila and Zara have moved into their own dances in my peripheral. I slowly stand not taking my eyes off Jaxson and his name escapes my lips, breathy. He jumps up onto the stage before I even finish saying his name and throws me over his shoulder.

"Jaxson, you're making a scene." He carries up the stage and turns towards the entrance of the dressing room.

We pass Penny dressed to dance and she hands me my phone. "It's been blowing up." She giggles at me as I mouth 'thank you'.

I swat at his ass. "Jaxson, put me down. It was one dance."

"No." That's all he says as he moves through the dressing room, out the door, and into the stairwell that leads to the apartment. Instead of heading up, he sets me on my feet and pushes me up against the wall with his hand collaring my neck but not squeezing, just holding me so I'm looking up at him. "What were you thinking, Sadie?" His eyes blaze as he looks down at me and it's doing all kinds of things to me.

"The girls wanted me to dance with them." I lean into his hold and rock my hips, looking for more.

He gives me what I want, stepping into me, and I gasp at the feeling of his warm muscular body pressed against me. "I told you what would happen if you were one of my dancers. Is that what you wanted? A reaction from me?"

I nod, even though that's not why I did it. But I'm definitely loving it now. "I can't have you getting arrested for assault." I rise up on my toes, rubbing our bodies together until my lips are next to his ear. "I only want to dance for you."

"Why can't I resist you." His lips slam against mine and I melt into him, returning the kiss, and wrapping my arms around his neck. Kissing him is just like I imagined. I can feel it all the way to my toes and yet it still feels like I can't get enough. We break apart, staring at each other, and I want to pinch myself to make sure it's real.

"I don't want you to resist me."

"Sunshine." He hisses as he grips my hair, pulls my head back, and kisses me again. I run my fingers through his long hair and grip it with a little pull. Fuck, I want him.

He pulls back. "You're too addicting."

"Then don't stop." I try to kiss him but his hold on my neck stops me.

"I'm not going to reward you for doing something risky."

"Then punish me." I rock my hips against his and moan at the stiffness of his erection.

"Head upstairs, Sadie." He steps back from me and drops his hold on my neck.

Instead of turning to the stairs, I step towards him. "I can still work."

He blocks the door with his arms crossed. "Not after the brawl of horndogs you caused."

I roll my eyes at his ridiculousness. "It wasn't a brawl. You're the only one to throw a punch."

"Don't fight me on this. Go upstairs."

"So bossy," I tease as I start up the stairs. A loud smack and my right butt cheek stinging has me looking back at him. Did he just spank me? His heated smile tells me he did and liked it.

I definitely liked it too. He can spank me anytime. I give him a wink before running up the stairs. When I reach the door, I look down at him and he hasn't moved.

"You do look great in that." His eyes scan over me like he's wanting to see what's underneath.

"Does that mean you want me to send you the picture I took of myself earlier?" His heated grin tells me his answer. He doesn't move as I open the door and close it behind me.

Callie the babysitter looks shocked at seeing me. "Damn, girl."

I shrug and smile at her. "Thanks. I've been put in timeout for the night. You can head home."

I grab my pajamas and head to the bathroom to change. Callie waits to leave until I'm out and says goodbye. Wanting to check on Phoenix, I stick my head into his dark room but find the bed empty. I head towards Jaxson's room, opening the door slowly, expecting to see a sleeping Phoenix but he's wide awake and watching TV.

"Phoenix." I push the door open and give him a 'really' look.

"Sadie," he calls excitedly and pats the bed next to him.

Moving towards the bed, I slide in and he scoots to the middle. "You should be asleep, Little Man."

"I'm not tired." He says that like he wouldn't be in trouble if his dad walked in right now to see him awake.

"How about I read to you?" I reach for the book on the side table and hold it up.

"I'd like that." I turn off the TV and turn on a side lamp and we both lay down, getting comfortable.

Phoenix falls asleep before I even get halfway through the book and I smile down at him curled next to me. Shifting slowly to not wake him, I go to get up, but he reaches out for me with a soft whine. "Don't go."

"I'm not going anywhere." Laying back down, he snuggles into my side. Not wanting to wake him with the TV, I grab my phone and pull up my messages with Colton and Tanner.

Tanner: You're looking for trouble Blossom.

Colton: Damn Dove you look sinful. There's no way Jaxson is missing this.

Me: He found out and wasn't happy. Punched a guy.

Colton: Not surprising.

Me: We kissed.

I type nervously. I know I'm with them, but I want Jaxson too and I don't know how they'd feel about that.

Colton: Still not surprising.

Me: You're not mad?

Tanner: We'd only be mad if you didn't want the kiss.

Me: I wanted it.

Colton: Do you still want to kiss me?

Me: Yes. Both of you.

Colton: That's all I care about.

Tanner: Just do me a favor and don't add any more men to this relationship. I already have to share you with my horny twin and the old man.

I chuckle.

Me: No one else.

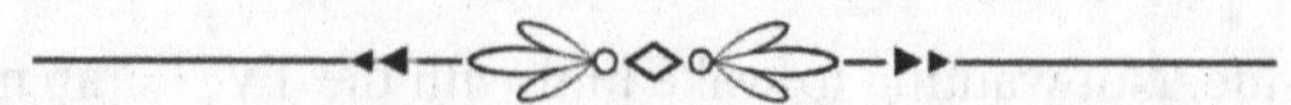

"Hey." A quiet whisper and the soft touch of fingers running through my hair wakes me, and I turn towards the touch to see Jaxson sitting on the edge of the bed in pajama pants and a white tee.

"Hey. Everything okay?"

"Yeah. Just let me grab him." He nods to Phoenix.

"Leave him. Come on, lay down. Get some sleep." I pat the empty side of the bed and he opens his mouth to say something, but I interrupt. "Whatever I say."

He chuckles and I watch him reach out, turn off the light, and then I feel his lips press against the side of my head. Turning towards him, I press my lips to his in a quick kiss. "Goodnight."

"Goodnight." His breath brushes against my lips before he stands and walks to the other side of the bed. I settle back into the bed as it dips on the other side and I feel Jaxson grab my hand and set it on his chest. I fall back asleep with a happy smile on my face.

Chapter Twenty-Nine

Tanner

Riona looks happy as Enzo twirls her around to *Jingle Bell Rock* and at one point years ago, I wanted her to smile at me like that. Now, with us at her annual holiday party turned engagement party, and my mind filled with a rainbow haired beauty, I'm glad she never did. Stella's smile is what I live for. The way her eyes brighten, cheeks flush in the slightest, and lips pull wide with the ends turned up has me weak. It's not a full smile with her cheeks puffy and teeth showing. It's a smile that says she's happy, content, and exactly where she wants to be. A smile I look forward to seeing on her face the next time I have her in my arms. The urge to call her has me reaching into my pants pocket for my phone, but I don't pull it out. She doesn't need me bothering her at work.

"What's got you pouting?" Colton walks over and leans on the wall next to me.

I want to say I'm not pouting but that's what he wants. "Nothing."

He chuckles. "Come on man. It's a celebration and it's Christmas. Put a smile..." My phone vibrating in my palm is a welcome distraction so I don't have to listen to my brother's annoyingly cheerful banter. Stella's name lights up my screen just above a message bubble. Unlocking the screen, my breath catches at the picture Stella sent of her in a gold glittery bra and pantie set.

"Fuck." Colton hisses in desire next to me and I know he's looking at the same image I am.

Stella: Shh... Don't tell Jaxson.

I'm tempted to let him know so one of us can enjoy the show.

Me: You're looking for trouble Blossom.

Colton: Damn Dove you look sinful. There's no way Jaxson is missing this.

He smirks over at me. "We might need to find our way down south soon."

I side eye him with a matching smirk. "Doesn't hurt to get more contacts and buyers."

"Yeah, finish the year off strong."

Colton types something on his phone but mine doesn't vibrate when he slips his back into his pocket. "You texted Jaxson."

"Hell yeah. The old man gets to watch it live; I at least want the security footage." I chuckle at my brother and his self serving logic but I'm not going to deny I want a copy as well. She looks so carefree and alive when she dances and in that outfit... Yep, can't think of that right now.

I adjust myself in my pants and button my jacket, hiding what just the thought of her does to me.

"Colton. Tanner," Killian calls out for us as he steps out of the room, signaling with a head tilt to follow. Colton and I push off the wall in unison and stride out of the room after Killian. We don't say a word as we follow him into Riona and Enzo's office but that's only until the door closes behind me.

"What's with cloak and dagger?" Colton crosses his arms over his chest as Killian turns to us. The only reason he'd bring us to this room is because he doesn't want anyone to hear. My brother and I helped Matteo soundproof this room.

"I just got a call from one of my dealers. He had someone he didn't know approach him tonight to pass a message to me." Killian pauses as he runs his fingers through his hair and you can see the hesitation on his face.

"The suspense is killing me, man." I roll my eyes at my brother's impatience and attempt to lighten the mood.

"This man said that the Russians are screwing us over. They haven't sent us the guns we ordered. Instead, they're using our funds and documents we set up for customs to smuggle their drugs to the Volkovs."

"How did this man know about the shipment?" I ask.

"That's what I'd like to know, but he slipped from the dealer. Look, I know you want to enjoy the festivities." Colton chuckles at

203

the ridiculous statement as he checks over his gun. We love our friends, but the parties and galas have never been our thing. "I need you to receive this shipment and check it yourself. I don't want to start a fight with the Russians right now, but I will."

A fight isn't what we need right with the holidays, the wedding, and everything going on with Stella, but it's a fight we will win if it comes to it. Ivan Volkov should be trying to stay far away from us right now after the shit he, Lorcan, and Maxim pulled. He's the only one still alive but we can fix that. "We'll head out now."

I go to leave but Killian speaking stops me. "Keep your eyes open and guns loaded. Something about this doesn't sit well."

"We're not planning on dying tonight, Boss. Don't worry so much. Go enjoy the eggnog." Colton pats Killian's shoulder as we all head back to the main room.

A look of disgust washes over his face. "I hate that shit. I'll have a few fingers of bourbon for you." Killian raises his imaginary glass to us as he goes back to the party and we continue out the front door.

"Fuck, it's cold out here. This intel better be good. I don't want to be freezing my balls off for nothing." Colton leans against our car as he rubs his gloved hands together and then covers his mouth and nose, breathing deeply.

It's been snowing since we got to the docks about an hour ago and my brother decided standing outside in it was better than sitting in the heated car.

"Get your ass back in the car." I roll up the sliver of window I have open so we can talk to each other or he can talk to me. He might not get in right now, but eventually, he'll get bored and get in. I watch him through the melting snow on the defrosted windshield as he comes around the car to the passenger side.

"That was rude." He slides into his seat and immediately takes off his gloves and holds his hands to the vent.

"You could've stayed out there. The shipment should be here any minute."

He glares over at me but doesn't say anything as he cranks up the heat and fan. "It's not snowing in New Orleans."

"No, it's not." Whatever he's wanting to talk about isn't about snow and I have a feeling it's about a certain text conversation we had with Stella after getting here.

"Are you really okay with Stella being with Jaxson too?"

"We knew this was coming. The way she talks about him and the way he protects her, it was going to eventually."

"You're not worried about her wanting their little family more than us?" I look confused at my brother. He was the first of us to notice something between them and if he wasn't okay with it, he should've spoken up before now.

"No, and you know she won't either. What's this about?"

"Just checking to make sure you're okay about it. You haven't told me what's going through your head about the fact that Stella has kissed someone else and has feelings for them."

"I would give Stella anything, so if she wants Jaxson in addition to us, I won't tell her no. What I feel for Stella won't change with him and his son in the picture. It's more people to love her and she deserves all the love."

"Alright. I'm okay with it too." Colton has always been more into sharing than me.

I chuckle. "I know. If you weren't, you would've told him to fuck off when we first met him."

Colton chuckles too. "True."

A boat horn rings through the night sky as a spotlight lands on the dock ahead of us and Julian's men start moving to help tie off.

"Nothing is getting off that boat until we inspect it." Colton and I get out of the car and walk in unison to where the boat ramp is lowering. Julian's men start up the ramp in front of us and we're right on their heels. They know we're here for the shipment but they don't know our suspicions.

"Which ones are ours?" Colton asks as we step onto the cargo ship filled with shipping containers and wooden crates.

One of the men looks down at his papers and then points to four wooden crates. "Perfect." Colton strides over to them with a crowbar that he had to pick up somewhere. "We'll let you know when these are ready to be removed."

I follow after him. "Where did you get the crowbar?"

Colton turns his wrist, revealing two. "Found them while I was wandering around earlier." He hands me the second one as we approach the crates.

Together we pop off the four lids of the different size boxes. As expected, wood wool covers the top of our supply but with a quick sweep of my hand, it reveals smaller metal boxes. Ammo fills the first box I search through.

"This is good," I call out to Colton.

He nods, holding up a handgun. "Same."

Moving to the longest box, I find three rocket launchers and an ample supply of rockets. Irritation fills me as I realize it was fake intel. I look at Colton who's going through the last crate. When he looks up at me, I know he's thinking the same thing as me. He gives me a subtle nod in agreement and we both leave the crates as is and head back to Julian's men. Grabbing the wad of cash from my pocket, I toss it at the guy closest to me. "Close those up and make sure everything makes it to our warehouse."

"Let's get the fuck out of here," Colton says behind me, and based on the jitter in his voice, I can picture him hunched with his arms across from the cold, looking pissed that we're here for nothing.

Heat hits my face as I get back into the car and I silently thank myself for keeping the car on. Pulling off my gloves, I look over at my brother. "Call Killian."

Colton's phone rings through the Bluetooth as I press the accelerator to slowly move through the snow covered docks. "What did you find?" Killian answers as the sounds of the party dwindle in the distance.

"Everything's good. No drugs, just our order," I answer Killian before Colton gives him a more colorful answer.

"It was fake intel, man. We've been freezing our asses off for nothing. I want this guy so I can tie him up in the middle of nowhere so he can freeze to death." I shake my head at my brother as I pull out onto the vacant street that runs in front of the docks.

"Tanner, look out," Colton yells just as headlights turn on out of nowhere, revealing a truck speeding towards us.

Chapter Thirty
Sadie

The bedroom is still cloaked in darkness as my phone vibrates continuously on the nightstand, waking me. Who could be calling me this late? I groan in irritation as I pull away from a still sleeping Jaxson and Pheonix. The ringing stops before I can grab my phone and the screen lights up with a missed call from Riona. I unlock my phone to call her back when a text comes through.

Unknown: You had those twins following you like lost puppies, wanting to please you, but you know you're mine. You haven't let them touch you, have you? Waiting for me. Don't worry I've put down the strays for you.

An awful chill runs through me and I rush out of the room with the phone to my ear as I try calling Tanner and Colton, but both go straight to voicemail. Jaxson appears from the room as I try Riona next while pacing the living room.

"What's wrong?" His voice is sleepy.

Before I can answer, Riona picks up. "Stella. It's Tanner and Colton."

"No. No. No. No." My knees go weak and I fall toward the floor but Jaxson is there to catch me. "Don't tell me they're dead. Please, Ri." Jaxson carries me over to the couch and holds me in his lap.

"Oh my god, no. They were in an accident but they're doing okay. A lot of bruises, some cracked ribs and minor concussions. Nothing serious compared to what their car looks like."

Thank God. He didn't succeed. "It was Cyrus. He did this." Jaxson looks at me confused at how I know it's him.

"Stella, the guy that t-boned them wasn't Cyrus. He's actually worse off than the twins." I can hear the doubt in her voice.

"He's involved. I just got a text from him practically admitting it."

"Fuck, another one. We all need to get new phones."

Another? What's that supposed to mean? As much as I want to ask, now isn't the time. "Can I talk to them?"

"They're both sleeping and visiting hours are over. I'll have them call you once we're allowed in to see them."

I shake my head even though she can't see me as I try to get off Jaxson's lap. "Don't bother. I'll be on the first flight out."

"No," both Jaxson and Riona say.

"You can't go." Jaxson holds me to him.

"He's right, Stella. It's a trap. He can't find you so he hurt someone you care about to draw you out."

"I should be there." I feel deflated because I know they're right, but I want to be with them. They were hurt because of me and now I can't be there to help them, take care of them, or hug and kiss them.

"They want you safe more than anything." Jaxson pushes my hair behind my ear and I lean into him.

"They're hurt because of me," I whisper.

"Not a chance, Stella. This is all on Cyrus. Listen, I got to go look into this other guy. I promise to call as soon as visiting hours open."

"Thank you, Ri." We hang up and I wrap my arms around Jaxson's neck. He holds me as we're both silent and I'm spiraling in my head. I left New York so no one there would get hurt but they still did. He tried to kill them. I look up at Jaxson to see him looking at the wall across from us. I don't want him or Phoenix to get hurt, but I know leaving won't save them now. I can only save them if I go to Cyrus, but I don't think I have the courage for that.

"I need you to promise me something." Jaxson looks down at me and I continue, "If it comes to yours and Phoenix's safety or mine, you let me go. You choose yourselves. I would do anything to keep you safe."

His hand slides into my hair and I feel his confliction at my request. "I can't promise you that. I would do anything to protect you and Nix." He uses his grip on my hair to pull my face to his and our lips lock in a slow desperate kiss. Shifting on his lap so I'm straddling him, I press my body against him and rock my hips where they meet his.

"I'm not going to be able to survive if something happens to either of you." I start kissing down his neck.

"Nothing is going to happen." His hands slide down my back and grip my ass, pushing me further into him as I rock my hips against his growing erection.

"Then promise me." I bring my face close to his so our lips are skimming against each other.

He stares into my eyes for a few seconds before he growls, "Whatever you say," and flips us so I'm laying on my back and he's hovering over me.

He leans forward until our noses touch, but I can't look away from his golden brown eyes. "Phoenix will always be my number one, but I will fight for you to the end if he's safe."

Before I can tell him that isn't what I asked of him, he presses his lips to mine. I want to pull back and make him promise his safety too, but I know he's not going to, so I'll ask for something I know he'll give me. "I need you."

"Where do you need me?" he whispers as he kisses down my neck and along my shoulder. "Here?"

I hum at the feeling of his lips against my skin but it's not what I need. I arch up and grip his hair, pulling him lower. He chuckles and sucks my nipple through my shirt, bringing it to a point. "Ah, here."

"Yes," I moan.

His hand slides under my shirt, across my stomach, and to my other breast. He pinches my nipple and it hardens from the pain, matching the one he has soaked. Needing to feel his warm skin under my palms, I fist his shirt on either side of him and pull it up his body. I whimper when his shirt gets stuck on his shoulders and I feel Jaxson's smile against my breast. "What do you need, Sunshine?"

"Please Jaxson. I need to feel you. Your warm skin, hard muscles, everything." He sits up, pulling me with him, and I push his shirt over his head. I'm in awe as I run my fingers over his chest, feeling his short hair tickle my palms, and down his defined abs. He's sculpted just for me.

"My turn. Let me see you." He grabs the end of my sleep shirt and slowly pulls it up and over my head. "You're so beautiful." His eyes take in every inch of my exposed skin as he runs the tips of his fingers down my arms. My skin buzzes from his touch as I stare up at him, waiting.

"Jaxson," I whisper, begging him for more, for everything.

His eyes jump back to mine and a sexy smirk forms on his face. "Do you need me, Sadie?"

"Yes," I pant.

"You need me to touch you." He places his hand flat on my chest and I know he can feel how fast my heart is beating as he pushes me back down. "You need me to kiss you." Leaning forward, his mouth hovers over mine but he doesn't kiss my lips. His head drops lower, kissing the swell of my breasts. "You need me to make you come."

His hand runs down my stomach and his fingers toy with the edge of my pajama shorts. I raise my hips, giving him permission, and his fingers slip underneath the elastic band to find me without panties and he grins up at me.

"You definitely need me here." His fingers skim over my lower lips, feeling how wet he's making me.

I buck against his hand, desperate for more. "Please. Take them off."

He gives me a cocky smile and I can almost hear him say 'Whatever you say.' His fingers hook into the sides of my shorts and I lift my hips, helping him remove them. Jaxson sits back on his knees as he drops my shorts to the ground and looks over my naked body. "I could look at you like this all day."

"Hopefully you'd do more than look." He chuckles as I run my hands up his forearms.

His eyes darken as he leans forward. "I won't just be looking." Our lips crash together, desperate for each other. I can't wait anymore. I need him. Tangling my fingers in his hair, I hold his lips to mine as I hook my leg over his hip, pulling him on top of me. A moan escapes me, feeling his hard length against my sensitive clit. "Give me what I want, Jaxson."

"Not just yet, Sunshine." He grips my hip, holding me down. "There's something I want first." His heated smirk as he lowers his face to my breast has my clit throbbing but when his hand once again skims down my stomach, the anticipation has me ready to explode.

Spreading my legs wider, I rock my hips, trying to get him where I need him. His fingers brush over my clit and I suck in a breath with how sensitive I am. His thumb presses into my bundle of nerves as he rubs tight circles and I let out a breathy moan as I arch into Jaxson's face and rock my hips pushing his fingers further into me. "I want you to come on my fingers." Jaxson looks up at me from my breast with his hand hovering over my core. "Squeezing them tight, before I make you come on my cock." He pushes two fingers deep inside me and my heated walls pulse around them.

"Yes, please." My nails run across his scalp from the pleasure as his tongue flicks over my harden nipples at the same rhythm he rubs my clit and fucks his fingers in and out of me. My breaths turn into pants as I build higher and higher and I know this orgasm is going to rock my world.

"You shine all the time but glow like this. It's something I could watch all day."

"Oh god." I grind down harder on his hand as I bring my hand to my other breast and knead it. "More. I need more."

Jackson takes my breast in his hand and pinches my hardened tip as he lowers himself down my body. I hum in lust as my core pulses around his fingers and he growls loving my reaction.

"So wet for me." He pushes my legs wider with his mouth hovering over my exposed sex. "I bet you taste as good as you look."

He pulls his finger out of me and licks me back to front before pushing three fingers back inside and I whimper at the stretch. A heated smile comes across his face. "I could get lost in you. Your taste. Your smell. Your touch. I can't wait to feel you wrapped around me."

"Yes. Yes. Yes." I'm so desperate for my release.

"Then come for me, Sadie." He lowers his lips to my clit as he pumps his fingers inside of me, hooking them up so with each swipe my orgasm builds to an impossible high. His tongue flicks over my sensitive clit in a steady rhythm and I burst into a pleasurable free fall as I scream out his name and he covers my mouth with his hand. My orgasm feels like it lasts forever, pulling everything from me, until I slump into the couch.

The feeling of him removing his fingers leaves me feeling empty, and I whimper as I pull him up my body and crash my lips to his. I need him with me. My taste covers his lips and a shock of pleasure runs through me, making me moan.

"Are you going to give me what I want now?" I look up at him as I slide my hands down his back and push his pajama bottoms down until they fall to his knees, giving me a perfect view of his large dick that's standing erect and ready for me.

Wrapping my hand around him, I give it a few pulls before lining it to my entrance. Looking up at Jaxson's face, my eyes connect with his and I'm speechless at how this man is looking at me. It's like he wants to devour me, love me, protect me, and give me everything in just one look. "Jaxson," I whisper. "I want it all."

He leans forward capturing me in a passionate kiss as he pushes inside me slowly and we moan together. I wrap my arms and legs around him, bringing his body closer to mine so I can feel his warm skin against me as we rock in a slow loving way that matches the heat of our kiss. As our kiss gets more desperate with pleasurable need, Jaxson meets that need with each powerful thrust. My nails scratch over his back as my pleasure builds again and I break our kiss. "Oh god."

"Being inside of you is even better than I imagined, Sunshine. You're so tight and warm. Fuck." He leans back and brings my legs over his shoulders and the new angle hits me just right.

"I'm so close. Fuck. Make me come." I arch my back as I grab onto the couch and he thrusts into me faster, hitting that beautiful spot. Mumbled words spill from my lips as he rubs my clit, sending me straight over the edge. Throwing my head back, I moan as my second orgasm hits me and Jaxson reaches forward and covers my mouth again, muffling my screams as he fucks me through my pleasure and then comes with a growl that's so sexy, I clench around him wanting more.

We're both breathing heavily as he moves my legs from his shoulders and lifts me so I'm straddling his lap. My arms wrap around his neck as he kisses across my shoulder. "You okay?"

I nod, not lifting my head. "Yeah. That was amazing. I've never come so hard."

"Does that mean I have bragging rights over Tanner and Colton?"

Lifting my head, I look into his eyes. "I haven't slept with them. Cyrus was the last person I was with."

He pushes the hair from my face and kisses me softly. "I'm glad I was able to show you what mind blowing sex is really like." We both chuckle and I lay back on his shoulder, feeling exhausted.

"Come on." He grabs my clothes off the floor and then lifts me in his arms, carrying me to the bathroom. The counter is cold as he sets me down on it but I don't pull away as he runs a washcloth under warm water. "I should've asked before coming inside you."

Placing my hands on either side of his face, I tilt his head towards me, making him look into my eyes. "I didn't want it any other way. As long as you're clean and I'm clean, that's all I care about."

"Does that mean you want to have my baby, Sunshine?" He crowds me against the counter with a possessive look on his face and I know I'm about to burst his bubble.

"I can't get pregnant, Jaxson. Just another thing he took from me." I had always worried about what kind of damage Cyrus inflicted after he forced two miscarriages that first year by beating me because he couldn't prove the babies were his. When I found out from the doctor who helped me after being rescued from that mansion, it almost killed me. After years of therapy, it's something I've made peace with, but it doesn't stop the tears from pooling in my eyes.

Jaxson runs his fingers through my hair and leans down to kiss me. "I'm sorry he's taken so much from you." I give him a weak smile and he places another kiss on my lips before stepping back. "Come to bed when you're ready."

He closes the bathroom door behind him and I take a few deep breaths and blink the tears away before turning and looking at myself in the mirror. A smile pulls across my face as I take in my messy hair, flushed cheeks and the red mark Jaxson left on my shoulder. I look well fucked. A chuckle escapes me as I shake my head at myself.

A couple minutes later, I step out of the bathroom, back in my pajamas, and walk into Jaxson's room. As I approach the bed, I notice Phoenix isn't in it and a horrified feeling washes over me. Oh my god did he see us having sex? Had we woken him up?

Jaxson chuckles at my horrified look. "He's out cold. I just moved him to his room." He reaches out and pulls me onto the bed and into his side. I snuggle into him, draping my arm over his chest and my leg over his. His arm wraps around my body as he kisses my head and we lay there in silence for a few seconds as I take in what happened tonight.

Looking up at Jaxson, I whisper, "They're going to be okay, right?"

He leans down and kisses me. "Yeah, they'll be fine. Colton will be calling you just to flirt tomorrow and Tanner will call just to make sure you're okay."

"They know we kissed."

Concern fills his eyes. "We're they upset?"

I shake my head. "Not at all. Tanner just asked that I won't be with anyone else and his words were 'I already have to share you with my horny twin and the old man.'"

We both chuckle. "I'm not that much older than you. Just six years."

"I'm not complaining about the extra years." He definitely knows how to use them.

"Because you know it means I have more experience." He runs his fingers under my shirt and up my side and I suck in a breath. God, he gets me hot so fast. I grab his hand and pull it out.

"They have a lot of experience as well." At least that's what I'm told and I'm hoping to find out soon. Jaxson holds me tighter against him and I listen to his heartbeat as he takes a deep breath.

"You'll get to see them soon." I know he's right, but I feel torn in half about it. I want to see them so badly but if I'm able to, that means Cyrus is gone and they'll be expecting me to come back to New York. I'm just not sure I'm ready to leave New Orleans.

Chapter Thirty-One

Jaxson

Sadie hasn't been quite herself the last few days. I can tell she's worried about Tanner and Colton, even though she talks to them at least once a day, and about what Cyrus is going to do next. Especially when I had to tell her about the first text she received. Manuel has decided to come back, which has me on high alert since his focus is all on her, watching her from the VIP area and trying to get her to come over.

With Christmas tomorrow, I want to give her a fun day filled with joy so she can forget for at least a few hours all the trouble around her. And with Nix out of day camp for the holiday, what better way to do that than to get out of the apartment and show her our city. The only way to start a day exploring New Orleans is to get some beignets and there's only one place on Bourbon Street to try.

Madame Loretta's. Sadie and Phoenix giggled the whole time they ate the sugary fried dough, making powdered sugar mustaches.

Now Phoenix is happily pulling her from booth to booth at the Christmas Art Fair and pointing out all his favorite decorations. She hasn't looked happier. They stop at a man doing a caricature drawing and I step up beside her, wrapping my arm around her waist. She looks up at me smiling and I lean down to kiss her.

"Dad, can we do it?" Phoenix points to the artist as the couple he was drawing stands.

I smile at Sadie. "What do you say?"

She looks down at an excited Phoenix. "I say yes."

"Yay." He runs up to the empty chair and Sadie is close behind him. Handing some money to the artist, I take the seat next to Sadie as Phoenix climbs into her lap and she beams at him. My son doesn't even realize how happy he just made her by choosing to sit with her. They've bonded over the last few weeks and his favorite part of his day is having breakfast with her. They even shared a waffle today before we left so their routine wasn't broken.

The artist starts drawing and my phone vibrates in my pocket. Shifting to the side, I pull it out and see a text from the extra hands I secretly brought today.

Thing 1: You have two lurkers.

Thing 2: Manuel's friend.

I push my phone back into my pocket and smile down at Sadie and Phoenix. "Everything okay?"

"Everything's perfect." Wanting to make sure this picture is perfect for her, I smile at the artist until he's done.

He rips the paper off the easel and shows it to us. "How do you like it?"

It perfectly envisions us. Sadie and Phoenix are smiling forward and I'm looking down at them. "I love it." Sadie looks in awe as she reaches out for it and brings it closer so Phoenix can get a closer look.

"So cool." Phoenix is fascinated with himself.

I chuckle. "Alright let's get up so the next people can go." I take the picture, roll it up, and the artist hands me a rubber band.

"Thank you." Sadie smiles at the artist and helps move Phoenix along. The next booth has crochet stuffed animals and Phoenix has forgotten all about the drawing as he zeroes in on a stuffed dinosaur. My phone vibrates in my pocket again and I turn my back to them as they admire the toy.

Thing 2: Lurkers have been taken care of.

Thing 1: They won't be bothering her anymore.

Good. Hopefully, they hid the bodies well. Looking back at Sadie and Phoenix, they're walking out of the booth with the dinosaur securely in Nix's hand.

"Dad, look what I got. I'm going to name him Dino." He holds it up for me.

"We haven't paid for that, Nix." I try to move him back into the booth so he can put the toy back, but Sadie stops me, touching my arm.

Her smile is soft as she looks up at me. "It's okay. I bought it for him."

"You didn't have to do that." I know Phoenix's puppy dog pout when he wants something is convincing, but she can say no.

"I wanted to. It's his gift from me."

"Yeah. My Christmas gift." Phoenix hugs the toy to his chest.

"Then he should wait until tomorrow to have it." I give him a pointed look.

"When I was growing up my grandparents always let me have one gift on Christmas Eve. This can be his." She takes my hand, linking our fingers, and the argument vanishes as she leads me to the next booth. It's a good feeling walking hand in hand with her, like I want to do it for the rest of my life.

A playground up ahead catches Phoenix's attention and he looks back at me excited, silently asking permission. Giving him a nod, he takes off running, heading directly to the monkey bars and I wrap my arm around Sadie's shoulders as we watch him. My phone vibrates in my pocket again but I don't pull it out as I look behind us, finding two familiar faces. My day with her is up. Leaning next to Sadie's ear, I whisper, "Looks like we have some visitors."

Chapter Thirty-Two

Sadie

"Looks like we have some visitors," Jaxson whispers in my ear, and I look up at him confused. He nods back over his shoulder and I look back the way we just came. I search through the crowd finding a couple of families, a small group of women, two men, and a few couples. Who is he talking about? Wait... I look back over to the two men and instantly recognize the identical men who are smiling at me.

Oh my god! I run over to them and throw myself into Colton's arms. He lifts me off the ground and I wrap my legs around his hips and kiss him. His body stiffens and I pull back from the kiss to see the healing cut above his eye pulled tight with the hint of pain on his face.

225

"Oh my god! I'm so sorry." I try to unwrap my legs from around him but his hold under my thighs keeps me in place. "I'm hurting you. Put me down."

"Not until we finish that kiss." He leans forward but I turn my face and his lips kiss my cheek. I smile at Tanner and he gives me a wink. Colton, realizing I'm not going to give in, starts lowering me back to my feet. Once my toes touch the ground, Colton turns my face back to him and kisses me silly. He kisses me like he's missed me as much as I've missed him. "I'm going to request that you greet me like that always."

I chuckle, giving him another quick kiss. "I'll work on that but I have one more greeting I need to get to." Colton slides his hands from my waist and I move over to Tanner who pulls me close and I wrap my hands around the back of his neck. "Hi." A hint of a bruise draws my attention to his hairline and I lightly brush his hair away to get a better look.

"Come here." His fingers tangle in my hair and he pulls me into a soft and intimate kiss and I forget about the worry that was bubbling up. They're here.

"It's good to see you, Blossom." He places a kiss on the tip of my nose.

"I could say the same. I'm so happy you're here." I look back at Colton. "Both of you."

"Well, you get us all to yourself for the day." He reaches out and takes one of my hands.

Tanner places his hand over mine on his chest. "Just for a day. We have a buyer's meeting in Mexico that we need to be at tomorrow afternoon."

"And decided to leave a day early to make a covert detour." Colton leans forward and kisses my shoulder.

"We're here for the date you promised us." Tanner gives me a sexy grin and I'm all for whatever he has planned.

"And we plan on using every second we have with you." Colton has a flirtatious glint in his eye like he's imagining all the dirty things he wants to do to me.

"Then we better go say goodbye to Jaxson and Phoenix." I turn around and a few people are staring at us. "Plus we're drawing an audience."

"Just wait until they see you kiss Jaxson." Colton gives me a teasing smirk as he hooks his arm over my shoulders.

Tanner links our fingers as we move across the fair to where I left Jaxson. Jaxson smiles peacefully at me as we approach, telling me he's okay with this and my heart soars. Jaxson has always known about Tanner and Colton, and Tanner and Colton know things have grown with Jaxson, but to have all three of them here and not pulling me in separate ways has my heart warming.

"So, whose idea was this?" I look at all three of them and Tanner tilts his head towards Jaxson.

Jaxson shrugs like it's no big deal. "I knew it was bothering you that you couldn't go to them, so I brought up the idea of them trying to find a way to get here."

I move out of the twins' holds and wrap my arms around his middle. "Thank you."

He runs his fingers through my hair, tilting my face up so I'm looking at him. "It was selfish really. I just wanted to see you smile again."

I can't help it, my smile grows. "I've been smiling."

"Not as bright as you are now." He leans forward and kisses the corner of my smile making it widen even more. "Now go have some fun."

"I have to say bye to Phoenix." Not wanting to call him over, I unwrap myself from Jaxson and head to the jungle gym he's playing on. "Phoenix." The little man who has become one of my favorite people looks over at me from the top of the slide. He gives me an excited wave before sitting down and pushing himself down the slide. When he gets to the bottom, he jumps off and comes running at me.

I crouch down with my arms open and he slams into me with a big hug. "Did you see me, Sadie?"

Jaxson said he wanted to see me smile, and his son always seems to be able to do that. "Of course, you slid down that slide so fast."

"Come watch me do it again." He unwraps his arms from around me and tries to pull me, but I stop him.

"Hold up, Little Man." Phoenix looks back at me. "My friends are here to see me so I'm going spend the day with them, but

I wanted to let you know I'll be home for breakfast so don't eat your waffle without me."

"I promise." He beams at me, holding up his pinky and I wrap mine around his.

"Okay, go finish playing." Phoenix runs off and I stand, turning back to the three men that have their eyes locked on me.

Jaxson has his arms crossed, showing off his muscular arms in his black long-sleeved shirt and he stands broad in his jeans looking like a bodyguard. My bodyguard. Tanner stands with his hands in the pockets of his dark dress pants with his white button up sleeves rolled up, and I imagine this is how he would look coming home from work if he had a regular job. My serious man. Colton has his hands in the front pockets of his dark jeans with his green button up, open a few buttons at the top, and a dirty smile on his face. My flirt.

I wrap my arms around Jaxson's neck as I approach and his go around my waist. "Thanks again. I'll see you tomorrow." He leans down and gives me a quick kiss.

"Enjoy yourself, Sunshine."

We release each other and I turn to Tanner and Colton. "So where are you taking me?"

Colton hooks his arm around my shoulders again and starts leading me away. "Are you ready to be swept off your feet?"

I look back over my shoulder and give Jaxson a smile before looking at Tanner who places his hand on my lower back. "I can't wait."

Chapter Thirty-Three
Sadie

It's been such a great day with Tanner and Colton. They took me on a picnic in City Park and then we strolled around the city until they pulled me into a boutique shop and told me to pick out a dress. A dress that was just as amazing as the holiday jazz cruise they took me on. There was a lot of dancing, drinking, and laughing. It was just perfect, but the night isn't over, at least I hope not based on our flirting, touching, and stolen kisses.

Tanner holds me close as we walk into their hotel lobby and I can't help my smile as I take in the lighted greenery that fills the open space along with holiday music. My smile isn't because of the lobby, it's the two men who have stolen my heart over the last few months. Being with them again makes me feel whole.

Colton brushes up next to me as we head to the elevator and runs his fingers down my exposed back along the edge of my dress.

Sparks trail down my spine following his touch that stops at the top of my ass, but I can feel it all the way to my needy core. Giving him a heated look, I bite my lip silently telling him what his touch does to me. His eyes darken as he leans closer. "I can't wait until I can remove this dress."

"It's going to look perfect laying by the door," Tanner whispers next to my ear as he pulls me into the elevator, and chills run through me at the thought of them stripping me. His fingers tangle in my hair as he presses his body to my front and captures my lips in a deep passionate kiss.

Colton steps up behind me, sandwiching me in between them as he grips my hips and skims his lips up the side of my neck. "We're going to strip you naked, lay you out on our bed, and have you screaming our names as you come."

Their words alone have me hot but adding in their touch and kiss, I would let them strip me here in this elevator. Tanner starts kissing down the other side of my neck, but before my whimper escapes my lips, Colton is sealing his lips to mine. Reaching back, I tangle my fingers in his hair and he smirks against my lips as he kisses me with hunger.

The ding of the elevator barely registers in my foggy lust, but Colton pulls away and I pout at the loss. He chuckles and pulls me with him out of the elevator to the double doors right across from it. "Are you desperate for us, Dove?"

I reach out for him instead of answering as the three of us walk through the doorway into their penthouse suite. As soon as the door clicks closed behind us, the tension between us heightens and I hold my breath, waiting for what they're going to do. In unison they close the distance between us, Colton in front and Tanner behind me. Goosebumps break over my skin as they push my dress down my arms, letting it fall off my body, leaving me in just my black lace thong and heels.

Tanner presses in behind me and grips my hair, holding it to the side, giving him better access to my neck. "You're beautiful, Blossom. So sweet." He swipes his tongue over where my neck meets my shoulder and I moan tilting my head more. "So loving."

Tanner runs his fingers up my spine and a shiver runs through me as Colton tilts my chin up towards him. "So perfect for us."

Colton lifts me off the ground, bridal style, crashing his lips to mine, and carries me through the suite to set me down at the end of the bed. "Ours."

I raise on my toes and skim my lips over his. "Yours."

His hand goes to the back of my neck, holding me in place as he closes the distance between us. I lose myself in his heated kiss, loving the way his lips feel against mine and I want more of him against me. Sliding my hands up his chest and over his shoulders I push his blazer off. It hits the floor as I start unbuttoning his shirt, but I must not be quick enough because Colton takes over. Some of his buttons pop off as he pulls his shirt open and I chuckle at his eagerness.

My hands run over his bare chest, feeling his warm skin under my palm and I lean forward and press a kiss over his heart. Looking up at him, I want to tell him he owns a piece of mine but he's not the only one. I turn towards Tanner to find him shirtless with his pants undone, and for the first time, I see the bruises that scatter up his left side and across his chest. My heart hurts seeing the damage of their accident and I reach out, softly brushing my fingers over the darkened skin.

"I'm fine. It looks worse than it feels." He wraps his arms around me, pulling me against his chest, and I melt into him as his lips cover mine. His hands slide to my ass and grip it as he presses his hardened cock against my stomach. I hum against his lips, loving his need for me, and I reach in between us, sliding my hand into his boxers. Before I can wrap my hand around his erection, he grabs my wrist, stopping me.

"Not yet, Blossom." He pulls my hand out of his pants and kisses my fingers. "I want to watch you first." He turns me back to Colton and nips at my earlobe. "I'm going to watch my brother worship your body." His hands slide over my skin, not touching me where I want him, as he tells me what's going to happen and I start to pant with need. "Make you come multiple times. He's going to show you how you're the only one he wants."

"And you?" I'm breathless from Tanner's words and touch and Colton standing in front of me, looking at me like I'm a dessert he's been craving as he strokes himself. His abs are tight as his arm flexes with every stroke and it has my mouth watering for him.

"You fill my thoughts every second of every day." His words have my heart soaring and I want to pull him into a kiss to show him how much I know what he means, but he pulls away as Colton steps into me.

Colton smirks down at me. "There is no turning back after this, Dove. I'm never letting you go."

I smirk at him. "Promise?"

"You know it. Now get that perfect ass on the bed." I step out of my heels and give him my back as I climb onto the bed. His hand runs over my ass with me on all fours and I smile back at him.

"Let's get these off." He hooks his fingers into the side of my thong and pulls them down my thighs, and I crawl the rest of the way out of them. Turning onto my back, I lay out with my legs straight and prop myself up with my elbows. Tanner has taken a seat in the armchair by the french doors leading to the balcony with his dick in his hand as he slowly strokes himself. Seeing him like this has me licking my top lip. I want to crawl over to him and take him into my mouth. He smirks at me like he knows exactly what I'm thinking.

Looking at Colton, I find him staring down at me. "Are you going to just stare at me? If you both like to watch, just let a girl know and I'll get myself off." I slide my hand down my stomach as I widen my legs.

"Don't you dare, Dove." Colton climbs on the bed, over me, grabs my wrists, and holds them over my head with one hand. "I would love to watch you get yourself off, but let's save that for one of our fun late night calls." His fingers skim over my sex before pushing one and then two fingers into me and I arch my back with a moan, taking his fingers deeper. "I'll be the one making you come tonight." He presses his lips to mine.

I spread my legs on either side of his body and rock my hips, riding his fingers as he pumps them in and out of me. Colton lets go of my wrists as he slides his hand down my body to my hip, holding me in place. His kisses follow down the middle of my body until his shoulders are in between my thighs and he smiles up at me as he wraps his arms underneath my thighs and grips my hips. "I bet you taste as good as you look."

"Stop talking and find out." I reach out, running my fingers through his hair, and push his head closer to my needy core. His lips vibrate against my sensitive clit as he chuckles and I hum out as I feel the pleasure all the way to my toes. Colton doesn't let up as he takes a long taste, running his tongue from my needy hole to my throbbing clit and flicking it.

He hums against my clit and I arch my back, loving the feeling. "Oh god, more."

"I'm going to give you so much more." Colton's grip on my hips tightens as he pulls me closer to him and focuses his attention on my bundle of nerves. With each flick of his tongue, my pleasure builds higher and higher and I want the release Colton is bringing me close to.

"Colton, please," I beg, not sure what I'm asking for, but Colton gives it to me. His tongue rolls over my clit as he pushes two fingers inside of me and I explode all over his tongue and fingers, screaming out his name. My afterglow has me smiling up at him as he covers my body with his and I run my fingers through his messy hair.

"You definitely know what to do with your tongue." I reach in between us and wrap my hand around the base of his erection. "Now show me what you can do with this."

His lips press against mine as I slide my hand up his cock and rub my thumb over the tip, collecting his precum, before sliding it back down. A squeal escapes me as Colton rolls us so he's underneath me. "How about you show me what you can do with it?" He thrusts up into my hand as he gives me a cocky grin.

"You want me to… ride… your… cock?" I lean forward and place kisses down his chest and over his bruises as I say those last three words. I rock my hips over his erection drawing a deep groan, and a wicked smile pulls across my lips, loving the way he wants me. I continue to spread my warmth over his cock, waiting for him to tell me he wants me sinking down on his dick, but it doesn't come from him.

"Fuck yourself on his dick, Blossom. Show us how you want it." A shiver runs through me as I look back at Tanner and slowly slide myself on Colton's cock. Tanner leans forward naked with his erection hard against his stomach, holding my stare as I take every inch of his brother.

"Give him a show, Dove. Perform for him," Colton whispers in my ear. Looking back at Colton, I wrap my arms around his neck and pull him into a kiss. Colton's hands run down my sides and I rock my hips slowly, matching our kiss. "You were made for me, Dove."

A moan slips from my lips as I lift my hips, rising up his cock to the tip and lowering myself back down slowly. Colton kisses down my neck as my breasts rub against his chest and his grip on my hips tightens as he sets our pace.

"I haven't worshiped these yet." He licks in between my breasts. "They look so beautiful bouncing as you take my cock." My nipples harden at his gaze as he runs his hands up my sides to my breasts and cups underneath them, pushing them up. His eyes darken as he flicks his tongue over the pointed tip and wraps his lips around it, giving a gentle pull.

Pleasure courses through me and I let my head fall back, bracing myself against Colton's thighs, allowing him full access to my bouncing breasts. With the new angle, his dick hits me in the best way and I roll my hips as I ride him in a slow but deep way taking every inch of him. I lose myself in all things Colton. His cock stretches me perfectly. His roaming touch. His mouth on my breasts. His dirty mouth.

"Fuck, Dove." I clench around his cock as my body vibrates with pleasure. "You feel so good squeezing around me. Are you going to come all over my cock?"

"Yes. Yes. Yes," I chant as I ride him faster, chasing my own high, and when my orgasm crashes through me, I grip Colton's hair and pull him to a kiss. His mouth covers my screams as he grips my hips and thrusts up into me. My orgasm only seems to intensify as he continues to fuck me until it's just too much and I scream out his name and let it all go.

His arms wrap around me, holding me up, and I feel him release inside me as he groans out, "Fuck… Stella." I wrap my arms around him as I rest my forehead against his, catching my breath. His hands run up and down my back, soothing me, and I open my eyes to find him looking up at me. "You're my only one, Dove."

My heart warms with love at his words, and I lean forward giving him a loving kiss. "I'm yours, Colton. You own a piece of my heart. Please don't break it."

Colton knows the last person I gave my heart to abused it for his own wants, so when he says, "I would never," I know he's telling me the truth.

Chapter Thirty-Four

Tanner

Finding Cyrus is taking longer than I wanted, which means it's taking longer for Stella to come home. Before all this, I knew she was special to me. But when she left, something deep inside of me was missing, and having her here I feel complete. Watching her with Colton, I know he feels the same. The way he looks at her tells me he's fallen for her too.

I lean back in the chair slowly stroking my erection as Colton and Stella whisper to each other. They hold each other close and for the first time ever, I feel a hint of jealousy of my brother. Not that I don't want him to have her, but more I want her wrapped around me too. As if she knows what I'm thinking, she looks back and smiles at me.

Lifting my free hand, I hook my finger at her, calling her over. Her smile brightens before she looks back at Colton and gives him a quick kiss. She crawls off his lap and slowly walks over to me. I grip the arms of the chairs fighting the need to reach out for her, allowing her control. Her knees straddle my thighs as she climbs onto the chair and slides her hands up my chest, and I lose my battle, gripping her hips, pulling her down so her heat slides along my cock.

"Did you like the show?" She smiles at me, rocking her hips along my erection as she lovingly runs her fingers through my hair.

"I could watch you all day, Blossom." Gripping the back of her neck, I pull her into a kiss as I show her how desperately I need her.

"I have a secret I want to tell you," she whispers against my lips and then kisses along my jaw until her lips skim my ear. "I like watching too."

Well, fuck me. So many ideas fly through my mind because I plan on exploring this kink with her. She leans back to see my reaction and my grip on her hip tightens as I thrust up against her. "I knew you were made for me."

I stand from the chair, gripping the back of her thighs, and carry her to the bathroom. Setting her down in front of the vanity, I press into her back as our eyes connect in the mirror. "Watch me fuck you, Stella." I look to the full length mirror to our left and smile as it perfectly reflects her ass against my cock. Stella follows my gaze and her heated smile has me ready to slide in deep. I kiss up her spine as my hands slide down her arms to her wrists, where I wrap my fingers around them and move her hands to the edge of the counter.

Her eyes connect with mine again in the mirror over the sink as she's bent over and the need in them matches mine. I grip my erection and run it along her sex, covering my cock in her slickness. "I can't wait to explore this with you, Blossom."

Slowly I press into her entrance and her warmth swallows me, pulling an animalistic growl out of me. "When you're back in New York, I know the perfect club." Pulling out to my tip, I thrust back in and she moans out. "I'm going to find one here too. I can't wait to feel how wet you'll get watching someone else scream out in pleasure." I grip her hips as I pick up my pace and I love how her breasts sway with my thrusts. "Your body was meant to be viewed by only our eyes."

She seems to melt at my words, and I grip her hair, turning her face to the full length mirror as I fuck into her with a need I've been suppressing for months. She pushes back into me, meeting each of my thrusts with a moan and I'm losing control. Letting go of her hair, I lean forward, pressing kisses to her shoulder as I reach around her and rub circles over her clit. She tightens around me and I nearly come from the amazing feeling.

"Come for me, Blossom. You have me ready to explode, but I need to feel you come around me first."

"I'm so close, Tanner. You feel so good," she moans as she lifts her head and our eyes connect in the mirror.

I lose control with our eyes connected as I fuck into her, drawing out both our pleasures. Her orgasm shows first in her eyes as they squint slightly and then a vibration runs through her as she screams out and her grip around my cock has me coming right along with her. Wrapping one arm around Stella and bracing my other on the counter, I hold the both of us up as our combined orgasms make us weak.

As my high subsides, I kiss up Stella's back until I reach her neck and then I scoop her up into my arms. My lips press to hers as I carry her to the shower and turn the warm water on. Setting her on her feet, I hold her to me and place kisses all over her face. "I love you, Blossom."

Her eyes widen in shock at my admission, but she smiles up at me as I wait for her response. She rises on her toes and presses her lips to mine. "I love you, too." I seal my lips back to hers and push her against the glass shower wall.

"Can I come in now?" Colton's voice has me pulling back from our kiss as we both chuckle.

"Yeah."

Colton smirks at us and I know he heard what we said to each other, but he doesn't seem bothered. He pulls her with him under the showerhead and grabs the body wash. "Let us take care of you and then we can snuggle up in bed."

As we work together to wash her up, Stella's exhaustion starts to overcome her as her eyes start to droop. Colton takes her in his arms, carries her out of the shower, and sets her on the counter to dry her off. She rests her head on his shoulder as he does it and I wrap a towel around my waist. Once he's done, I step in and carry her to bed. She climbs into the middle and Colton and I each take a side of her. Colton wraps himself around her from behind as she curls into my side and I run my fingers through her wet hair.

"I've missed you guys. I wish you could stay." She slides her hand across my chest, resting it over my heart, and I place my hand over hers.

"This will be over soon and you won't need to hide anymore." Colton kisses her bare shoulder as his arm goes around her waist.

"What if I'm not ready to leave New Orleans?" I know she's talking about Jaxson and Phoenix.

"Wherever you are, we'll find a way to be with you. Don't worry about it now, Blossom."

"Nothing can keep us away from you, Dove." Stella doesn't say anything as she slips off to sleep.

I look at my brother and he gives me a nod, agreeing we'll do anything for her, even if it's stepping down as Killian's Chiefs. We'll always be a part of the Murphy Clan with being the heads of the Flynn family, but not being at Killian's side gives us more freedom to be away from New York. But like I told Stella, it's not something to worry about right now.

Chapter Thirty-Five

Sadie

Waking with the sun shining through the white curtains and being in Colton and Tanner's arms is one of my new favorite ways to wake up. A smile forms as I stare up at Tanner who's still sound asleep. He looks so peaceful as he dreams. Carefully rolling over, I turn in Colton's hold to find him still asleep as well. He looks like he's having the best dream based on the cocky grin he has on his face.

Not wanting to wake them, I carefully slide out of their holds and climb off the end of the bed. Looking back at them, I have to hold back a laugh at Colton holding onto Tanner's arm. He's not going to like waking up like that.

Leaving them to sleep, I head to the bathroom to get ready. Dressed in my clothes from yesterday, I head back into the bedroom to say goodbye. I don't want to leave them, but I made a promise to Phoenix.

Moving to Colton's side of the bed, I lean over him as he now lays on his back and place a kiss on his cheek. As I pull back, his arms wrap around me and pull me on top of him, rolling so I'm once again in between the both of them.

"You better not be sneaking out on us, Dove. It's Christmas." Colton holds me close as he nuzzles his face into my breasts.

"I didn't want to wake you." I run my fingers through his hair. "Merry Christmas!"

"Where were you going?" Tanner's sleepy voice sounds behind me as I feel him press against my back. I look back at him, mouthing the holiday greeting before he presses his lips to mine.

"Nowhere. She's going nowhere. I need my Christmas gift." Colton's hands slide up my shirt and I try to wiggle away from him.

"Stop. I promised Little Man I'd have breakfast with him."

Colton smiles up at me and I know a bad joke is about to come out of his mouth. "If Jaxson isn't enough for you, Dove, you can always have mine for breakfast."

Tanner groans behind me and I shake my head in disappointment. "That's gross. Phoenix. I'm talking about Phoenix."

Colton gives me a cheeky grin. "Well, Jaxson's little man did create the Little Man."

"Too much Colton. Just too much." He chuckles and I can't help but join him. With him distracted, I roll us so he's on his back and I'm straddling him. "I really have to go."

"Give us ten minutes, Blossom." Tanner sits up and gives me a quick kiss. "We want every second possible with you."

Colton sits up as well and kisses me. "And we still need to give you what we brought you." He lifts me off his lap and I sit cross legged in the middle of the bed as they move around the room.

I tilt my head to the side, confused that they brought me something. "What did you bring me?"

Colton smiles at me as he pulls on some boxers. "Just some things you might be missing."

"We had the girls grab some stuff from your apartment." Tanner walks out of the bathroom with a travel bathroom bag in his hands and his sweatpants hanging low off his hips. God, he looks good. "My eyes are up here." Tanner points to his face and I take my time scanning up his body to his face.

"Yes, but your eyes aren't the only mouthwatering thing about you."

He smirks at me. "Don't start something you can't finish."

"Stay another night and I can finish it." I'd love another night with him. This time I would worship them.

"I wish we could, but we can't move this meeting." Tanner leans forward and gives me another kiss.

"Alright, I'm ready." Colton comes out of the bathroom dressed in sweats and a t-shirt and throws his things into a bag. "Put a shirt on man, we have to go."

Colton throws the shirt Tanner had out at him and Tanner catches it and pulls it over his hand. With his bag over his shoulder,

Colton comes over to me and holds out his hand for me. "Your chariot awaits."

I chuckle as I slide my hand in his and allow him to pull me up and off the bed. I follow Colton out of the room with Tanner close behind me.

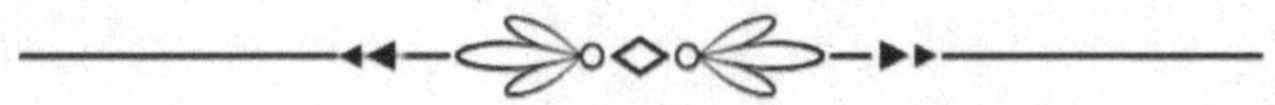

Phoenix is waiting for me, in the living room, playing with Legos, with two Eggo waffles sitting on a plate beside him. "Merry Christmas, Little Man. Sorry I'm late." Jaxson's leaning against the island as I walk by and I stop to give him a quick kiss. "Merry Christmas."

"Merry Christmas, Sunshine." He swats my ass as I continue past him and I playfully glare at him as I walk towards his son. Sitting across from Phoenix, with his Legos in between us, I grab a waffle as I watch Jaxson, Colton, and Tanner head downstairs. What's that all about?

"Cheers." Phoenix draws my attention back to him as he taps our waffles together.

"Cheers." I smile down at Phoenix and enjoy my time with him. He shows me the massive Lego set Santa brought him, telling me all the things he can build. We're working on a car when the guys come back up and join us.

Tanner kisses me on top of my head as he goes to the chair and Colton lifts me off the ground and sets me in his lap as he sits on the couch. "Hey."

I try to get off his lap to continue working on the car, but Colton holds me to him and whispers, "You can help him later. I only get so much time with you." I stop fighting his hold and melt into him.

Phoenix looks between all of us, confused. "Why are you kissing them when you kiss Dad?"

"Oh..." Well, that wasn't expected. I look to Jaxson, who's sitting next to me, for help, but he's too busy holding back his laugh just like Colton and Tanner. This isn't funny. I elbow Colton on his uninjured side, making him cough.

Phoenix keeps his gaze on me and I smile down at him. "I know it's confusing because it's expected that I only kiss your dad, but what I have with Colton and Tanner is special too."

Phoenix perks up. "I'm special too, right?"

"Yes, Little Man. You're the best kind of special. You're my favorite kid of all time." I lean forward wanting to hug him, but Colton holds me in place with a playful smile.

Phoenix beams up at me and then his dad. "I'm more special than you." I cover my mouth with my hand to muffle my chuckle but Colton and Tanner both let out their laughs.

"He's my favorite too," Colton announces as he holds his fist out to Phoenix and the little boy who has stolen a piece of my heart jumps up and bumps his little fist against it.

Jaxson stands from the couch. "Alright, Nix, it's time to get ready. Grandma is waiting to celebrate Christmas with you."

"Yayy." Phoenix runs to his room to put on the outfit Jaxson has already set out.

"We're going to need to leave soon too, Dove." Colton places a kiss on my shoulder and I give him a sad smile.

"Come on. Let's say goodbye downstairs without young eyes watching." Tanner walks over to me and holds out his hand. I place mine in his and Colton lifts me from his lap and sets me on my feet.

None of us move quickly down the stairs, but when we step off the last step, Tanner pulls me against him and holds me tight. I wrap my arms around his waist. "I'm going to miss you so much more now."

"I'm going to miss you too, Blossom. We'll be back as soon as we can."

I rest my chin on his chest and look up at him. "I love you, Tanner."

He slides his fingers into my hair. "I love you, too." His lips slide over mine in a kiss I want to last forever, but unfortunately, it doesn't. Tanner loosens his hold on me as another hand touches my lower back and I lean into Colton's touch. Tanner places a kiss on my nose before releasing me and Colton pulls me into him.

He tilts my chin up and smiles down at me. "Give me a smile, Dove. It's the only thing that will make me feel better." I put a smile on my face, but it doesn't quite feel real. "Nope, that won't work." He slides his hand down my sides and starts tickling me.

I squeal out as I try to get away but his hold on me is solid. As I wiggle in his arms, my cheeks start to hurt from the wide smile on my face and I look up at Colton. "I love you."

Colton stops tickling me and smiles brightly. "A smile and a I love you. You just made my week." He leans forward and skims his lips over mine. "I love you too, Dove." Pushing up on my toes, I press my lips to his and show him how much I love him for all that he is. Wrapping my arms around his neck, I press my body against him and his hands slide down my back and grabs my ass.

"Nix is coming in 3..." Jaxson calls from up the stairs. "2..." I pull back from our kiss. "1..." Colton moves his hands from my ass just as Phoenix jumps off the last step.

"Boo." He chuckles with glee as he runs past us and heads outside with Jaxson right on heels to get him situated in the car.

The door closes behind them and I pout as I reach out for Tanner and he takes my hand in his as Colton hooks his arm over my shoulder. "I guess it's time for you to go."

We head to the door and as Colton pushes it open, I hear yelling. "How dare you go after my men?" Colton and Tanner push the door wide open and step in front of me with their guns raised and I see Manuel pointing a gun at Jaxson. I gasp as I step back and fear washes over me as I search for Phoenix. Finding him hiding behind the front of Jaxson's truck next to me, I move over to him and hold him behind me.

"I know you killed them. They were following her." He points to me and a sense of uneasiness washes over me knowing

Manuel has men watching me. "They've missed their last two check-ins."

"You need to leave, Manuel." I peek through the Tanner Colton wall to see Jaxson also holding a gun at his side. "I told you to leave her alone."

Manuel seems to realize he's not at the advantage anymore and starts backing up. "You can't stop this, Jaxson. Watch your back." He walks backwards towards the busy streets with his gun aimed in our direction. Once he hits the sidewalk, he takes off running and out of sight.

I stand from the front of Jaxson's truck and step out with Phoenix clutching my leg. My three men turn to us as they put their guns behind them and Phoenix lets go of me and runs to Jaxson. "Dad."

Jaxson lifts Phoenix in his arms and I can hear him crying into his dad's shirt. Colton and Tanner surround me as I watch Jaxson with his son. "Are you okay?"

I don't answer as I watch the little boy I care about cry because he's scared, and he's only scared because Manuel wants me for something.

Chapter Thirty-Six

Colton

Manuel ruined our goodbye with Stella. Instead of having a goodbye with loving kisses and sexy promises, we said goodbye to her as she climbed into Jaxson's truck with a look of guilt on her face. Guilt she shouldn't be feeling. Guilt I won't be feeling as I torture screams out of him for even thinking he can look at her, let alone sending men to watch her. To take her.

Anger builds inside me with each mile we drive away from her. "Manuel needs to be handled sooner rather than later." Tanner grips the steering wheel tighter as he quickly glances at me.

"If we weren't twins, I'd be worried that you could read my mind."

"We don't need to be twins for me to see how much you want to strangle him with how tight your fists are." He nods down at my hands on my legs.

I release my fists and stretch out my fingers, seeing red nail imprints on my palm. "What do you say we make a pit stop after our meeting on the way back? We're the ones who made his two men disappear, let's do him the same favor."

"We can't without talking to the Russos. He's their underboss."

"Good thing we're friends then." I reach into my pocket and pull out my phone. There's only one brother I'm calling for this. Matteo.

The crazy fool handles their personnel but he's also the easiest one to rile up especially when it's about the safety of his girl, our girl, or any girl. He's Riona's knight whenever she has a new lead about a sex trafficking ring, kidnapping, child abuse, or sexual assault.

"What's up, Colton? Shouldn't you be with your girl instead of calling me?" Killian's the only one who's supposed to know that we didn't fly straight to Mexico.

There's only one way he knows. Ash told Ri. "You shouldn't know where I am so maybe Ri should learn to keep some secrets."

He chuckles like what I said is ridiculous. "Why are you calling me?"

"I'm just giving you a courtesy call to let you know by tomorrow morning you'll have one less underboss."

Matteo growls. "What did Manuel do now?" Oh, so he knows he's a problem.

"He pulled a gun on us all this morning, ranting about his men being missing, men we killed." Irritation fills my voice just thinking about the idiot.

"Well, that's pretty minor considering we're looking into his possible involvement in sex trafficking with his interest in Stella."

Minor, really? "It was in front of Phoenix and Stella and she's blaming herself."

Matteo takes a deep breath. "Look, I'm sorry, man. I know what it feels like to want to rip apart the man who's hurting your girl, but you can't do anything with him yet. If we're right, Riona wants the whole organization and he'll lead us to them."

Why wait? We all have ways to pull the truth out of people. "We could torture it out of him." He sighs and I know I'm not getting his approval. "Keep him away from her. If he so much as looks at her, I'm ending him."

"Understood. It won't be me you'll be fighting if you don't at least get a location before ending him."

Oh, I'll get something for Riona. "Trust me, it won't be quick."

I hang up with a curse as Tanner pulls into the airfield. "Doesn't sound like we're returning here in a few hours."

"We're not. I'll give Ri a week and then I'll force the answers she wants from him before I slaughter him like a pig." A week to plan all the depraved things I'll do to him.

"Then I guess we can tell Stella that we'll be back soon."

Two positives.

Chapter Thirty-Seven

Sadie

I wish I had the resilience of a six year old. After spending Christmas at his grandma's, Phoenix was his bubbly self without any of the fear I saw that morning. I guess the presents helped. Me, even days later, I still have the lingering feeling something bad is going to happen and it's all going to be because of me. I've been distancing myself from Jaxson for the last couple of days because of it. I know he knows it, because whenever he's close, he pulls me into his arms and kisses me until I melt into him.

But Jaxson isn't the only one I'm pushing away. I've stopped answering Tanner and Colton's calls and I'll only talk to them through text which has them more concerned each day, but I need to keep all of them safe and at a distance.

The only thing about separating myself from them is it makes it harder and harder to be happy. I'm so used to Colton's flirty jokes,

Tanner's smile as he listens to me talk about my day, and the feel of Jaxson's arms around me in bed that without those things, I feel numb. So numb that I exhaust myself everyday dancing in the empty club trying to feel anything good, but it's only sadness and pain that I'm able to express.

The music playing over the speakers is slow and haunting and I twist my body around the pole, transitioning from trick to trick without letting go like I'm trapped to it. Trapped like how Cyrus wants me. Trapped by the obsession Manuel has. Trapped with fear that the people I love the most are going to get hurt.

"Sadie. Sadie. Sadie." I'm jolted out of my spiraling thoughts to find myself hanging upside down and spinning. The only person I can't seem to keep away from because he's the brightness to my dark days comes running through the empty club with Jaxson behind, carrying his backpack.

"Wow, cool." Phoenix looks at me in awe as I right myself on the pole and slide down.

"Hi, Little Man. How was day camp?"

"Look at what I drew." Phoenix holds up a crayon drawn picture and I squat down at the edge of the stage to get a closer look. He drew him and me with different colored dots bundled together next to us. "It's us at the Farmer's Market." Ahh, so the dots are fruits and vegetables.

"This is very good." I smile at him and he beams up at me.

"I can't wait for tomorrow. We're going to have so much fun." This little boy can always bring a smile to my face.

"Yes, we are."

"Can I fly?" Phoenix bounces on his toes as he looks between me and the pole I was just on.

"You want to spin?" He nods excitedly.

"No hands." He holds his hands out and twirls.

I giggle at his enthusiasm. "You have to ask your dad."

I look up at Jaxson who's sitting in one of the front row chairs and he smiles at me with a nod. "You need to listen to everything Sadie says though. No fooling around."

He nods several times. "I promise."

Jaxson is silent for a second acting like he's thinking and Phoenix is vibrating with anticipation. "Alright then."

"Yay." He jumps in excitement and then turns to me, holding up his arms.

I reach out, grab him under his arms, and lift him onto the stage. "Jaxson, can you please get the foam pad? Just to be safe." Jaxson stands with a nod knowing I want to make sure nothing will happen to Phoenix.

He disappears backstage and I look to Phoenix. "Alright Little Man, I have one rule. You only move when I say. This is all about balance and if you move without me saying, we could fall. Okay?"

He nods with his eyes focused on me. "Let's do a little test spin." I sit down on the floor facing the pole with Phoenix in front of me. "I want you to grab the pole here." I touch the pole right at his eye level and his little hands don't even close all the way around it.

"Now you're going to keep your hands there and jump up and wrap your legs around the pole like it's a rope swing." I place my hands on his waist. "I got you. Are you ready?"

"Yeah." The skin between his eyebrows wrinkle from his focus on the pole.

"On 3. 1…2... 3." Phoenix jumps up and I lift him holding him up until he wraps his little legs around on the pole. "Alright squeeze your legs tight." Phoenix makes a cute grunting sound as he tries to squeeze his legs as tight as possible. Tentatively, I loosen my hold on him, testing his grip, and he doesn't slide down.

"Alright hold tight I'm going to spin you." I grip the pole underneath him and twist it. His giggles are so infectious that I'm laughing with him, but he gets distracted and starts sliding and I grab him around his waist. "Okay. Feet on the floor." Phoenix does as I say and then lets go of the pole as well.

"Looks fun." Jaxson is standing next to us with the mat behind him. I stand up and pull Phoenix back and against my legs so Jaxson can wrap the mat around the pole.

With the mat down, I let go of Phoenix and he wobbles as he steps on it and reaches for the pole. "Let's fly."

I chuckle as I step up behind him and in my peripheral, I see Jaxson jump off the stage. "I'm going to pick you up and I want you to grab the pole like before. Hands and legs and squeeze really tight. Don't let go until I say."

He nods with a cute serious look. "Got it. Don't let go."

"Good. You ready?"

"Yes!" With my hands on his waist, I squat behind him. "Jump for me in 3... 2... 1." Phoenix jumps and I use the momentum to lift him so he's in front of my face. "Okay. Tight."

He does his little grunt again and I move quickly before he starts slipping. With my hand above his, I push off the ground to the side and swing around the pole so I'm facing him and we're spinning slowly.

"Hold tight." I remind him as I get myself up the pole and underneath Phoenix. My hold mimics his as I take his weight with my thighs clenched and my ankles lock around the pole. "Alright, Phoenix, you can relax your hold, but don't let go." His death grip loosens as he smiles at me.

"You ready to fly?" He beams as he nods excitedly. "I need you to slowly straighten out your legs towards my face. One leg at a time and your hands stay where they are."

He stays very focused as he does what I say and I shift my hands lower so I'm leaning back. Once his legs are straight, I say, "Cross your ankles." He does as I ask and I lay an arm over his legs and grip his shorts to secure him. "Lay back slowly, Little Man, and fly."

Phoenix lays back on my thighs and spreads his arms wide giggling. "I'm flying."

I chuckle at his happiness as we very slowly spin around in circles until we've lost the momentum and stop spinning. "You want to drop now, like a roller coaster?"

He tilts his head up with wide eyes. "Yes!"

"I need you to grab onto my shorts and loosen your legs around the pole." He does what I ask and I shift my hold, so my legs are straight out and I'm holding the pole above and below us. Phoenix relaxes against my body. "Let's scare your dad. Hold on."

I loosen my hold on the pole and we drop a few feet as Phoenix squeals and I hear a curse from Jaxson. Tightening my grip again, we stop just above the stage and laughter erupts from me as I relax into the mat. That was a lot more fun than I thought it would be.

Phoenix laughs with me as Jaxson jumps up onto the stage. "You scared the shit out of me." I hear the chuckle in his voice and I smile up at him.

"Gotcha."

Phoenix yells, "Gotcha Dad," as he sits up and holds up his arms. Jaxson leans forward and picks him up and sets him on his feet.

"You sure did." He shakes his head at his son. "How about you say thank you to Sadie and head upstairs?"

Phoenix throws himself at me, tackling me back to the ground in a hug. "Thank you. Thank you. Thank you. It was so much fun."

I hug him back chuckling. "You're welcome. You can fly with me anytime."

He stands back up and starts to run off stage but Jaxson yells after him, "Don't run."

Phoenix slows down and disappears down the back hallway.

"You made his year." He holds his hand out to me and I place mine in his and let him pull me up. I fall into his chest and he wraps his arms around me. "You've made my year too."

My heart hurts at his words because I can't tell him how much he has changed my life and keep him at a distance. I reach out, placing my hand on his cheek, and he leans into my touch. "I should go shower."

I step out of his hold and head upstairs. Phoenix is in his room when I walk by and I close the bathroom door behind me and stare at myself in the mirror. Tears fill my eyes from the pain of walking away from him and I look away, not being able to face myself right now.

Removing my clothes, I step under the showerhead and let the tears fall down my face with the water. Arms wrap around my waist and I'm pulled back against a tall frame. "You can keep trying to pull away from me, but I know you don't really want to. Stop trying, I'm not letting you go." Jaxson places a kiss on my shoulder and I turn in his hold and wrap my arms around his waist.

"You should." Keeping my forehead pressed to his chest, I close my eyes, hating that my shit is following me. "You're just going to get hurt. Phoenix was crying a couple of days ago because Manuel had a gun pointed at you over his obsession with me."

"That's not your fault, Sunshine. Phoenix is fine." His hands run slowly up my back and I internally fight the soothing feeling.

"You could've been killed."

He tilts my face up to his. "Manuel was just trying to scare me."

"Well, he scared me."

He swipes his thumbs over my cheeks, wiping away my tears as he stares into my eyes. "I promised you I'd keep you safe. Let me keep my promise." I rise on my toes and press my lips to his. He tangles his fingers in my hair and holds me to him as he takes over the kiss and pushes me against the wall. "Plus I hear women love heroes."

I chuckle. "How about you let me show you how much I love heroes." I kiss down his neck, pushing him back to the far wall, and continue down his body as I kneel in front of him.

"I'm loving this appreciation so far."

"Just you wait." I lick up the underside of his hardening cock before wrapping my lips around his tip and sliding my hand down his length. My lips follow my hand as I take him in my mouth, all the way to the back of my throat. He holds my hair back away from my face and I look up at him as I suck up his length and then take him again tightening my lips around him. His eyes roll into the back of his head as he jerks in my mouth and I moan at how sexy he looks.

"Fuck, Sunshine." He bucks forward hitting the back of my throat and his uncontrolled need has me clenching my thighs together as a rush of pleasure courses through me. I grip his ass as he tries to pull back and take him further down my throat, wanting him to take what he wants.

"You want me to fuck your face, Sunshine? Use you for my pleasure?"

With our eyes connected, I moan my answer and fire burns in his eyes. His grip in my hair tightens to almost painful, holding my head still, and he thrusts into my mouth. Yes. This is what I want.

He fucks my mouth over and over, chasing his own orgasm just like he said he would. My own need for his and my release has me kneading his balls in one hand while my other slides down my body to my aching clit. I jolt at the first touch to my clit with a groan and Jaxson curses. "You have me so close, Sadie. Are you going to take my come, swallow it down your pretty throat?"

I moan my pleas as I tighten my lips around his cock and suck him deeper. "Look at you so needy. Loving every second of giving yourself to me." I rub my clit faster, chasing my orgasm that's on the edge of bursting.

"I want you to come as you taste me sliding down your throat." My eyes roll into the back of my head as Jaxson thrusts into my mouth, again hitting the back of my throat and forcing me to swallow around him as his orgasm shoots down my throat. His taste covers my tongue as he pulls back and I come with a deep moan that has me breathless.

Jaxson lifts me off of my knees and slams his lips to mine as I'm still swallowing his release but he doesn't seem to care. My back hits the shower wall as my legs wrap around his waist. I can feel Jaxson's dick hardening against my still needy core and it's like my body takes over as I rock my hips, feeling aftershocks from my orgasm.

"Dad!" Phoenix calling out to Jaxson and knocking on the door is like a bucket of ice water being poured over us.

I look at Jaxson wide eyed, hoping he locked the door because there was no way I was explaining this to Phoenix. "What, Nix?"

"You said you'd play Legos with me." His whine is easily heard through the door.

Jaxson sighs as he rests his head on my shoulder. "I'll be out in a few minutes."

Silence is the response on the other side of the door and I unwrap myself from him as he holds my waist.

"Go." I step away from him.

"We'll finish this later." He gives me another kiss before stepping out of the shower and wrapping a towel around his waist.

"Can't wait." I give him a flirtatious grin before turning into the warm water and grabbing my body wash.

"Hey, Sunshine." I look back at him. "I'll be your hero any day."

Chapter Thirty-Eight

Sadie

The club has been busy tonight with it being New Year's
Eve. There was Russo business at the start that had us all on edge.
For me, it was Manuel's presence, for the others it was having all the
underbosses here and not wanting to upset them. I guess when
you're friends with the woman their bosses love, all apprehension
goes away. So, when their meeting ended about an hour ago, you
could almost hear the collective sigh of relief, but I wasn't a part of
it. The other underbosses left but Manuel stayed, lounging back in
his normal seat. And he didn't sit alone for long. His friends slowly
started joining him.

I stopped looking over there a while ago even though I know
he's been tracking me as I move up and down the long bar. Penny
walks up to the side of the bar and I smile over at her. They're about
to have a shift change with the current dancers and waitresses

switching so Penny is holding down the floor. "Can I have three bourbons, two Jack and Cokes, and a vodka martini?"

"Yeah, I got you." Starting with the martini, I pour the vodka, vermouth, and olive brine into a shaker with ice and pop the top on it. I feel my phone vibrate in my pocket so as I shake the martini, I pull it out hoping it's a text from Colton or Tanner. They're at Killian and Aisling's wedding and I've been begging for photos since I can't be there.

Unknown: Sadie is such a pretty name. It's like you're calling to me. You want to be my Lady.

As I read the message everything around me seems to stop. He knows my name. A loud whistle rings through the club and I look up to see my worst nightmare sitting in the VIP area next to Manuel with a pleased smile on his face. Cyrus is here. It feels like a hand is wrapped around my throat as I try to breathe but I can't.

Cyrus stands from his chair, holding my stare, and I know I need to run. No, I need to find Jaxson, but I can't seem to move. He walks around the table he was at and tears fill my eyes as I beg my legs to move. I can hear Penny's muffled voice like she's yelling at me from a different room, but I can't look away from him.

A hand wraps around my wrist as a male voice asks, "Hey lady. You okay?"

Hearing *Lady* jolts me out of my frozen state and I jerk back from the hold on my wrist, dropping the shaker, and it crashes to the floor. Looking back at Cyrus because I need to keep him in my sight line, I find him standing at the entrance of the VIP and there's no way to escape.

The bar exit and the VIP entrance are too close to each other, so I move in the only direction that'll keep me away from him. I can sense people staring at me and can hear my co-workers calling out my name as I walk backwards down the bar putting more distance between us. He can't get me right now. No one is going to let him back here. My back hits the far corner of the bar and I'm finally able to find my voice. "Leave me alone." I don't yell it out, but I know he heard it over the music because I can hear his response.

"Never." The sound of his voice again sends a chill down my spine. He steps out of the VIP area and turns away from me, heading down the hallway to the exit.

When I can't see him anymore, I slide down the cabinet, wrap my arms around my knees, and bury my face as I let out a sob. I can feel someone crouch in front of me. "Are you okay?" Jake calmly talks to me. "Do you need anything?"

I shake my head no, about to tell him I need a minute when a loud bang sounds from the other end of the bar, and I look up scared, thinking Cyrus has come back, but it's Jaxson, moving towards me with the folding counter wide open behind him.

"Sunshine." Worry is written all over his face and I know he can see the fear in mine. Jake steps in front of him, stopping him from getting closer.

"Look some guy freaked her the fuck out."

If I wasn't so scared, I'd chuckle at his description of what happened. I am freaked the fuck out. Jaxson looks down at me and I answer his unspoken question of who. "He was here. Cyrus found me." Jaxson's whole body stiffens as he looks around the club, but I know he won't find him.

"He left," Jake tells him. "And Manuel left right behind him."

Jaxson continues scanning the club until he's positive it's safe. "Let's get you upstairs."

Jaxson reaches out his hand and I set mine in his and let him pull me up. His arm goes immediately around my shoulders and I turn my face into him so I don't have to see all the attention I know the scene I created has gotten.

Jaxson doesn't stop until we're in the stairway that heads up to the apartment and the door locks behind us. "Are you okay?" He holds me at arm's length, making sure I'm physically not hurt before he pulls me against his chest, and I wrap my arms around him sobbing.

"He found me. He knows my name." My hands shake, still holding the phone, and I show him the text.

He takes my phone and stuffs it into his pocket. "He's gone. You're safe."

"I'm not safe, he knows where to find me." Oh my god, he knows Manuel. "You're not safe. You need to let me go." I try to push away from him, but he holds me tighter. "He's going to kill you."

"No." Jaxson's voice commands attention, and I look up at him with tears running down my cheeks. "I'm not letting you go. You're not running. Promise me that when I leave, you won't run. You won't give him what he wants."

I want to tell him I can't promise because I know if I stay, he'll come back and force his way to me. I'm no longer safe and neither are they, but I also know he's right. If I run tonight, he'll be waiting for me and it'll be like running right to him. "I promise."

Jaxson slams his lips to mine in a desperate kiss before pulling back. "Go upstairs and try to relax. I promise he's not getting to you."

I nod, not knowing what else to do, and head up the stairs. I do know one thing, there's no way I'm relaxing.

After sending the babysitter home, I grab a knife from the butcher block and carry it over to the sitting chair. With my back in the corner and a good view of the front door, I bring my knees to my chest and grip the knife on top of my knee. I'm not going without a fight.

Chapter Thirty-Nine
Sadie

My head droops forward as my eyes start to close and I jerk back up and shake my head to wake up.

"I told you I'd always find you, Scarlett."

Cyrus steps out of the dark corner across the room from me. I jump back with a gasp and he disappears. My heart races as I search the open space for him. Where did he go?

"We're forever linked." He reappears on the other side of the couch from me.

"Leave me alone," I hiss, holding the knife out in front of me.

He vanishes again and I push back in my seat, using the knife as a pointer as I scan the room. Tears run down my cheeks as I panic. Where is he? A figure appears next to me with a whisper, "Sadie."

I swing the knife towards him as I yell out, "Nooo."

He grabs my wrist, stopping me from slashing him and I throw a punch with my other fist, connecting with his shoulder. "Fuck. Sadie, it's me. *Sunshine*."

The haze of my nightmare starts to fade and instead of Cyrus next to me it's Jaxson, crouched down holding my wrist out with the knife pointed at his face.

"Oh my god." I let go of the knife and it falls to the floor. Tears continue to roll down my face but from guilt instead of fear. "I'm so sorry." I pull away from him. I could've killed him. "I thought you were him. He was here."

"It's okay, Sunshine."

"I could've killed you. Oh my god, what if it was Phoenix?" He tries to reach out for me, but I jump from the chair and move away from him.

"You were in a nightmare. You didn't mean it." He stands and tries to close the distance between us, but I move backwards. "I have to say I'm surprised by your fight." He gives me a playful smile as I back into the island and he closes the distance between us. "That punch was great form."

A small smile starts to form on my face. "I took some self-defense classes after I moved to New York."

He rests his hands on either side of me. "What about weapons?"

"I can hold my own." My smile widens as confidence builds inside me.

"You definitely are good with a knife. Can you handle a gun?"

I nod. "I'm not a sharpshooter but I can hit a target." Riona gives any of us lessons on self-defense and weapons handling when wanted. I took them quite regularly five years ago. Not so much now.

He scoops me in his arms. "Then he doesn't stand a chance. Now let's get some sleep. You can't slay a monster with no sleep."

I wrap my arms around his neck, taking the comfort he's giving. "I'm scared."

"I know, but don't look at it as what he could do now that he knows where you are. Look at it as we know where he is and you have a whole army ready to take him out."

He sets me on the bed and I curl under the covers and watch him remove his clothes until he's only in his boxers. I roll into his side once he's lying down and his arms wrap around me.

"He's the one that should be scared." I whisper the words, hoping they become real, but I know he's not scared. He thinks nothing can touch him. He's above everyone and nothing gets in his way or what he wants.

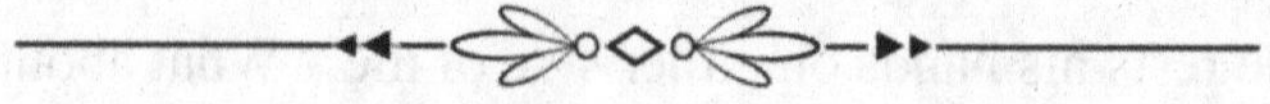

Screams wake me up and I fumble out of the empty bed. "Phoenix."

I run out of the bedroom to find Phoenix lying on the floor motionless with blood spreading around him. "*Phoenix*," I scream as I run to him and crash down on my knees next to him. I pull his loose body into my lap to find the front of his shirt covered in blood and a long cut down his stomach. The knife I was holding last night lays next to us covered in blood and I press my hand on the wound.

"No. No. No Please don't die. *Jaxson*!" I look around frantically for Jaxson.

"He can't help you." Cyrus steps over a pair of legs that are sticking out from behind the island and I recognize Jaxson's boots.

"Nooo. Jaxson." I squeeze Phoenix to my chest as I cry out, "Help!"

"No one is coming. You're all mine now." An evil smile pulls over Cyrus' lips as he walks to me.

I gasp awake, shooting up into a sitting position, breathing hard and I look around the dark room. Jaxson. Phoenix. I turn on the lamp next to me and frantically run my hands over Jaxson's chest. "What's wrong?" He's groggy as he looks at me.

"Nothing." It was just a nightmare. They're okay. "Sorry." I turn off the lamp and lie back down. Jaxson's light snores fill the room and I try to slip back to sleep but I can't. What if the scream I heard was real? What if he has Phoenix? What if Cyrus has gotten into the apartment? I need to just check that everything is okay. I slide out of bed and quietly out of the room.

The apartment is silent and cloaked in darkness as I walk through the open space, making sure all the windows and the front door are locked. My phone sitting on the counter catches my attention and I walk over to it. Unlocking it, I find the message Cyrus sent me, but it wasn't the last one.

Unknown: I've been searching all over the country for you.

Unknown: Imagine my surprise when you were the girl Manuel has been bragging about.

Unknown: You came right to me. It's too bad you had to involve the bar manager and his son.

Unknown: No one touches what's mine.

Real panic sets in my stomach at his threat towards Jaxson and Phoenix.

Me: Don't touch them.

My hands shake as I respond to Cyrus. As my blue bubble pops up, regret fills my stomach for responding.

Unknown: Return to me willingly and save them.

I can't go back to him and be forced back into his prison of pain. But I can't let anything happen to them. I won't let them die for me. They can move on; I would die if anything happened to them because of me. Before I let my fear take over, I respond.

Me: Give me a day.

"Sadie?" Phoenix's little voice startles me.

I quickly lock my phone and hide it behind me. "Phoenix. What are you doing up?"

He rubs his eyes. "I had a bad dream."

"Oh no." I squat down and open my arms. Phoenix runs into them and I give him a big hug. "Everything is okay now."

"Will you come sleep with me?"

"Of course, Little Man." I stand with him in my arms and carry him back to his room. His little twin bed is tight with the two of us but with my back to the wall, I hold him in my arms as I run my fingers through his hair. As he falls back asleep, I make a silent promise to myself that in the next twenty-four hours, I'm going to show them how much I love them and wish I could have this life with them.

Chapter Forty

Sadie

Even with a cute Phoenix snoring next to me, I couldn't sleep. If I only have a day with them, I want it to be the best day ever because it's going to break my heart leaving tonight. Without waking Phoenix, I climb out of bed and head to the kitchen. I want to make Phoenix real waffles. Finding the waffle maker and mix in the pantry, I pull them out and start mixing up the batter and getting the coffee ready.

Wanting to wake Jaxson first, I take a cup of coffee with me to his room and set it on his nightstand. Sitting on the edge of the mattress, I lean over and place a kiss on his lips. He smiles at me as I pull back. "Good morning."

"Morning." He grips my shirt and pulls me back to him for a deeper kiss. I melt into him and he rolls us so I'm underneath him. "Why are you up?"

"I'm making breakfast, but I wanted to talk to you about something."

"I'm listening." He starts kissing down my neck as his hands go under my shirt.

My back arches under his touch. "It's about the Farmers' Market."

"Phoenix will only be upset for a little bit that you can't go anymore." He kisses each of my breasts over my shirt as his hands slide up my sides.

My voice is starting to get breathless from his touch and I grip his wrists stopping him. "I'm still going."

Jaxson looks up at me confused. "What?"

"I'm still going on the field trip."

He looks at me like I lost my mind. "No, you're not. It's not safe."

It's safe for today but I'm not going to tell him about the deal I made. "I'm not going to lock myself in this building because of him."

He sits up and I follow. "It's only until we get Cyrus. He knows where you are. You're only safe here."

"I'm not asking to go alone. Come with us." Reaching out, I place my hand on his cheek. "Phoenix has been excited about this for weeks and I won't upset him because of Cyrus."

"I can't go." He pulls away and gets off the bed. "I have meetings here this morning."

"What meetings?" I move off the bed as well, following across the room as he pulls on his pants.

"We're handling Manuel today. The Russos want him gone."

We're? Jaxson isn't a part of that side of business. Is he dirtying his hands again because of me? I want to tell him he doesn't have to, but I know it won't stop him. "I'll call Matteo and he can get some guys to watch us."

He sighs as he turns to me and frames the side of my face with his hands. "This isn't a good idea, Sadie, and I want to tell you no but..."

"Whatever I say," I whisper with a smile on my face as I lean forward.

"Yeah, something like that." He pressed his lips to mine. "You're carrying a gun and if something happens you leave immediately. Nix has a SOS on his watch that comes directly to me. If you feel an ounce of something being off, press it."

I wrap my arms around the back of his neck and lean into him. "I promise his safety is my first priority."

He pushes my hair from my face and I can see his worry even though he's allowing this. "What are you making for breakfast?"

His lips press to mine as I answer, "Waffles, of course." We both chuckle and I lean further into his kiss.

I dropped Phoenix off at the school bus taking the kids to the Farmer's Market, but I elected with some of the other parents to drive separately. There was just not enough room for all of us on the bus.

"Sadie!" Phoenix calls out my name as he jumps off the bus. "Did you see me waving?" I drove right behind the bus and Phoenix was waving at me through the back window the whole ride.

"Yes, I did. Did you see me waving too?"

He nods excitedly and I chuckle. The teacher calls for everyone's attention and I hold out my hand for Phoenix to take and his little hand wraps around three of my fingers. After the teacher tells us the rules and splits up the groups, Phoenix pulls me behind him and his group of five friends. With each booth we stop at, the kids listen intently to the farmer as they describe their fruit or vegetable and how they grow them.

I step back with the other chaperones in my group when we get to the honey booth. Just the thought of tasting honey had Phoenix letting go of my hand and pushing through his friends, so he's front and center at the table. "He's very attached to you. How long have you been with Jaxson?" one of the moms, Karen asks.

"It's still new but I live close, so I get to spend a lot of time with Phoenix." I smile over at her, not saying I live with them because I'm sure that would appall her.

"Wow, moving fast," Sarah, the other mom, adds with a little judgment.

I give a tight smile instead of telling them to fuck off. "So, what do you do when you're not chaperoning?" Karen starts talking about an at-home candle business she has and I zone her out as I look down at a happy Phoenix who's so entranced with the man telling him about the beehives.

Someone taps on my shoulder drawing my attention away from Phoenix. "Excuse me, Sadie?" A man in biker gear with a bike beside him stands behind me and I look at him confused.

"Yes?"

"I have a delivery for you." The personal delivery man reaches into his messenger bag and pulls out a black velvet box that's the size of my hand.

"Who's this from?" This doesn't feel like something Colton, Tanner, or Jaxson would do.

He looks down at his invoice. "Doesn't say. Have a good day."

The messenger jumps on his bike and rides away without waiting for a response. Slowly I lift the lid of the box and a black leather choker with red cloth roses sits inside. Without even reading the note, I know who it's from, and it sends a chill down my spine.

Wear your crown, Lady.

Your Lord is watching.

I look up from the choker and scan the crowd looking for him, but the only people I recognize are the two guys Matteo sent. I asked them to keep their distance so they don't catch the attention of the school. One of them must see the panic on my face because he starts moving closer, but I shake my head, telling him no.

"Ooo. What do you have there?" Sarah coos as she tries to get a look but I slam the lid shut and stuff the box in my purse.

"It's nothing."

"Sadie." Thankfully Phoenix coming up to me with a honey straw stops her from saying anything else. "Taste it." He holds out the straw where the tip is covered in his saliva.

I pour some honey on my finger and hand the straw back to him. Together we taste it and I hum out, making Phoenix laugh. "This is really good."

"Can we buy some?" He looks back at the booth, eyeing the jars.

"You like it that much?"

"Yes." He nods. Of course, he likes it. It's like eating sugar.

"Okay. We can use it on our waffles."

"Really!?" He jumps up excitedly.

"You'll have to try it tomorrow." My smile drops a little knowing I won't be there for him to try it. I buy a jar from the vendor, and with Phoenix's hand in mine, we move to the next booth.

I keep my eyes on the crowd knowing he's here somewhere. He wouldn't say he's watching if he's not. Not caring about socializing with the two moms, I stay close to Phoenix, listening to the farmers.

We come up to the floral section of the market and I stop in my tracks when I see Cyrus and two other men standing at the entrance and they aren't just enjoying the view. No... I was stupid to think he'd give me the day.

I reach for Phoenix's shoulder stopping him as well. "Little Man, we need to go." I start to pull him in the other direction and he pulls back.

"But we haven't seen the flowers." Looking back at the flower entrance, I see them walking towards us. Quickly I pick Phoenix up and start moving through the market at a fast pace.

"I'm sorry, Phoenix. We need to get home." We pass our two guards and without saying anything, they move with us keeping between us and Cyrus. We get to the truck and I can hear footsteps approaching. My heart races as I open the backdoor and set Phoenix inside. "Get in your seat, Little Man."

A grunt sounds from behind the truck and I look back to see our two guards fighting the men that were with Cyrus. "Buckle yourself in." Where is he? I close the door and open the driver's door. Once inside I lock the doors and look back, checking on Phoenix and hoping to see our guards standing and the others on the ground. When all I can see is Cyrus' men, I hit the accelerator and race out of the parking lot.

Once out on the street to head back to the apartment, I hit Jaxson's contact. The sound of the ringing comes through the sound system and with each second he doesn't answer my panic heightens.

"What's going on, Sadie?" Phoenix sounds upset from the back and it tears me up inside that I put him in danger. Jaxson's voicemail picks up and I hang up and try again.

"I saw a bad man at the market and we needed to leave. We're going so we're safe."

"Dad will keep us safe." Phoenix's confidence in his dad makes me smile for a second.

"Yes, he will." In the rearview mirror, I see two SUVs weaving through traffic. He just needs to answer the phone. His voicemail picks up again and I hang up.

Trying to keep my voice calm so Phoenix doesn't know I'm panicking, I ask, "Phoenix, can you hit the SOS button on your watch? I can't get your dad to answer my calls."

"It's only for emergencies." I hit the accelerator as the SUVs get behind us and I turn off the street, taking the exit for the highway.

"This is an emergency." Panic is present in my abrupt response as I weave through traffic. A light ring comes from the back seat and I silently pray that he answers. I don't know what to do right now. I can't let them get Phoenix too. His watch cuts off and I feel tears filling my eyes. Where is he?

A hit to the back of the truck has both Phoenix and me screaming and I grip the wheel tighter as I try to pull away. "Sadie I'm scared."

"I know, Little Man. I'm trying to get us away. Try your dad again."

A black SUV pulls next to us on the driver's side and I quickly take the exit we were about to pass to avoid their attempt to ram the side of us. The exit leads me onto a two lane highway but I haven't lost them. I need to get Phoenix somewhere safe and away from Cyrus. If I can lose them for a few minutes, I can find a place to hide him. I need help.

I press on Colton's number as a hit near the back tire catches me off guard and the truck starts to spin. I try to right us as Phoenix screams in the back but I feel the truck running off the road by the dip of a ditch and then we stop abruptly with a loud bang. My head hits the window from the impact and ringing starts in my ears.

"Phoenix," I scream out for the little boy who shouldn't be in this position, and I can hear his cries over the ringing.

Looking out the window, I see men coming through the field we're in and I fumble with my door handle to get out. My door creaks open and I slide out with my back against Phoenix's door, pulling out the gun Jaxson gave me. With my vision blurring, I start shooting at every figure I see as I move along the truck to open Phoenix's door. "Phoenix!" I swing the door open to find him screaming in his car seat and I reach over him to unbuckle his seatbelt. "Are you okay?"

He nods with tears running down his face and he reaches out for me. I grab him around his waist and quickly carry him around to the other side of the truck while shooting off a few more shots. With us hidden, I see we've hit a tree on the edge of the woods. Sitting Phoenix down, I crouch in front of him. "Nix, I need you to run. Run as far as you can and hide." I pick up his wrist and point to the watch. "Your dad will find you. He's probably on his way."

"No, I can't." Tears stream down his cheeks as he shakes his head.

"I need you to be a big boy and run for me. Run so hard." Tears run down my cheeks as well and I pull him in a hug. "I love you, Phoenix." I let go of him as I hear Cyrus calling out for me by a name I haven't answered to in years. "Now *run*." I push him towards the woods and watch him for a few seconds before sliding back around the truck with my gun raised. Someone reaches out and grabs my wrists and I'm pulled into the chest of a man as he bends back my wrist until I drop the gun.

Cyrus appears in front of me with the wicked smile that fills my nightmares. "Hello, Lady."

I try to kick out at him, but I'm pulled away. "I had a day."

"Never agreed to that. You know I like the chase." He tries to touch my face, but I lean as far as I can away from him.

"Fuck you."

His hand swipes out and slaps me across the face. My cheek burns as I glare at him. "You don't talk to your Lord like that. It seems you've forgotten your lessons." He looks at the men that are closing in around us.

"Go find the boy," he orders, and I lose it.

"No! Leave him alone." I throw my body forward catching the man holding me off balance and then slam my head back connecting with his face. He screams out as he lets me go and I lunge for Cyrus but the handle of a gun hitting the side of my face knocks me to the ground and everything goes black.

Chapter Forty-One

Jaxson

"What are you doing here?" I look up from my phone as I sit at the empty bar to find Manuel standing at the end of the hall entrance.

"I do believe I run this club." I give him a cocky smirk as I stand, leaving my phone on the bar.

"This is business and you're not welcome." He gives me a cocky grin, thinking he's better than me.

I chuckle. "This is business, but you're the one not welcome anymore."

Colton and Tanner appear behind him, without his knowledge, blocking any attempts of escape as Dante, Matteo, Enzo, and Riona walk out from the back.

287

Manuel's condescending smile drops at the sight of our bosses and my smile grows. "Dante. Matteo. Enzo. Welcome to New Orleans."

Matteo chuckles. "Thank you. We plan on having a good time here." He looks over at Riona with a devilish smile and she returns it.

"Well, let me show you around. I know..."

"That won't be necessary," Enzo interrupts him.

"The only thing we want from you is information," Dante says as we all surround Manuel.

Colton pushes a chair into the back of Manuel's knees, forcing him to sit. "And your death."

Dante holds up his hand, stopping Manuel from saying a word. "I don't want to hear your lies. You made a mistake about going after Sadie. She's a friend we sent here for protection. Can you believe my surprise when I found out one of my men was a threat to her, especially since we don't deal in sex trafficking?"

"You see our fiancé despises sex trafficking and kills those who deal in it," Matteo says.

Riona steps forward with a knife twirling on her finger. "You're going to give us everything on the group you're working for or I'm going to skin you alive. Do you understand?"

"Fuck you, bitch." Manuel tries to pull a gun out from his back but Tanner holds a knife to his throat, stopping him.

"I wouldn't do that if I were you." Colton and Tanner remove his two guns and any other weapons he has on him.

Tanner grabs his shoulders and pulls him back against the chair as Matteo's fist connects with his cheek. "Watch your mouth."

Enzo steps in front of Manuel. "Let's start with Cyrus. Tell us where he is."

Manuel smiles up at him. "Cyrus. He showed up in town about five years ago and built an empire that rivals yours." He glares at the Russos. "All for revenge and his Lady." He smirks at me. "His Lady that he will never give up." His phone chimes and a laugh falls out of him. "I hope you said goodbye to her this morning."

I grip his shirt in my fist. "What's that supposed to mean?"

Colton's phone starts to ring and I look up at him. His eyes connect with mine and I know it's Sadie. He answers on speaker and sounds of screams spill from the phone. Both hers and my son's. My fist connects with his face before I even register I'm moving. "Where are they?" I'm pulled back from him by Colton and Tanner and I shove them off me. "Get off of me."

If they were in trouble, she was supposed to call me. I search my pockets for my phone, coming up empty until I glance at the bar, finding it there. I push through the twins, grab my phone, and curse at all the missed calls and SOS signals from Phoenix. "Fuck."

I pull up Phoenix's app to see his tracker moving just off the interstate and I head for the back entrance. "Let's go. I have Phoenix's location." Colton and Tanner are close behind me and I look back at Manuel surrounded by our bosses. "I want him alive when I get back."

Tanner takes the exit that I'm showing Phoenix is off of and as we pass the middle of nowhere gas station, police cars line the side of the small highway up ahead. He slows the truck as we come up on a field. "Don't stop."

Slowly we drive past the field where I see the tire tracks that lead to my crashed truck but seeing the two driver side doors open gives me hope. I recognize some of the cops surrounding my truck, but I don't see Sadie or Phoenix.

Looking down at my phone, I see Phoenix's signal in the woods. "Pull up ahead. Phoenix is in the woods." Tanner pulls off the road just past the field where there's an unmarked drive.

Making sure not to draw the attention of the police, we exit the SUV and quietly trek through the woods to where Phoenix is. My phone shows we're right on top of where he should be and my heart sinks. Trees surround us and I spin calling out his name, hoping to see his blonde head stick out from behind a tree. Colton and Tanner spread out on either side of me as we search.

"Jaxson," Tanner calls out for me, and I turn in his direction to see regret on his face as he holds up Phoenix's watch with a broken band. Cyrus has my son and the woman I love. He's made a terrible mistake. I'll tear this city apart to find them.

Chapter Forty-Two

Sadie

Soft tiny fingers running through my hair pull me from my unconsciousness and I crack open my eyes to see Phoenix lying in front of me. I tighten my arms around him. "Phoenix."

"Sadie," he cries when he sees me awake. "I'm scared."

I hold him tighter to me and I look around us to see we're in a dirty room with no windows and only one door. We're lying on a metal twin bed frame with a thin mattress and one blanket. A tightness around my throat has me reaching up and touching the metal shackle that's locked to my neck. Looking up, I follow the chain to where it connects to the wall. Fear runs through me, but I don't let it overtake me because I need to protect Phoenix.

I rub his back as he cries and I kiss the top of his head. "I know you're scared, Little Man. I am too, but we have to be brave." I reach for his wrist to find it bare.

"They took it," he whispers like I'd be disappointed.

"It's okay. Your dad won't let anything happen to you. Just be brave, Phoenix." I hope I'm right.

"I'm a big boy. I'm brave."

"Yes, you are." I run my fingers through his hair. "I need you to listen to me, Phoenix." He looks up at me with tear soaked cheeks and I wipe them away. "When they come back, I need you to hide under the bed, up against the wall, cover your ears, and close your eyes. You will stay there until they leave no matter what you hear. Do you understand?"

His bottom lip quivers and I know he's upset by what I'm asking. "But what about you?"

"I'll be okay, promise. Tell me you will do as I ask."

"I'll hide."

"Show me how you'll cover your ears and close your eyes." Phoenix does as I say, looking cute with a scrunched up face. I tap his nose with my finger and he opens his eyes. I smile down at him and he drops his hands. "Very good. You're so brave."

To distract Phoenix from the nightmare we're in, I tell him stories of a king battling an evil dragon to save his son, a young prince who finds himself lost and uses his courage to find his way home, and a princess that wanders the world trying to find her lost kingdom. I'm in the middle of the last story when the sound of footsteps stop outside our door. "Phoenix, go under the bed. Do as I said."

Phoenix scurries under the bed as the sound of the lock on our door flips over. I stand at the edge in front of where Phoenix should be and push the skirt of my dress down. The shackle around my neck tightens as I reach the end of the chain, but I don't fall back on the bed. I'm going to face him standing.

Cyrus walks into the room alone and the door shuts and locks behind him. His eyes roam over me and I feel gross in his line of sight, but I take the moment to look him over as well. Not in attraction but to remember how human he is. He might inflict pain, cause terror, and haunt my nightmares, but he's human. He ages, and not well. He has weaknesses. He bleeds.

"You're still so beautiful, Scarlett. How is it you've gotten even more gorgeous?" He strides towards me and I fight the fear of what I know is about to come and not step back.

"Not being raped daily and being loved can do wonders for a person. I recommend it. I see your ugly monster has come to the surface. Your charming looks are long gone." I look at him in disgust.

His hand whips out and connects with my cheek and it knocks me onto the bed. A whimper comes from underneath me and Cyrus chuckles as he grips my hair and pulls me back off the bed. I fight in his hold, jamming my elbow into his side and throwing my head back, causing his own fist to punch his face. He growls in frustration and throws me onto the mattress.

His body crashes on top of me before I can catch myself and I throw punches at him trying to get him off but they're weak with him on top of me. He grabs my wrists and holds them above me with one tight grip that I know will leave bruises. With his other hand, he starts pulling the skirt of my dress up, and I kick out trying to stop him as tears run down my cheeks.

"Don't do this, Cyrus. I'm not yours anymore."

He tears my panties off me and I try to close my legs, but he's already in between them. "You're wrong." His belt coming undone jingles and I shake my head slowly hoping he'll stop. "You'll always be mine."

He thrusts into me and I scream out from the pain. I try to buck him off but he weighs too much. His hand goes around my neck and my airway closes. "Stop fighting or I'll use the boy in every way I use you."

Terror runs through my veins at his threat and I let my body go limp because I won't let this monster touch Phoenix. Cyrus loosens his grip on my neck and I suck in a breath. "You can be so good to me, Lady. Giving me what I want." He fucks into me and I stare up at the ceiling as tears continue down my cheeks and a familiar feeling of numbness starts to overcome me. "I will remove their touch from your body so you only remember me."

That'll never happen. Memories of Jaxson, Colton, and Tanner will be the only thing keeping me alive. Just like now, I escape to the thoughts of Tanner's loving words, Colton's mischievous smile, and Jaxson's safe touch.

"Look at me, Scarlett." I don't move my eyes from the ceiling. His grip on my throat tightens again, more than before, and my eyes widen as I look at him with panic. He smiles with victory and slams his lips to mine. The bed squeaks louder as he fucks into me harder and I close my eyes as tight as my lips, hoping this will be over soon.

"You feel just as amazing as ever. No woman has ever felt the same as you." He grunts as his thrusts start to become erratic and I know he's about to come. His head hangs between us as he feels his pleasure and I try to pull away from him so his mark isn't inside of me, but he grips my hips, holding me in place as he thrusts deep and comes.

Disgust feels me as he dirties me with his release. "No woman has been worthy as much as you to stand next to me. I'm a king here and you will be my queen." He presses his lips to mine and I turn my face away from him. His hand grips my face and turns it back to him. "My men will bow for you tonight."

Cyrus pulls himself out of me as he lets go of my wrists and I curl into a ball and pull my dress down over my bent legs. He climbs off the bed and heads to the door. "I'll come collect you later." I don't look back at him as my tears pour down my face and I bite my fist to stop the sobs from coming out. The lock clicking back into place has a wave of relief washing over me and I silently pray that my men will save me soon. I can't survive being his again.

The bed dips and my body locks, fearing he's still here but the sight of the tiny hand that pulls the blanket over me has me relaxing. Phoenix. I want to pull him into my arms and hold him, but

I can't let him see me like this. I can't touch him with Cyrus' release leaking out of me.

"He's not a special friend," Phoenix whispers as he hugs me from behind.

"No, he's not." I silently cry into my hands.

Phoenix runs his fingers in my hair and whispers, "Once upon a time, there was a boy who didn't have a mom. All his friends had one so he wished on his birthday for his mom to come. One day he found a pretty woman sleeping on his couch and he knew she would be his mom when she accepted his waffle."

Chapter Forty-Three
Sadie

A hand running down my cheek pulls me from a dreamless sleep. "Wake, my queen. It's time for you to meet your subjects." I gasp awake at the sound of Cyrus' voice and move away from him. He smiles down at me like he's waking the love of his life and I feel sick. I look away from him to find myself in a different room. A lavish room with grand furniture including the large plush bed I'm on. The water.

Water was dropped off for us after Cyrus left and while we sipped it slowly, it must've had some sort of sleeping aid in it. "Phoenix. Where is he?" I move to the other side of the bed and stand looking for the boy I have to protect.

"He's fine." Cyrus stands from where he sat on the edge of the mattress and I press myself to the wall behind me and run my hands down my sides making sure my dress is down but the silk under my hand has me looking down. I'm in a white silk slip that barely goes past my ass. A different tightness on my neck has me reaching up and my fingers brush over a thin choker.

"Where is he?"

"He hasn't been touched. I left him sleeping in his cell." I stare at him, not sure if I believe him or not, but all I can do right now is hope he's telling the truth. "We need to go; the show is about to start."

Cyrus goes to the wood door and opens it. Two men walk in and head straight for me. They grab me aggressively and I fight their holds as they pull me from the room. "Let go of me." Cyrus walks ahead of us down a long hallway that is lined with doors just like the one Phoenix and I were behind. "Phoenix," I call out, hoping to hear him, so I know he's okay.

Cyrus spins around fast and grabs my face. "You will be quiet and not say a word or I will punish that boy you call out for, do you understand?"

I nod and glare at him. He lets my face go and I jerk my arms from the guards' hold. "I can walk by myself."

Cyrus takes a deep breath in frustration but doesn't react to my disobedience other than a nod to his men. He turns on his heel and continues down the hall and I follow a few feet behind him with the two guards closely behind me.

At the end of the hall sits a set of large wooden double doors with two men standing in front of them. As we approach, they pull the doors open and we step out onto a stage that's lit with candles. The audience is cloaked in darkness, only looking like dark shadows.

Cyrus stops at center stage and I'm stopped by the guards behind me just off to the side of him. I look back at them with a glare and they let go of my arms. The stage is wide but not empty. There are two boxes at least ten feet tall covered by a curtain to our left and a similar one to our right and I have a bad feeling about them. Cyrus looks back at me but it's not only his eyes that I feel on me. "Welcome to the Underground, my Lady."

I look out to the anonymous crowd and it sinks in what this is. Cyrus has gone from sex slavery to selling skin. He turns back to his audience and steps forward. "Welcome back, my friends. Tonight is a very special night with a once in a lifetime chance but before I get to the surprise, let's look at the product."

He waves to his left and the curtain furthest from us lifts. "We have the pure." A glass box that reminds me of the mansion's basement sits underneath the curtain with a girl who looks no older than sixteen sitting curled up in the corner of the box in a white slip like mine.

The next curtain starts to rise revealing a striking woman with pale skin, dark hair, and feminine curves under her white slip. "The desired."

Cyrus looks to his right and the last curtain starts to rise. "The forbidden."

A little boy standing at the front of the box is revealed and my heart drops. "Phoenix." The guards' fingers brush over my arms as I pull away from their attempt to grab me and race to Phoenix's prison. I try the handle and of course, it's locked, but it doesn't stop me from trying. I call out his name as he hits the glass yelling mine.

Two sets of hands grab me and pull me away from him. He cries as I fight the guards. Cyrus appears before me and I growl in anger. "You promised not to touch him."

"And I won't. His buyer will," I scream as I try to lunge at him, but the guards pull me away. Cyrus backhands me across my face and the hit throws me back against the guards.

"Your surprise tonight is the sacred." He turns back to the crowd and has his arm extended to me.

"One time only. Right here in front of all of you. She needs to be taught a lesson. She needs to be reminded of what happens when she disobeys me." He smiles wickedly at me and flashes of my punishments from years ago fill my mind.

I look to Phoenix who's staring back at me with tears running down his cheeks. He can't see that. I close my eyes and raise my arms as much as I can to signal to cover his ears and when I open my eyes again Phoenix is curled in the corner with his eyes closed and hands over his ears.

"Let's start the bid at $10,000." Cyrus' voice sounds cheerful at the thought of me being raped, abused, and tortured, and all for money.

I look out to the crowd wanting to face the vile men that bid on me. I wait for someone to call out or for some sort of movement, but nothing happens. "I said we're starting at $10,000."

Cyrus reaches for me by grabbing my hair and pulling me to the front of the stage. "I promise she's worth the..." An object emerges from the darkness and flies right at us. I duck as far as I can to the side, to avoid it, and when I look to see what it is a smile pulls across my face as I recognize the engraving on the knife embedded in his shoulder. She hit her target.

Gripping the knife, I pull it out, breaking Cyrus from his shock. He screams in pain, letting go of my hair to clutch his shoulder and I smile at him. "I told you I wasn't yours." With the knife in my grip, I swing out and slice his throat. His screams turned to gurgles as blood gushes from his open wound. He falls to his knees as he clutches his neck and I stand over him. "My turn to kill who you love."

Chapter Forty-Four
Colton

Hearing the screams of Stella and Phoenix and seeing the wreckage has my sanity cracking. I'm buzzing to get my hands on Cyrus but Manuel will have to do for now. I storm into the club with Tanner and Jaxson on my heels to find Manuel, shirtless, with his hands and his ankles tied to the center pole with plastic covering the ground. Manuel has round bruises covering his upper body along with bloody gashes where his nipples and belly buttons used to be. Matteo's standing in front of him with a bat in his grip, ready to swing. I jump up onto the stage and take it from him.

"We've just been having fun," Matteo says as he steps back but I don't really care. All I care about is making him feel the pain that I feel knowing Stella is in the hands of the man who has hurt her so much.

Manuel will feel all the pain she's felt at the hands of Cyrus, and if he's lucky I'll kill him quickly, so he doesn't have to live long with it. I swing the bat into his side with all my power and the sound of bones crushing is music to my ears. I swing back to go again but Jaxson moves past me and lands a punch to Manuel's face, slamming his head back against the pole.

"Where are they, Manuel? I swear to god if anything happens to them you are going to wish you were dead."

Manuel tries to smile with his busted lip and swollen eye. "After tonight, who knows where they will be."

I swing the bat, hitting him across his stomach and he grunts in pain as he tries to bend forward. "What's that supposed to mean?"

Manuel chuckles in between his coughs. "They'll be sold at tonight's auction. Well, maybe not Sadie."

He reaches out for the bat and I hand it over to him. "Just don't kill him until we get answers."

Jaxson takes the bat and I leave him to weaken Manuel until I'm ready to draw blood and answers.

Tanner stands with Riona, Dante, Enzo, and Matteo, watching the show. "What kind of toys did you bring?" I jump off the stage in front of them.

"Just a few favorites." Riona smiles down at her draggers that lay in a line on the table in between us but it's the duffle bag I'm curious about.

"My favorites too." Matteo lifts the bag and sets it on another table. "I got pain, screams, and terror." Matteo holds up brass knuckles, a machete, and pliers but I also see gardening shears, baseballs, a hammer, and a torch.

"We can have some fun with these." I grab the hammer and weight in my hand. "How do you want to play this?" Manuel's screams fill the space but he's still not ready to talk.

"How about I ask the questions and you all inflict the punishments?" Riona suggests.

"That's not your style." Riona has always had a love for torture.

"I love Stella, but I won't assume that she's mine to protect anymore and Phoenix is Jaxson's son."

I look at Tanner and he grabs the pliers from Matteo. Not needing to look back at the old man raging behind me to know she's his, I say, "They're ours to protect."

Manuel yells turn to begs and I smile at my friends. "Stop... please." His breaths are short and I hope Jaxson has punctured a lung.

Grabbing the brass knuckles, I turn back to the stage. "Nice job, old man." I throw the knuckles and he catches them. "Time to get some answers."

If I didn't hate the man, I'd be impressed by how long he held out before giving up the location of the auction. After an hour of torture with his nails pulled, hands and knees shattered, beaten continuously, and a few teeth removed, he sang. Giving us everything. The time, location, rules, and invite list. Riona gushed over some of the names on the list. Men and women she's had on her radar but haven't found the proof to go after them. If they're here tonight, she'll be able to mark them off her list.

Tanner and I walk through the dark cemetery and I have my head on a swivel, expecting to see a ghost or two watching. I'm sure they can sense the monsters walking through where they've been put to rest. "Stop freaking." Tanner shakes his head at me, not believing in my ghost theory.

If we were anywhere else, I wouldn't be so on alert. "You watched *The Originals* with me. New Orleans spirits are no joke."

He chuckles. "You're ridiculous."

"You better watch your back disrespecting the spirits." I smirk at him.

"Come on, let's get inside." The mausoleum in front of us has torches lit on either side of the door, signaling this is the entrance. Tanner walks through the decorative glass doors and I turn back to the cemetery.

"We'll add a few evil souls to your world tonight, make sure they suffer."

Tanner calls out for me and I give the haunted air a smile before jogging up the few steps and joining Tanner inside. In the middle of the space, an opening on the floor reveals a stairwell going down. I look at my brother and we both nod as we wrap our hands around our guns and head down the steps.

The stairwell isn't long, just enough steps to lead us to a hallway that we're barely able to stand tall in. The hallway is lit with torches just like the ones outside but it's not long. A few yards in front of us stand two guards. As we approach, the guards don't move, just like Manuel said. They only need the passcode.

"Court is in session." Tanner gives the passcode and the guards grab the handles to the massive wooden double doors and open them wide. We walk into the room side by side as we button our suit jackets and I look to the back of the room only lit by the candles on stage. Riona and her men sit in a booth in the back corner, Jaxson sits at a small table next to them, and we head to the booth on the other side of him.

The place is full and I feel disgusted that I'm even in the same room as these people, acting like one of them as I order a drink from a man that looks like he needs to be set free.

A couple in front of us whisper to themselves but they're not quiet. "Hopefully the desired is a man. We haven't had our fun in a while." The woman smiles at her husband and he leans forward, kissing her.

"You know me so well. Breaking men is so much more entertaining."

Tanner growls in anger telling me he heard them too, and I hold up my fist. He smiles at me and holds up his as well. We shake them up and down four times. Rock. Paper. Scissors. Shoot. I throw my hand out flat for paper and Tanner holds out two fingers for scissors. Cursing under my breath, I throw my head back in defeat and Tanner lightly chuckles. "Man." Damn. I guess I'll get the woman.

The waiter drops off our drinks and disappears through the double doors we entered. Let the show begin. The red curtains that run along the front of the stage pull open, revealing three box shapes with curtains lying over them and the crowd quiets as they face the stage.

The double doors in the center of the backstage wall open revealing Cyrus in a tux. He steps forward and Stella appears in a silk slip that's similar to the one she wore when I first laid eyes on her. She looks even more beautiful than she did then, but like then you can see how much she doesn't want to be in it, how much she doesn't want to be here, how much she doesn't want to be near him.

He looks back saying something to her, but her eyes are straight forward scanning over the crowd. You can see the second she realizes what this is and I'm not waiting another second.

Without needing to signal the others we all move with blades in our hands. As my knife slices through the neck of the woman in front of me, my other hand covers her mouth. Cyrus starts his show, "Welcome back, my friends. Tonight is a very special night with a once in a lifetime chance, but before I get to the surprise, let's look at the product."

The six people in the row in front of us bleed to death in our arms without a sound as he reveals the first box, "The pure," showing a scared teenage girl. We take the next row with the same precision. These monsters lose their lives as the desired is revealed. I release my latest victim as the final curtain is pulled up with Cyrus announcing, "The forbidden."

Myself, Jaxson, and Stella all realize who's in the last box at the same time and as Stella yells out for Phoenix, I lunge at Jaxson, getting in front of him and holding him back.

Not wanting to risk the attention of him fighting me, I pull him into a hug and whisper, "Calm down. Nothing is going to happen to him. Let's end this." Stella's screams and Phoenix's cries for her break my heart and I know he's feeling this a thousand times more, but surprise is how we're going to save the both of them.

Jaxson stops fighting me and I let him go and give him a nod. He returns it and I turn back to the stage to see two men dragging Stella back to where she was and Phoenix is banging on the glass. Cyrus has a cocky smile on his face like he loves their reaction to each other.

Light gurgling sounds come from my right and I look over at Tanner to find him taking out two men. The man in front of me looks over as well and I lunge forward, ending his life before he can say anything. "Your surprise is the sacred." Cyrus looks so proud of himself as he addresses his dwindling crowd.

We only have one row with four people left. My guess is these are the worst of the worst. "One time only. Right here in front of all of you. She needs to be taught a lesson. She needs to be reminded of what happens when she disobeys me." I crouch behind my final guy with Tanner and Jaxson taking the men on either side of mine and Matteo has the lady at the end. Riona is behind us with Dante and Enzo ready to take out the people on the stage.

Stella's focus is on Phoenix as she closes her eyes and tries to cover her ears. Phoenix instantly goes to the corner and does what she did. She thinks she's going to be raped and abused and all she's worried about is Phoenix, making sure he doesn't see it. She's too good for us but I'm not letting her go.

"Let's start the bid at $10,000." The man in front of me goes to lift his paddle and I slice my knife across his throat with my hand over his mouth. As his life ends, his paddle falls into his lap and I'm thankful it doesn't fall onto the concrete ground.

"I said we're starting at $10,000." Anger fills Cyrus' voice as he steps back, grabs Stella by her hair, and pulls her next to him. "I promise she's worth the…"

Something flies by me on my left and lands right into Cyrus' shoulder, cutting him off, and the smile on Stella's face tells me she knows we're here. I watch Stella pull the knife out of Cyrus' shoulder and cut across his throat as I hear two gunshots go off, killing the two guards that were holding Stella.

Breaking into action, I pull out my gun and aim for the doors we entered as those guards burst into the room. Tanner and I each take one and then turn back to the stage as more shots ring out. Two men from the side of the stage fall to the ground along with two men coming from behind the stage double doors. All seems to calm after that other than Jaxson running to his son and Stella going to town on Cyrus' chest with Riona's knife. A smile forms on my face watching her as I climb up the side steps with Tanner behind me. We pass the two other captives knowing Riona and the Russos will get them.

Tanner and I stand over our bloody woman with pride at her slaying her monster. "Blossom," Tanner calls out to her and she immediately stops stabbing him and smiles up at us.

"I just wanted to see if he had a heart." We both chuckle as Tanner holds his hand out to her.

She places her free hand in his and he pulls her up and against his chest. "He doesn't." He crashes his lips to hers and she melts into him.

"Dad." Phoenix's shaking voice fills the silent space, as Jaxson gets his prison open and he crashes into his father's arms.

Looking back at Stella, she's watching them with relief on her face but the guilt is what has me pulling her against me. "You did good with him, Dove. You kept him safe."

Her arms tighten around my waist and she presses her forehead to my chest. "Not good enough." Her words come out in a soft whisper like she didn't want anyone to hear them and I want to argue that she did but she's only going to hear it from Jaxson.

"Come on, let's get out of here."

Chapter Forty-Five

Sadie

It doesn't feel real. Cyrus is dead. We're safe. I'm free. No more living in fear that he'll come back. No more worrying about falling in love and him taking them from me. No more putting my life on hold. Looking up at Colton, who has his arm around my waist, holding me to his side as he leans against an SUV while we wait for Riona to sort out the mess in the catacomb, I whisper, "It's over."

He smiles down at me. "Yes, it is. No more hiding. No more staying away. I hope you're ready to have us here all the time."

Tanner squeezes my hand as he stands across from his brother. "We'll be wherever you are."

Jaxson stands in front of his son who's sitting inside the other SUV next to us. I hate myself for having put Phoenix here. I

311

shouldn't have gone to the Farmer's Market. I shouldn't have thought Cyrus wouldn't harm him.

Phoenix's face is red from crying, from feeling fear no person should ever feel, and it's all my fault. "Nix, did they hurt you? Touch you?" Jaxson checks over Phoenix's arms since that's the only exposed skin since he's still in his school uniform.

Phoenix shakes his head. "Sadie had me hide whenever the bad man came. She told me to close my eyes and cover my ears when he hurt her." He shows his dad what he would do and tears fill my ears because he shouldn't have needed to hide like that. "But I could still hear because the bed was squeezing and she was crying. I followed the rules though and didn't come out until he was gone."

No. I didn't want him to hear that. I should've done better keeping that away from him. Jaxson looks at me for the first time and I look away from his pity and bury my face in Colton's chest. Jaxson will never forgive me. "I want to go back to New York."

Colton's other arm wraps around me as I feel Tanner moving close behind me. "Whatever you want, Blossom."

A piece of my heart tears off at that phrase, thinking I'll never hear Jaxson say, 'Whatever you say', again.

Colton runs his fingers through my hair and pulls so I look up at him. He wipes the tears from my cheeks. "Let's get out of here. Riona can meet us back at the house."

I nod with my chin hitting his chest. He moves me over to the passenger door of the SUV Jaxson and Phoenix are at and opens it for me. I climb in without looking back at them and as soon as the door closes, I rest my head on the window. Tanner gets into the driver's seat as Colton takes the one behind me and they both reach out for me at the same time. Tanner places his hand on my knee and I intertwine our fingers. Colton squeezes my shoulder and then twirls some of my hair as we leave the parking lot. I zone out during the drive, not watching the city pass by but reliving the past day.

I'm so caught up in what could've happened if they didn't find us that I don't even realize we've stopped in front of a historic french style home until Tanner is knocking on the window. I blink the haze from my vision and lean back so he can open the door. Silence fills the car and I realize we're the only ones left; the others must already be inside. He reaches out, placing his hand on my cheek, and I lean into his touch. "You're safe, Blossom. Nothing is going to touch you again."

I don't know how he can read my turmoil but I'm thankful he can. "Can you rewind the last twenty-four hours and stop it from happening?"

"That's not something I can do because then Cyrus would still be alive. I know he hurt you, but I will help you heal and hopefully forget."

Forgetting sounds great. "I'll take that."

"Then let's start with a shower."

I nod and place my hand in his as I slide out of the SUV. He pulls me through the small iron gate in front of the house, and I look up at it admiring the white with black accents, large front porch, and second floor balcony. This is what I picture a classic New Orleans home looking like. "Is this the Russos'?"

"Yeah. We're all crashing here tonight." We walk through the black wooden door and dark wood continues inside on what looks like a freshly glazed floor. The black and white theme continues into the sitting room to the right and the kitchen to the left. I follow Tanner up the stairs to the second floor and there are two doors on either side of the hall. The one to the right of the stairwell is open and I look in to see Jaxson putting Phoenix to bed. I quickly look away and follow Tanner to the room across from them.

The bedroom door closes behind us and I'm drawn to the sound of water running through the open door on my right. Following the sound, I find Colton standing over a large claw foot bathtub, pouring soap into the water. I smile at the gesture. "I didn't have you for a bath guy."

Colton smirks back at me. "This is for you, but I'll happily join you."

"Good, I don't want to be alone." Tanner moves behind me and slides the jacket he gave me when we walked out of the mausoleum off my shoulders as I watch Colton remove his clothing. He has a cocky smirk on his face, knowing I'm enjoying the view.

"Like what you see, Dove?"

"Maybe. Lose the pants so I can know for sure." He chuckles as he drops his dress shirt to the tile floor and goes for his belt.

"How about I get you naked?" Tanner whispers next to my ear and a chill runs down my spine as goosebumps break across my skin. His fingers run along the top of my shoulder, grabbing the thin silk straps and pulling them down my arms, slowly revealing my body to them. The slip hits the ground at the same time Colton's pants and boxers do. My eyes scan over the sexy man in front of me and I reach out for him. He pulls me against him and presses a kiss to my lips.

"l love you, Dove."

Tanner steps behind me and I feel his bare chest on my back. "I love you, Blossom."

I look back at Tanner and seal my lips to his. "I love you both."

Water splashes and I look back to Colton to find him standing in the tub with his hand out for me. Reaching for his hand, I step into the bath and we both sink into the water with him at my back.

"We want you to relax tonight." Colton's hands massage my shoulders and I relax back into his chest.

"Let us take care of you." Tanner pulls a stool next to the side of the tub with a wash sponge in his hand. He sinks the sponge into the warm soapy water and I reach out, wrapping my fingers around his forearm that's leaning on the tub.

"We're here for you. If you need to talk about what happened, we'll listen, we'll hold you, we'll always love you. Our love for you can only grow." Colton kisses the side of my head.

A sinking feeling in my stomach has me looking away from them. I didn't want them to know that Cyrus touched me again, that he once again overpowered me, and took what he wanted.

Tanner turns my face back to him. "You don't have to talk about it now. If or when you're ready, we're here for you. Nothing you tell us will make us love you less."

"It'll be quite the opposite," Colton adds.

I sit up from Colton's chest and turn so I'm able to look at both of them. "You're saying you love me more because Cyrus..." I won't finish that sentence. I'm not ready to say it out loud.

"We're saying we love you because you're a survivor. You survived him. We love you because your only concern even with the awful things Cyrus did to you or when he tried to sell you was Phoenix and making sure he wasn't scared by it. We love you because you've taken your own freedom." Colton tangles his fingers in my hair and pulls me to him. Our eyes connect as our lips skim over each other's. "We don't want you to hide this from us because you're afraid of how we'll react."

"I only want to focus on us. He doesn't get to interfere in my life or our relationship anymore." I press my lips to Colton's and his hand moves to the back of my neck, holding me to him.

Shifting in his lap, I straddle him and deepen the kiss. His hands slide down my body and a hum of excitement flows through me. A hand tangles in my hair and I pull back from Colton's lips to smile at Tanner.

He presses his lips to mine. "Let us clean you and we'll give you what you want."

I nod, wanting the releases that my body is buzzing for. Colton takes the sponge that Tanner had and slides it over my shoulder and down my arm. Tanner tilts my head back and uses the hand nozzle to wet my hair. "Close your eyes, Blossom. Just feel us."

Obeying, I close my eyes and soak in the feeling of them. Colton drops the sponge and continues running his soapy hands over my upper body, giving my breasts extra attention. I arch into his touch and moan as Tanner massages shampoo into my scalp. Running my hands over Colton's shoulders, I lock my fingers behind his neck and rock my hips against his hard cock. Colton's hands grab my hips, stopping me. "Just feel, Dove. We promise to make the wait worth it."

I groan. "Then hurry up."

They chuckle and I can feel the vibrations from Colton but his grip on my hips keeps me from seeking out my pleasure. Lips skim over my ear and Tanner whispers, "Be good."

A shiver runs down my spine and I can't stop myself from sinking further into Colton's lap. Tanner rinses the shampoo from my hair as Colton washes my stomach, wraps his hands around me to my back, and slides down to my ass. Hoping they're finally done, I rock my hips along Colton's cock, thinking his grip was him encouraging me to move. "I'm not done yet." Colton nips at my collarbone and I gasp. "You like that, don't you?"

"Yes," I say breathless.

Colton's hands momentarily remove from my body and I can hear the sound of a bottle being squeezed. Seconds later, his hands are back on my hips and working their way down my legs. Lips press to mine and I turn my head towards Tanner pressing further into the kiss.

My skin tingles as Colton's hands move back up my bent legs to the apex of my thighs. Feeling his touch over my needy core has me bucking against him. "Your body is begging for a release, Dove. Should we give it to you?"

"Yes. Please make me feel good." I open my eyes and stare into Colton's.

"Oh, we won't disappoint," Tanner says as he pulls me back into a kiss just as Colton's thumb brushes over my sensitive clit. Moaning, I reach for both of them, digging my nails into their shoulders as I grind down on the length of Colton's cock at the same pace he's rubbing my clit. Hands move over the front of my body until they cup my breasts and pinch my nipples to harden points.

I let my eyes close again, not needing to know who's touching where and just wanting to feel the pleasure and excitement they give me. Colton's mouth latches on to one of my pointed nipples as a hand slides down the slope of my spine and I know it's Tanner. He pulls back from our kiss and kisses my nose. His hand glides over the curve of my ass and as his finger moves over my back hole, I open my eyes and stare into his.

"I want to take you here someday." He rubs circles over my puckered hole without breaking past the barrier. "Would you let me..." I'm a panting mess and my body is ready to explode from Colton's perfect stimulation on my clit and Tanner's unexpected curiosity. "While Colton fucks you."

"Yes. I'm all yours." I cry out as Tanner pushes his finger past the barrier that I've never willingly let anyone into and Colton flicks my clit faster. I erupt with a scream of pleasure and I dig my nails deeper, holding onto them until I come crashing back.

Falling into Colton's arms, he holds me through the aftershocks until I'm able to lift my head. Looking down at Colton's face, I smile at him as I press my lips to his. "Thank you."

"No thanks needed. I'll happily make you come whenever you want." He lifts me by my hips and Tanner wraps a towel around me as I stand in the draining tub.

I chuckle. "No, thank you for coming for me. Fighting for me. Loving me." Colton stands in front of me and they both help me out of the tub.

"We'll do anything for you, Blossom, but loving you is the easiest of them all. You're ours and we'll never let you go." I let Tanner dry me off before I wrap my arms around his neck and kiss him.

"My heart is yours. Today, Tomorrow. Forever."

Colton presses his lips to my shoulder. "Forever, Dove." He links his fingers with mine and pulls me out of the bathroom. I stop in the doorway when I see Jaxson sitting on the bed.

Chapter Forty-Six

Jaxson

Phoenix is okay. Shaken up from the car crash and being taken but oblivious to the real trauma of what happened and what could've happened, at least for now. Tomorrow I'll worry about finding help for him to be able to process this. Tonight, he sleeps soundless even after a day of horror while the woman I love is in the room across the hall being loved and cared for by her two other men.

She can't look at me and I know why. She called me and I didn't answer. I promised to keep her safe, and when she was in danger, I was more focused on Manuel.

Phoenix told me all about what happened. How she made him run after the crash. How she told him to hide when someone came. How she told him stories to keep him calm. She shielded him from all the bad. Protected him over herself.

I place a kiss on the top of my son's head and walk out of his room and across the hall. As soon as I open the door, I can hear the sounds of her moans coming from the bathroom. I want to join them, watch her fight the trauma she endured, and take her pleasure from the two she loves but instead of stepping into the bathroom, I head to the end of the bed.

I do peek into the bathroom as I pass and both twins look at me as Tanner blocks Sadie from my view. At least until he sees it's me. Both he and Colton smirk but my attention is on her. She looks like a goddess with her eyes closed, head tilted back, lips parted, and her upper body exposed over the water.

Sinking onto the mattress, I rest my arms on my thighs and fist my hands together. I stare at my conjoined hands as I listen to her. The sounds she makes as she's being touched, as she builds to a climax, as she comes is music to my ears. It's a sound I want to listen to for the rest of my life. I'm aching to get my hands on her, to hold her, to apologize for not being there for her. I squeeze my hands into fists, mad at myself.

I used Manuel as a punching bag and my cut knuckles show it, but while I wanted him dead at my own hands for his part in their abduction, I also used him for the anger I have for myself. I let them both down. They needed me and I made the mistake of not keeping my phone close, not turning the ringer on. It's a mistake I plan to never make again.

I look up from my hands as they walk out of the bathroom and my eyes instantly go to Sadie wrapped in a towel, with her cheeks flushed and her wet hair dripping down her chest. She freezes when she sees me and guilt fills me with her hesitation. Colton and Tanner kiss the side of her head before leaving the room, promising to find some food.

The door closes behind them and we're left in silence with distance between us. Tears fill her eyes the longer she looks at me and it kills me. "I'm sorry," I breathe out not being able to wait anymore. "I'm sorry I wasn't there when you needed me. I'm sorry I didn't have my phone on me when you were in danger. If I had answered, maybe he wouldn't have gotten you. He wouldn't have…"

"Jaxson." She whispers my name as she closes the distance between us and stops between my spread thighs. Her hand touches my cheek and I lean into her touch. "Why are you apologizing? This is my fault. I shouldn't have been on that field trip, exposing Phoenix to my danger. I was selfish, wanting a perfect day, and it turned into a nightmare."

I wrap my arms around her waist and pull her onto my lap so her knees rest on either side of my thighs. Her tears cover her cheeks and I wipe them away. "Sunshine, I don't blame you for what happened. It wasn't your fault. My love for you has grown over these last hours. You've protected my son like he was your own and when I heard he had gotten you, I felt my heart rip from my chest. I'm not sure how I'd live without you." I slide my hand into her hair and pull her closer so I can press my lips to hers.

She gasps against my lips as she wraps her arms around my neck, pressing her body to mine. "I wouldn't be able to live without you either. I love you, Jaxson." Her lips move over mine as she speaks, not wanting to break our kiss, but my next words need to be said with her eyes on me.

Pulling back from her, I look her in the eyes. "I love you, Sunshine. You are the light in my life. I want you here with us. I want you in my bed. I want you to help me raise Phoenix and I know I ask this when your heart also belongs to Thing 1 and 2." She smiles at me at their nicknames. "I'm not asking you to choose, I'm asking to be a part of your life with whoever and wherever you are."

She nods as her fingers slowly run through my hair. "Whatever you say." A sweet smile pulls across her face and I chuckle at her using the phrase I always say to her. Our lips press together again and I relish in the feeling of her lips on mine.

Chapter Forty-Seven
Sadie

Laughter and the smell of pizza flow up the stairs as Jaxson and I walk out of the room. I'm dressed in his dress shirt that falls to mid-thigh with him in just his undershirt and slacks. We follow the sounds down the stairs to find everyone in the kitchen. Colton and Tanner notice us first and their smiles have mine widening. I let go of Jaxson's hand as Riona looks over to us. We close the distance between us and envelope each other in a hug. "It's good to see you."

We pull back and I give her a grateful smile. "I'm glad you came."

"Always. How are you doing?" This is the third time she's saved me.

"I'm okay. Helps that he's dead."

"I'm proud that you took what you needed for peace." I look down at the ground at the mention of me killing Cyrus. I'm glad he's dead. I'm glad it was me that killed him. Watching his life leave his body was like being released from chains. But killing someone was never something I thought I'd ever do, and the fact that I did scares me. It shows me I'll do anything to protect myself and the people I love. A part of myself has hardened for what I'm willing to do while another opens to love. "If you ever need to talk about it or what happened, I'm always here."

"Thanks." I look back at my three men. "I think I have what I need to heal." She smiles and looks at her men.

"I know what you mean." Dante, Matteo, and Enzo smile at her.

Matteo grabs the pizza boxes. "Let's eat in the sitting room."

Colton wraps his arm around my shoulders as we walk across the foyer. "You're sitting with me." I smile up at him and chuckle.

"Where else would I sit, with Enzo?"

Colton growls as he pulls me on his lap. "Don't joke about that."

Rolling my eyes at him, I wrap my arm around his neck as I sit across his legs, leaning against the armrest. Tanner hands me a plate with a pepperoni slice on it and I mouth 'thank you.' He places his hand on my knee as he leans back next to us. "You're not going to get me a slice?" Colton looks dumbfounded at his brother.

Tanner rolls his eyes and hands over his plate. I smile at him, hook my legs over his closest to me, and slide my feet under his other. Jaxson sits on the other side of Tanner and I smile over at him. It feels good having us all together.

"What happened after we left?" Colton asks.

"Not much," Riona answers. "Made sure there was no one else down there."

"We found the waiter. He had been taken off the streets over a year ago. Was sold multiple times." Enzo pauses as it sinks in all the awful things that he went through. "Cyrus bought him about a month ago and beat him until he was obedient. He'll be coming back with us."

I smile at Riona, knowing that she'll make sure he gets whatever he needs. Find a life without horror and find a place in this world. It's what she does. It's what she did for me.

"What about the girls?" Jaxson asks.

"They were taken today just like you. They're shaken up but don't remember much in between being taken and waking in the glass boxes. We dropped them home and I gave them mine and our therapist's number if they ever needed anything."

"We left everyone else down there. It's fitting that they died in a cemetery. The catacombs have been sealed off so no one will be able to find them." Matteo smirks like he's pleased with him. "I hope the souls of that cemetery haunt those disgusting bastards for all time."

"See..." Colton nudges Tanner. "I told you the ghosts were watching."

We all chuckle and I lean into Colton. Cyrus will rot in that musty showroom. His blood will stain the wood. He will be forgotten. Never found. Never mourned.

"You okay?" Colton whispers as he runs his hand down my back.

Tilting my head so I'm looking up at him, I say, "Yeah I am." I mean every word of that simple statement. I don't have to run or look over my shoulder anymore. I have a family. I have three men I love and a little man I adore. And I'm finally free.

Epilogue

Jaxson

One month later

Music blares through the club as I walk in through the backdoor after dropping Phoenix off at my mom's for the day. Instead of heading upstairs, I continue through the hallway that opens to the club. The bar and seating area are empty as I walk into the open space, but I wasn't expecting anyone to be there. It's the stage my eyes instantly go to. Sadie swings around the pole in my sweatshirt and pants. They drown her body, but I don't think she's ever looked sexier.

A smile pulls across her face when she spots me and her feet touch the ground, stopping herself. "I've been waiting for you."

"Oh yeah?" I strip off my jacket and drop it over one of the chairs. Whatever she has in mind, I'm game.

"Yeah." She hooks her finger at me, beckoning me to her. "Have a seat." She walks around the back of the chair that's placed at the beginning of the walkway to the center pole.

I jump up onto the stage and pull Sadie up against me. "What are you up to?" My finger goes under her chin, tilting it up so I can press my lips to hers. Sadie pushes up on her toes, deepening the kiss. Her hands slide down my chest and to my sides where she grips my shirt. I tangle my fingers in her hair, holding her to me as she turns and pushes me into the chair.

"I have a dance just for you." Her lips press to mine one last time before she stands in front of me with a seductive smile.

A new song starts over the speakers as she messes with her phone. Leaning back in the chair, I spread my legs wide and rest my arms on the armrests. Watching her dance is one of my favorite things. When there isn't Russo business needing the club, she comes down here to dance as I work on the books. She's always a welcome distraction during that time but I've never gotten a personal dance.

Sadie walks backwards with a lustful sway to her hips that matches the tempo of the song. Her hands slide up her body to the zipper at the front of my sweatshirt and she pulls it down.

She lets the sweatshirt fall off her body revealing a blush pink lace bra. "You're wearing my sweats to remove them."

"I figured you'd like what's underneath it better." Sadie gives me her back as she bends forward, sending my pants down her legs. Her beautiful round ass in a matching thong shakes as she rolls her hips to the music.

"I like anything you wear Sunshine, but in this outfit, I want you closer. Let me touch you." I reach out for her, but she just shakes her head.

"You'll get what you want." Her hand wraps around the pole above her head. "Eventually."

She spins with her legs bent and then slowly straightens them into a split. Her wrists cross above her and she flips on the pole so she's facing it. Using her knees, she climbs up the pole and waves her body against it. Her eyes connect with mine and she smirks at me before falling back so she's hanging upside down. Her knees come to her chest as she twists and lands on her knees with her hands above her head facing me.

The breath I didn't realize I was holding as she partially fell with grace slowly releases and I smirk back at her. "You're trouble, Sunshine." Her hands release the pole and slide down the back of her head over her shoulders and down to her breasts.

"You like it." Yes, I fucking do.

She cups her breasts in her hands pushing them higher and together and when she releases them her bra falls open. Her breasts bounce as she slides the bra off her shoulders and I'm about to crawl my way to her. My need for her is getting to a breaking point.

She leans forward, placing her hands on the wooden stage and starts crawling to me. My hardened dick leaks precum at the sight of her breasts swaying as she closes the distance between us with her eyes roaming over me. I squeeze my dick as I adjust myself and she bites her bottom lip, tracking my hand.

"Getting uncomfortable, Jaxson?" She looks up at me from between my open legs as her hands run up my thighs. "Let me help with that." Her hand rubs along my erection, making me groan. She unbuttons my jeans and slides down the zipper. I lift my hips as her fingers hook the top of them and pulls both my boxers and jeans down. They bunch at my ankles, but I don't give a fuck.

Sadie smiles up at me as she leans forward with her hands on my thighs and places a kiss on the underside of my erection. "Fuck, Sadie." I tangle my hand into her hair and grip the armrest with the other to hold myself back from thrusting up towards her mouth. She places a kiss on the tip before licking the precum. Her humming at my taste sends vibrations straight to my balls.

My shirt slides up my body as her hands run up my sides and I grip the back of it, pulling it over my head as her lips press to my stomach. She stands with her ass out, kissing my chest, and I lose patience, pulling her on top of me. "You're mine now."

She rocks her heat against my painfully hard dick. "I'm not done with my dance."

Listening to the music, I say, "I'm pretty sure this is a different song."

She chuckles. "Have you not been listening?"

"Sunshine, everything around you disappears whenever I'm looking at you."

Her fingers run through my hair. "You don't want a lap dance?"

"I'd rather have you ride me." I slide my hands from her hips to her ass, gripping her cheeks and pulling her up against my waiting dick.

"I can work with that." Her lips press to mine as she slides her heat along my cock and I grip her thong, ripping it from her body. She wraps her hand around my erection and angles it to her entrance. Wet heat surrounds my erection as she slowly lowers herself down. Our breaths brush against each other's lips as we hold our stare. Sadie runs her hand down the side of my face and I lean into her touch. "I love you, Jaxson."

"I love you too, Sadie. More than I'll ever be able to vocalize."

Our lips crash together as Sadie slowly pushes up on her knees, sliding up my cock to the tip before sinking down again. My hands slide up her hips and I help her glide on my dick. Our kiss grows more desperate as our pace increases.

Sadie's head falls back as she moans and I move my lips down her neck. "Lean back, Sunshine." My hold on her hips tightens as she leans back, placing her hands on my knees. I thrust into her and she curses in pleasure at the new angle. Her walls tighten around me as I continue to thrust into her. Sadie's moans grow louder as she gets closer to the edge and it's a sound I want replaying over and over in my head. Leaning forward, I capture her nipple in between my lips and suck it into a pointed tip.

"Oh god, yes."

"Touch your clit, Sunshine. I want you to come all over my cock."

Her fingers rub circles over her clit and her walls choke my cock as I fuck into her, thrust after thrust. Sadie screams out my name as her whole body vibrates in pleasure, and I wrap my arms around her, pulling her chest into mine as I lose control, finding my own release in her warmth. "Fuck, Sunshine."

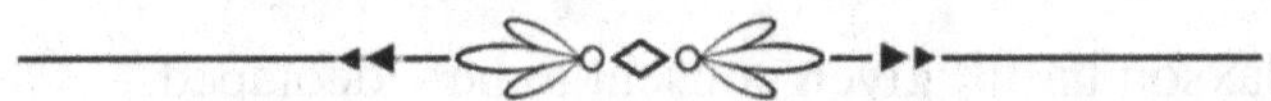

Colton

"Damn, Dove. You like a little dirt on your white feathers." Walking into the club just as Stella climaxes is definitely one of my favorite greetings. She looks back at me with her arms wrapped around Jaxson's neck and a wide smile. "I'm only dirty for you guys."

"That's what I like to hear, Blossom." Tanner stops next to me at the edge of the stage. "Is this something the two of us can join?"

Stella looks back at Jaxson and he gives her a nod. She stands from his lap and he holds her until she steps out of his grip.

When she reaches the end of the stage, I grab her hips and help her down. "Were you stripping for him, Dove?" She nods up at me as I lean down to kiss her. "I want the video."

She chuckles. "I turned off the cameras."

"Why would you do that?" I know she's not camera shy. Ever since she found out about my love of watching her on video, she has sent me several of her pleasuring herself. She's been loving the toys we've been sending her.

"Jaxson hasn't given consent to be videotaped."

"Fine." I give her a pout. "How about I record us together?"

"I'm okay with that."

"With me too." Tanner steps up behind her and kisses her shoulder.

"The three of us together?" Stella's pants in excitement

"Yeah, Blossom. Colton here." She sucks in a breath as he pushes a finger inside her core. "And me here." Her knees go weak as I imagine his finger at her back hole.

I scoop her up into my arms and carry her to the office. "Let's break in Jaxson's office couch."

"That's been broken in several times," Jaxson calls out and she chuckles into my shoulder.

"Not with us it hasn't," I whisper into her ear.

She smiles at me. "You can fuck me anytime on the couch. Any way you want."

"Fuck, Dove, I love when you talk dirty to me." Her chuckles fill the office as I step inside and place her on her feet. "I want you on top of me with my cock buried deep inside."

"Then we better get you out of these clothes." Her hands slide under my shirt and I suck in a breath at her touch. Our eyes lock as she pushes my shirt up with her hands skimming over my skin.

"You touch him, I touch you." Tanner steps up behind her and slides his hands over her waist and up towards her breasts. "Feel free to take as long as you want."

Her head falls back on his shoulder as she hums in pleasure from his touch. Tanner smirks at me over her shoulder as he runs his lips along her neck, silently gloating that she's in his hands.

Stella gets lost in my brother's touch, sliding her hands over my chest, realizing he's touching her where she's touching him. My shirt forgotten, she skims her fingers down my abs, guiding Tanner's hands to where she wants him.

Pressing my body against the front of hers, I brush my lips over hers. "You want his fingers deep inside you?"

She grips onto the top of my jeans. "Yes."

"You want him to make you come before you take my cock?"

"Please." She begs as she looks up at me.

"Unbutton my pants, Dove." Her hands fumble for the button and then the zipper. I step out of her reach before she pushes them down.

"Make her scream, brother."

Tanner takes her chin and tilts her head so he can kiss her. She moans against his lips as he grips one of her breasts with one hand and slides his other down her flat stomach and in between her thighs. Jaxson stands at the door to the office, and I smirk over at him as I pull my shirt over my head. "Enjoy the show, old man." Tanner spreads her lower lips open, giving me a perfect view of her pink and swollen clit. "So needy, begging to be touched."

"Yes, please. Please touch me," Stella begs.

Tanner doesn't deny her pleas and brushes his middle finger over her clit. She bucks against his hand, wanting more. He presses his fingers against her clit, rubbing tight circles over it and her knees go weak.

Tanner wraps his arm around her waist, holding her to him as his fingers disappear in between her thighs. I push my jeans and boxers down, letting them collect at my ankles as her breath catches from being filled. I sit back on the black leather couch, kicking off my clothes completely, and fist my hardened cock. Stella's eyes track my hand as I slide it up and down my erection at the same pace Tanner's fingering her.

"You like him inside you, Dove?" She whimpers as she nods. "Do you want to be filled by the both of us?"

"Yes. Yes. Yes," she chants.

"I bet even Jaxson would want to join. Do you want all of us?"

"Oh god, please."

"Come for Tanner. Scream out your pleasure as you squeeze his fingers with your warmth." She curses at my words as Tanner presses the heat of his palm against her clit.

"Soak my fingers, Blossom. I can't wait to use your release as lube." Tanner groans as he nips at her earlobe and she erupts, screaming through her orgasm and going limp in his arms. He scoops her up off her feet while placing kisses softly on her face as she comes down from her high.

When her eyes open, they connect with mine, and I smirk at her. "You ready for me?"

She nods as Tanner carries her over to me and I take her from him, settling her so she's straddling me. Her warmth against my wanting dick releases a deep growl in my throat. "Fuck, Dove. I need you."

She reaches between us, grabs my dick, and brings it to her entrance. "Then take it."

Tangling my fingers in her hair, I crush my lips to hers as I thrust deep inside her, causing us both to moan.

Tanner

Stella looks breathtaking with her skin flush, a lustful smile pulled across her face, and a pleasurable daze in her eyes. The moan she makes as my brother fills her has my dick aching, wanting to be buried inside her too. I grip myself, giving it a squeeze, knowing I'll be pushing through her tight back hole soon. Removing my clothes, I kneel behind her and place a kiss on her shoulder.

My eyes connect with Colton's, and without telling him what I need, he lays back, wrapping his arms around her so she's flat on top of him. Trailing my fingers down her spine, she arches back, pushing her ass towards me as she grinds herself on Colton's cock. My smirk grows at her presenting her ass to me. She looks back over her shoulder, watching me as I run my fingers in between her globes and circle her tight hole.

"Have you been using the plugs I sent you?" I let my fingers move south, gathering her wetness and bringing it back.

She moans, "Yes. They feel so good."

"She's not lying. She wore the largest one last night until I fucked her right here. She was so needy she came as soon as I was inside her." Jaxson runs his hand along the front of his desk as he leans against it.

Stella pushes back against my fingers with a moan like she's remembering the pleasure. "Please."

Pushing a finger past the barrier, her breath catches as her eyes widen in wonder. "Relax into Colton, Blossom. Let me get you stretched for my cock."

Her body complies, melting against Colton's as he pulls her lips back into a kiss and I slide further in. I finger her ass, only going knuckle deep a few times before adding a second finger. Her body stiffens as she stretches around them and I run my hand over her back to soothe her.

"Here," Jaxson calls out and I look over at him just as he throws something at me. Catching it, I smirk seeing its lube. "Do you even work in here or just fuck our girl?" Stella squeezes around me and Colton groans as I say, 'Our girl'.

"She's quite the distraction." That she fucking is.

Leaning over her, I squeeze the lube down my fingers and over her hole before easily sliding back inside her tight hole. My lips skim over her ear as I whisper, "You like being called ours, Stella?"

"Yes," she pants as I pump my fingers inside her, scissoring them to stretch her out.

"Don't worry, Blossom. We'll be making you ours tonight."

I add a third finger, making her hiss, and Colton runs his hands down her sides. "Breathe, Dove. If you can't take his fingers, you won't be able to take his cock."

"I can take it. I want it. Please, Tanner."

He grips her thighs, pulling her knees closer to him so her upper body is flat against him. "Show us you want it." Stella takes a deep breath and as she exhales, her body relaxes and I'm able to push my fingers all the way in.

"That's it, Dove." His hands run up her thighs to her ass where he spreads her cheeks apart for me. "You heard her. Give her what she wants."

The whimper she makes as I remove my fingers has me quickly lathering my cock with lube. "Take a deep breath for me, Stella." Placing my erect head against her barrier, I grip her hip as she sucks in a breath. "Let it out slowly." As she exhales, I push past the tight ring and slowly slide in. Her body tenses when I'm only halfway in and I lean forward, trailing kisses along her spine, waiting for her to adjust.

"Look at me, Stella," Colton whispers as he tries to soothe her, running his hands along her body. Her head tilts up and he pulls her into a slow kiss, making her melt, and I push forward sinking the remaining inches inside her.

"Oh fuck," Stella moans as she tries to squirm in between us. "I feel so …. stuffed."

Colton smirks at her. "Stuffed with our cocks."

She chuckles, squeezing around both of us, and a chorus of moans spills from the three of our lips. "Oh god, please."

Her hips rock in between us, telling us exactly what she needs, and I adjust my grip on her hips as Colton grabs her underneath her thighs. "Please what?"

"Fuck me, Colton… Tanner."

Giving her exactly what she wants, my brother and I slowly pull out of her and thrust back in. Stella grips the couch cushions, scraping her nails along the leather as her head falls forward and rests against Colton's chest. "Yes. You feel so good."

As I thrust into her, she slides up Colton's cock and he pulls her back down as I withdraw to the tip. Controlling the pace, I thrust in hard and deep, wanting her to feel every inch of us. She hums in pleasure as she rocks her hips, meeting us thrust for thrust.

"You're glowing, Sunshine, taking both of them." Jaxson draws her attention as he pushes off the desk and takes a few steps to us. He reaches out and brushes the back of his fingers over her cheek. "Can you take one more?"

"Yes. I need you too." She sits up, resting her forearms on Colton's chest as Jaxson pushes his open pants just low enough to release his cock. Stella reaches out, wrapping her hand around him as he tangles his fingers in her hair, holding her head where he wants her.

Stella/Sadie

His cock brushes over my lips, spreading his precum over them. Wanting a taste, I glide my tongue over my top lip and flick my tongue over the source.

"Fuck, Sadie. Open your mouth and wrap your beautiful lips around my cock." I smirk up at him before running my tongue along the length of him. Sucking his tip in between my lips, I hum. His grip in my hair tightens as he thrusts into my mouth, hitting the back of my throat. I let my eyes close as I relish the feeling of having all three of them at once. I feel so full but complete, like being with them makes me whole.

"Fuck, Dove. Watching you take all three of us is the hottest thing I've ever seen," Colton coos as his hand slides across my skin and in between us. "You have me ready to explode but I can't come until you do, choking my cock." His fingers press into my overstimulated clit, rubbing small circles over the nerves, drawing a long moan out of me that's muffled by Jaxson's dick.

Tanner picks up his pace as he pants next to my ear, and I let go of Jaxson's cock, reaching back and linking my fingers with his on my hip, so I'm touching all of them. The amazing buzz that has been rushing through my body since Jaxson got home once again builds fast.

"Come for us, Blossom. We want to mark you as ours." Tanner's whispered words send me over the edge, into the most intense orgasm where sparks flash under my closed eyelids and I feel like if they weren't holding me, I'd be floating.

"Fuck, you're squeezing my cock so good, Stella." Colton comes, groaning my name and filling my core. Tanner is next, shooting his seed into my ass as he bites down on my shoulder. I feel like jelly and I'm ready to collapse but I don't. Not yet. Looking up at Jaxson, our eyes connect as I feel his cock swelling in my mouth and I moan at the first taste of his release.

"Fuck, Sunshine." He fills my mouth and I swallow every drop before pulling back with a smile on my face.

Their hands roam over my body as I collapse onto Colton's chest and Tanner slowly pulls out. I whimper at the loss, but he scoops me up into his arms, making Colton's dick fall out and leaving me empty, and sits with me curled in his lap. "You okay, Blossom?"

I wrap my arms around his neck and nod against his chest. "I'm perfect."

"Yes, you are. I love you." He tilts my chin up and presses his lips to mine in a soft loving kiss.

"I love you, too," I whisper against his lips. Colton sits next to us with his jeans back on and I smile at him, mouthing 'I love you.'

He winks at me and mouths 'Same, Dove. Always.' Jaxson, fully dressed, holds up the sweatshirt I was wearing early and I slip it on. Resting back against Tanner, I stretch out my legs onto Colton's lap and link my fingers with Jaxson's as he sits in the office chair I first sat in when I arrived in New Orleans. Silence surrounds us as I enjoy having all of them together.

"Fuck, I forgot to record it." Colton breaks the silence and we all crack up laughing.

"I bet she didn't turn this camera off." Jaxson winks at me and I shake my head.

"Just the stage ones."

"Perfect." Colton gives me a mischievous look and I know he'll have the camera footage before he leaves.

"How long are you here?"

"Wanting to know if we'll be around when you're ready for us again?" Colton gives a cocky grin and I shake my head at him. "The answer is yes. We're here until you're packed. Then we'll be with you every day after that."

I'm confused. "Packed?"

"We have a surprise for you." Tanner kisses the side of my head.

Jaxson leans to the side and pulls out a piece of paper, handing it to me. Hesitantly, I take it and open it. On the paper is a Zillow ad for a townhome in the Chelsea neighborhood of New York City. "Is this for us?" My eyes stay on Jaxson as I watch for any doubt or uncertainty.

He smiles with a nod. "We're moving to New York." Tears fill my eyes from the excitement that Jaxson and Phoenix are willing to move to New York for me.

"With the new address, we figured you'd need this as well." Colton holds up a plastic card. Recognizing it's a New York driver's license, I take it from him and scan over our new address but it's the name at the top that takes my breath away. "We figured it was time to legally change your name from Scarlett to who you really are."

I smirk at the three of them. "I think you're a little premature on two of these names."

"It's inevitable, Blossom," Tanner says so matter of fact.

"Why wait to take our names?" Colton smirks.

"I don't need a fancy party to tell me you're my wife, but I'll give it to you whenever you're ready." Jaxson takes my hand and kisses my ring finger.

They're right. I'm theirs.

I'm Stella Sadie Flynn-Wright.

The End

Thank you so much for reading *Stained with Ash*. I would be honored if you had the time to write a brief review letting me know what you thought.

If you would like more of Stella, Tanner, Colton, and Jaxson please check out the bonus scene.

Linktr.ee/e.molgaardauthor

Keeping reading for a peek into *Ignite the Fire*, the first book in Riona's duet.

My name is Riona Murphy and I'm the daughter of the Captain of the Murphy Clan. As a mafia princess, I'm forced to have two faces. The fake innocent princess that everyone sees and the real ruthless killer that lurks in the dark.

At least that's the case until my best friend, Aisling, was taken. Now my mask is down and my daggers are clean. No one is going to stop me from tearing this city apart to find her.

My only problem, or should I say three problems, are the gorgeous Italians that have sworn to help me find her. With each day I spend with them, I find myself being pulled in by Enzo's sweet charm, Matteo's pure sex appeal, and Dante's dark stares.

When I let them into my bed, it was supposed to be just fun.
Temporary.

I definitely wasn't supposed to fall for them. Now I'm caught between two families. Pulling toward one while being pulled by the other.
Who will win? Me or my Captain?

Prologue

Riona

Tonight is the annual Murphy Gala. A night that all allies and enemies within the top crime families in New York come together without any violence. Really, it's a night to show everyone how powerful you are and we, the Murphys, are at the top. Which means my perfect princess face needs to be on point. I set my curling iron down, taking in the loose curls that fall across my shoulders, with my neutral makeup, showing off my pale skin, and making me look like an Irish Barbie.

God, I hate when I have to become this persona my father created. The innocent Irish princess that is perfect with a shy smile. It makes me look weak. And that's not me at all. I'm more of a straight hair, dark makeup and dark, skin-tight clothes kind of girl, with a fiery attitude and a lust for bloody justice. But I can't be me. Why? Nobody looks twice at a quiet, pure princess in my world, so their lips are always loose. And as the daughter to the head of the Murphy Clan, my power is knowledge. I collect everyone's secrets.

I start braiding my deep red waves in a loose side braid, finalizing my good girl look. "Riona."

"Yes, Father?" Through the mirror I watch my father, Lorcan Murphy, in his all-black tux that highlights his salt and pepper hair. For being almost 60 years old, his hair is the only thing that shows his age.

He walks into my bathroom and stands behind me. "You look very *pretty*." I narrow my eyes at him because he knows I hate being called pretty. It's so condescending when he says it. "I have a job tonight for you."

My green eyes connect with his identical ones in the mirror, and our father-daughter relationship immediately turns to business. "There's supposed to be no violence tonight."

His smirk from when he called me pretty disappears into a fierce glare. There is no talking him out of this. "It's my party. I can do whatever I want. Are you telling me you won't do it?"

"No. Who's the mark?" My power might be knowledge, but it's not my only one.

"Carl O'Brien. He's a traitor and a snitch. I don't want another day to come where he's breathing." Lorcan requires two things from everyone. Loyalty and keeping your mouth shut. You fail at one, you die. Carl failed at both.

I turn around, facing him, and lean back on the counter. "You want it done quietly?"

My father smiles at me with so much pride. "I knew you'd be the one for this."

"I'm your only assassin." Oh yeah. I'm my father's assassin. Secret assassin. Nobody knows outside the family. Hence the princess cover. "Do you want him going down here or a delayed death?"

"Here. But near the end."

"Yes, sir."

He gives me a nod and heads out of my bathroom. "Finish up getting ready and get what you need, then meet your brother and me in my office."

I give him a nod. "I'll be there in 15 minutes."

Wrapping a tie around the end of my braid, I head into my closet. My closet has two sides. One side is filled with my true style: leather pants, ripped skinny jeans, crop tops, low cut tops, and short dresses. The other side is for my fake identity. It's filled with evening gowns and conservative blouses and jeans.

Removing my robe, I grab tonight's emerald green evening gown, my signature color, off the hanger and step into it, pulling it up my body. I zip it up, stopping halfway up my back, and hooking the top at the back of my neck, completing the high neckline, A-line gown. The dress has a silk underlay with the top layer covered in lace flowers. Looking at myself in my full-length mirror, I place a sweet smile across my face, completing the image. I really do look like a princess, a Disney princess ready to find her prince. I chuckle to myself at that thought. I won't be finding any princes tonight.

Turning away from the mirror, a genuine smile comes across my face as I open a secret door in the back of my closet, revealing all my favorite weapons. Now these are the things that complete me. The first thing I grab are my favorite daggers and I strap them to my thigh. You always need to be prepared in this world. Then I pull open a drawer with my deadly jewelry to pick my green emerald ring that has a hidden needle in it. With careful hands, I let two drops of my choice of poison fall onto the needle and flip the stone over it before sliding it on my finger. My 15 minutes are coming to an end, so I step into my heels and leave my closet.

Stepping out of my room, I come face-to-face with my bodyguard, Steve. I don't really need him, but father insists, since it helps keep the princess image and that is what Steve thinks I am. He has no idea of my secret exit from the house for my more deadly missions. "Hi, Steve."

"Evening, Miss Murphy." He smiles brightly as he stands from leaning against the wall and straightens his black suit jacket. "You look beautiful."

I give him a strained smile as I look him over. He's always well put together, his auburn hair cut close, his face clean shaven, and not a wrinkle on his suit. He dresses perfectly for his job to blend in and be forgotten. "Thank you."

We both head down the hall toward my father's office. "Tonight you can hang back. Watch from afar." In order to get what needs to be done tonight I can't have a shadow.

"I'm supposed to protect you." There's concern in his eyes, but it's not needed.

"Tonight there's peace. There's no danger. Please stand in the corner. If I need you, I'll let you know. Plus, how am I going to be approached when I have a handsome man shadowing me all night?" I sweeten my smile so he'll believe my lie and he'll give me space.

"Of course, Miss. I'll keep an eye on you from a distance."

"Thank you, Steve." We stop outside my father's office door. "You can go to the party now. I'm walking in with my father and brother."

Steve gives me a nod and walks away. I give the door a single knock before pushing it open and walking in. My father and brother, Killian, are both sitting on the leather couch with a glass of whiskey in their hands. "You look beautiful, Riona. And I mean that."

"Thank you, Father."

"Yes, your princess face is fully in place." Killian mocks my fake appearance because he knows how much I hate it. "One day you'll be able to walk into these parties like the badass that you are."

"Yeah right. That's never going to happen. If anything is going to change, it'll be me walking in with my husband because father has sold me off for an alliance," I joke.

My father sets his drink down and stands up. "Well at least you know that's a possibility." He straightens his tux as he walks toward me. "But no matter who you marry, you'll always be a Murphy. Now let's go make our entrance. Show everyone how strong we are." Killian stands from the couch and straightens his tux. He looks just like our father, with his dark hair styled back and stern face in place. I loop my arm through my father's and Killian walks shoulder to shoulder with him on his other side as we head into our annual party.

My role as princess has been in full force tonight. I've smiled and spoken to all our guests. I've danced with all our allies and the sons of the other families in attendance. But my true mission for tonight hasn't had a chance to be planned out yet.

I'm currently dancing with Ivan Volkov's, the head of the Bratva, son, Maxim, and he is really driving me crazy. I've danced with him several times tonight and all he can talk about is how awesome he is at everything. And I mean everything. His not-so-subtle hints that he'd rock my world are absolutely disgusting and laughable. The word on the street is that he has a tiny cock and only lasts seconds inside a woman.

Finally, the song ends and I step out of his hold, but he quickly grabs my wrist, stopping me from leaving. "Where are you going? I'm not done dancing with you."

"I'm sorry, but I'm done dancing with you." His grip tightens to almost painful, and I hold back everything in me so I don't kill him for touching me like this. Instead, I have to play weak. Tears pool in my eyes as I blink at him timidly when I'm actually picturing his tall, lanky body hanging upside down and slitting his throat so his blood can stain his bleach blonde hair. "You're hurting me."

I try to pull away again but when I step back, I bump into someone. Turning, I find the one person I've been looking for all night. Carl O'Brien. He smiles down at me and then eyes Maxim's hold on my wrist. "May I have this dance?"

Maxim lets go of my wrist, storming off, and I smile up at the seventy-year-old man with gray hair and large belly. "Thank you."

He takes my hand, holding it in his and sets his other on my waist. I rotate my ring around as I place my hand on his shoulder. Looking past him, I see Steve making his way over. Our eyes lock, and I give him a head shake telling him to step back. Following orders, he stops walking toward me and heads for the wall. With Steve handled, I focus on dancing with Carl. "Are you having fun at the party?"

"Yes. Especially now. I've never had the pleasure of dancing with the princess at any of the others."

I fake being bashful by dropping my eyes and giving him a coy smile. "I'm not special."

"That isn't true." Carl tightens his hold on me and moves us in a quick circle, giving me the perfect opportunity. I fake a joyous laugh and trip over his feet as I scrape his skin with the poisonous needle.

"Oh my. I'm so sorry. The adrenaline from earlier must be draining me. I should probably go sit down." I act like I'm dizzy as Carl holds me like he's truly concerned for me.

"Absolutely. Let me help you."

"Oh no…"

Steve shows up at that moment. "I'll help her."

I give him a small nod and turn to Carl. "Thank you for the dance, Mr. O'Brien."

I step away from him and head to my father's sitting area with Steve hovering by my side, making sure people move out of my way. When we get to the couch, I give my father a subtle nod telling him it's done and sit down next to him. "Are you done dancing for the night, Riona?"

"Yes. It is quite exhausting." A server comes by with a tray of champagne and I grab a glass.

His eyes scan over the crowd. "Find any suitable suitors."

"Not the Bratva, Maxim. He grabbed my wrist when I wanted to stop dancing with him." I lean in closer to him. "Can I please poison him too?"

He chuckles. "Not tonight, Riona. But if he ever touches you again, kill him."

"Thank you, Father." We've always bonded over my darker side.

"Do you have enough energy to dance with your loving father?"

"Of course." I smile at him.

He stands, reaching his hand out and I happily take it. My father walks me to the dance floor, and we step into a familiar hold and start gliding across the floor. I've always loved dancing with him. It's the only time I can truly let my walls down because he's the only man to 100% have my back. My father twirls me in a circle and I let out a giggle. "What a beautiful sound. You should definitely laugh more often."

"This world is too dark for laughter."

"Your mother and I used to laugh all the time. When you find your person, you'll find the joy in laughing." The mention of my mother makes my heart hurt. She died fifteen years ago from an attack. Her and my father's second, Drew, were murdered trying to protect me, Killian, and his daughter, Aisling. They locked us in a room and ran, trying to draw our enemies away from us. They were forced into oncoming traffic and hit an 18-wheeler head on.

"One day. Maybe."

All of a sudden, a scream fills the room and all heads turn toward it. A lady I don't know is kneeling down next to Carl, who is on the floor, clutching his chest. "Someone call 911!" someone else yells.

My father's men all file into the room surrounding the body and I stand on the edge of the circle as Carl's son moves next to his father's body and tries to help him, but it's too late. Everyone watches as Carl O'Brien takes his last breath and moments later the EMTs come running into our ballroom and try to restart his heart. They won't be able to though.

People quickly start to disperse as the EMTs roll Carl's body onto a stretcher. Killian appears next to me as father tries to comfort Carl's family. "I guess the party's over."

Chapter One

Riona

"Riona!"

"Aisling!"

I can't help the smile that forms on my face as my best friend, my soul sister, calls out for me. "Where is that fine ass I've missed so much?"

I look over my shoulder as she steps into my closet, looking fantastic with her wavy strawberry blonde hair falling over her shoulders, her face void of makeup, showing off her freckles, and wearing a blue summer dress. Aisling and I grew up together, and after her mother died when she was an infant and her father died with my mom, my father took her in and raised her. "You're in the wrong room if you're looking for the Murphy ass you've been missing."

Lust fills her blue eyes as she thinks of my brother. While I had my best friend growing up, my brother had his lover, soulmate, future wife. They've been together for as long as I can remember and they're disgustingly cute together. "I'll see his ass later and it'll be naked along with the rest of him."

I scrunch up my face, grossed out. "You know you can't talk about my brother to me like that."

She chuckles and nods her head toward the knife I'm cleaning. "As your new attorney, I can't be a witness to this if you're cleaning off blood from someone you killed."

I look down at the knife and smile at my reflection on the blade. "It's not. Just my training partners. It was a small scratch. But it did bleed a lot." I give her a wicked grin as I set down the knife.

"So bad. How do you keep your training partners when you almost kill them?"

"I pay them well. And if they left, I'd have to actually kill them."

I walk over to her and give her a hug. "I've missed you, Ash. Congratulations on finishing law school. Sorry we couldn't be there for the ceremony."

"I skipped the ceremony because a very handsome brother of yours gave me a surprise visit." That explains where Killian disappeared to a couple of days ago.

"I'm sure he gave you more than one surprise."

She closes her eyes like she's reliving it. "Oh yes. All night long."

"Okay." I throw my cleaning cloth at her. "That is as much as I can take. Are you ready for a girls' night of celebrating?"

"Hell yeah. I need to get drunk. And so do you. Killian has said you aren't getting out as much."

I shrug my shoulders. "I've been busy."

"Well, you need to chill out. Killing takes a part of your soul. I don't want it to consume you."

I look away from her concerned face. "I know. Father is keeping something from me and every time I try to bring it up, he tells me to know my place like I'm not a part of this clan. Ever since the gala, he calls on me less and less. I'm getting bloodthirsty and killing slimeballs is the only thing that helps."

"Then we're going to let loose tonight and use your other favorite outlet." She gives me a wicked grin, telling me she's going to get me into trouble.

"Don't let Killian hear you say that."

"Oh please. A little jealousy won't kill him. Plus, I'll just be dancing. You're the one that needs to get laid." She turns to the side of my closet that holds my favorite outfits and runs her hands over the dresses that hide nothing. "Now let's find something that'll make all the men tonight beg at your feet."

Aisling holds up her shot. "To you finding a fine ass man tonight."

"To you finally stepping over to the dark side." I tap my shot to hers and, in sync, we tap the glasses to the bar and then take them.

"We grew up on the dark side."

"True. Now you get to dirty your hands by bending the law."

The bartender drops off two more shots and points to two guys down the bar. They raise their shots to us with hunger in their eyes. These two are a good start to the night. "Oh, tonight's going to be fun."

We both take the shots and then make our way to the middle of the dance floor. Within seconds, I lose myself in the music and the bodies surrounding us. I really did need a night where I can get out of my head for a while. Not be a mafia princess or assassin. Just a 23-year-old having a good time with her best friend.

I place both of my hands on Aisling shoulders as our bodies dance together. "Ohh... someone's finally onboard with having some sexy fun."

"Are you going to stop me?"

"Never. Wild Riona is one of my favorites." She looks over my shoulder with an excited smile. "It looks like your first contestant is stepping up now. Let's see if he is your lucky winner tonight." I roll my eyes at her acting like this is a game show.

"Hello, beautiful ladies! Can I be the meat to your sandwich?"

"No." Aisling and I both say at the same time while I let him see how grossed out I am by his pickup line.

"Fucking bitches." He glares at us before walking away.

"Contestant number one has been eliminated." We both crack up laughing.

"Hopefully there are better options than that. If not, you're going to warm my bed tonight."

I pull her into a swaying hug, and she pushes me off. "You wish."

We both chuckle but movement along the wall near the VIP area has my smile falling as I watch Maxim Volkov walk past the security guard that is holding the rope open for him and his guys. God, I hope he doesn't see me tonight. I can't deal with him. Ever since the gala, he's been coming on strong, constantly making passes at me.

Aisling looks around trying to figure out what caught my attention. "What is it? Do you see contestant two?"

"No, I see an entitled Russian asshole."

She rolls her eyes as she finds him in the crowd. "Ignore him. We're not mafia tonight so mafia problems don't exist." The song changes to something with a deep bass and I pull Aisling to me, and we dance in slow seductive movements. "I wish Killian could dance like this. It would be great foreplay."

"Oh please. It'd be the fastest foreplay ever. He'd pull you into a dark corner within seconds." They're the cute high school sweethearts that are all over each other every second of the day, even if they gross out the people around them. Specifically me.

A cute boy-next-door-looking guy moves his way over to us with his eyes on Aisling. "It looks like you have your first contestant."

Aisling looks over to the guy just as he reaches us. "Hi. Do you mind if I join you?"

"I'm actually taken." Aisling holds up her hand, showing her engagement ring Killian gave her last summer.

The cute blonde holds up his hand showing a wedding band. "Me too." He nods behind us and we both turn to see a muscular man standing on the edge of the dance floor at the railing. He smiles with a nod while raising his glass, giving his silent permission.

"Okay." Aisling shrugs her shoulders and takes the blonde's outreached hand.

I step back from them, pointing toward the bar. "I'm going to get us some drinks." Aisling gives me a nod and I turn away from her.

I have to move through what feels like hundreds of people to get to the edge of the dance floor, but once I do, I'm greeted with a massive crowd surrounding the large bar. Well, this is going to take forever. Walking the length of the bar, I try to find an opening. I'm just about to give up and head back to the dance floor when two guys walk away, leaving a small opening. I quickly slide into the spot before it disappears and lean on the bar top. Standing up on my toes, I look up and down the bar for the bartender.

"It's going to be awhile." I turn toward the deep voice, wondering if he was talking to me, and my breath catches at the tall dirty blonde hair and brown eyed man that is standing just inches away from me.

My skin tingles at his closeness and I fight myself not to lean into him. "Why do you say that?"

He leans on the bar next to me, brushing his arm against mine. A shiver runs through me as he leans across me to point to one of the bartenders. "That guy has only been working that end of the bar because of all the girls giggling over him." He points to the other end of the bar. "She hasn't left that end because she's talking to that guy."

Seeing exactly what he means, I lean back and take in this mystery guy that has me wondering if Aisling could be right about the trouble I could get into. "Well shouldn't there be a third bartender?"

"You'd think." A hint of disappointment flashes in his eyes like he's filing my comment away.

"How long have you been standing here?"

He looks down at his watch. "A couple minutes."

I move closer to him as I lean on the bar with my hip. "So how do we get our drinks?"

"I have an idea." A wicked sexy smile forms on his face.

I think I'd agree to anything right now. "Okay?"

"*You* need to get his attention." Or we could be taking advantage of the open bar top.

"Why me?"

His eyes roam up and down my body and I wish I was wearing a dress instead of this romper. Easier access for whatever he wants to do to me. "Because he won't be able to turn away from someone as beautiful as you."

My cheeks flush picturing what he could do to me out here in the open. I shake my head, wiping that thought away and focus on him and his plan. "How do you expect me to do that?"

"Make him think you're interested."

"Like this." I step closer to him, placing my hand on his chest. I feel his chest expand as I rise up on my toes and skim my lips up his neck.

His hand goes to my hip, fisting my romper and pulling me closer. "I'm not sure you'll be able to get this close to him."

I chuckle. "Good, it's not him I want to touch."

I pull away, standing flat on my feet, and turn back toward the bar. My Mystery Man doesn't remove his hand from my body, as he steps behind, pressing his body to mine so I can feel everything. I take a breath, forcing myself to watch the bartender, and not melt into the stranger behind me, as he finishes up a drink order. Before he could take another, I let out a whistle as I lean the top half of my body across the bar top, making sure my breasts look like they're about to fall out.

His head turns my way and I give him a little finger wave with a sexy come to me smile. "Hook, line…" The bartenders' eyes go directly to my breasts, and he gives me a cocky smirk before swaggering over to me. "And sinker."

My Mystery Man whispers into my ear, "You're a goddess, Beauty."

I bite my bottom lip to stop a moan from escaping. The bartender thinks it's for him and I play it up by running my finger along the edge of my romper down my chest, in between my breasts, to where my deep V stops. The bartender stops in front of me with his eyes zeroed in on my breasts. "What can I get you, dollface?" Ugh. Really. I have to fight myself not to scrunch up my face in disgust. "I'll take three gin and tonics and..." I look to my Mystery Man.

"Three Eagle Rares."

I cock my head to the side with a sweet smile. "You heard him."

The bartender isn't even fazed by my Mystery Man. He tries to show off by mixing my drinks and pouring the three bourbons but I'm not really paying attention to him. My attention is on the man behind me as I wait for his next touch. The bartender sets down our drinks and leans toward me. "What are you doing after this, cutie?" I lose my smile instantly and glare at him. Why don't guys realize that word is demeaning? I'm not a little girl or a puppy.

So I don't blow up on the bartender; I just turn away from him and walk away. But I do hear my Mystery Man say, "Not you, man."

I chuckle as I look over my shoulder to my Mystery Man. He smirks at me as he raises one of his bourbons.

Looking away from him, I move through the crowd back to Aisling. She smiles at me as I break through the crowd. "What took so long?"

I smile at her, excited to see how this night will end. "I might've found a true contestant."

"Oh my god! Where?" I look back to the bar, ready to point him out, but he's nowhere to be seen.

Chapter Two

Riona

"Here is the next round." Mike, Simon's big buff husband, walks over with four drinks. With my previous drink long gone, I could really use this one.

"Are you finally done watching?" Simon steps up to his man, taking two drinks from him and handing them to us.

They don't break eye contact as they instantly start dancing in sync with each other. "You know I love watching you."

Mike slams his mouth to Simon's. Oh shit. I look at Aisling and she is fanning herself. "That's hot." She looks at me. "Do you think I could get Killian to make out with a guy?"

I crack up laughing. "No. I don't."

Aisling pouts for a second then shrugs her shoulders. "I probably wouldn't like it. I'd get jealous."

I shake my head at her and take a sip of my new drink. Closing my eyes, I try to lose myself in the music and enjoy being normal. Feeling eyes on me, I reopen them and scan the crowd, hoping it's my Mystery Man because I haven't seen him again.

Instead, my eyes connect to another tall and handsome man with dark features as he makes his way toward me. As he approaches, I run my eyes over him, taking in his gray slacks and white button-up with his sleeves rolled up and the top few buttons undone. God, he is sexy. And sexy in a different way than Mystery Man. Mystery Man had his light touches and sexy smirk. This guy is steaming hot, in-your-face, sex appeal.

Mr. Sex Appeal approaches our group and Aisling looks him up and down as the guy smiles down at me and extends his hand out. Aisling smiles at me from ear to ear as she gives me a thumbs up and mouths 'contestant two'.

I slide my hand into his and he pulls me into his body. We move together instantly and all I want to do is run my hands all over him. So that's what I do. Looking up at him, I watch his face as I run my hands up his arms, over his shoulders, and down his chest. He is all muscle. He also isn't shy about touching me either. His eyes flare with desire at my touch and as his hands run down my sides and rest just above my ass. "Do you know how beautiful you are?"

My body heats at his question because there is something about it that is about more than my looks. Mr. Sex Appeal takes one of my hands in his and turns me so my back is to his chest and our conjoined hands are across my stomach, holding me to him.

His scruff rubs against the edge of my ear as he whispers, "All these people can't keep their eyes off you. But they can't touch.

They all want to bow at your feet, Princess." For the first time ever, someone calling me princess sends a shiver of desire through me.

I squeeze his hand as I melt into him, feeling how hard his muscles are. And I do mean *all of him*. I grind against his hardening length and he curses next to my ear. "God. You make me want to say fuck it."

"So, say it. What's so wrong with going after what you want?"

He growls next to my ear before kissing the spot right behind it. "So many things." He unlinks our fingers. "Thanks for the dance, Princess."

His body moves away from mine and when I turn to look for him, he's gone. How did he disappear so fast?

I stand there looking through the crowd of people dancing to hopefully see his retreating body.

"Hey. Where did contestant two go?"

"I don't know." How have I let two gorgeous men vanish on me?

I look back to Aisling and she's looking down at her phone. "Killian is here. He wants me to meet him outside."

"Go. I'm going to head to the bathroom." I point behind me to the back corner. "Meet you back here?"

She nods and we go in separate directions. I start my way through the dancing crowd for the second time tonight. Right as I get to the edge of the crowd, a guy bumps into my shoulder, knocking me off balance a little, but he grabs my hand to steady me. Looking up at him, my breath catches at the sight of his bright blue eyes that contrast against the dark shadow over his face. But before I can say anything, he turns away and the crowd swallows him.

I shake my head, snapping myself out of another strange encounter with a sexy mysterious man. I'm heading in the direction of the bathroom again when I realize there is something in my hand. A piece of paper. I slowly open it and a shiver of worry runs through me.

Maxim is coming for you.

Looking up from the paper, I do a quick spin, looking for Maxim or the guy who gave me the note. I can't find either of them and for the first time tonight I wish I had my weapons. At least Killian is here now. I just need to go to the bathroom and get back to them because he is definitely carrying.

The bathroom is surprisingly empty when I push the door in. So empty that I do a double check to make sure there isn't a sign on the door stating out of order. With the door empty of a sign, I take the blessing and choose the biggest stall. One thing I hate about rompers is that you have to completely undress to go to the bathroom. And since I can't wear a bra or panties with this outfit, I have to get completely naked.

I quickly go to the bathroom and redress because I'm feeling vulnerable right now. The state of undress, the quiet, the threat of Maxim is making me want to get around people again. Just as I get my romper back into place, the bathroom door opens, letting in the sound of the club and then silence fills the room as the door closes again. A cold chill runs through my body at the sound of boots walking toward me. Black boots appear under my door stall and I take a few steps back because I know they aren't going to wait for me to open the door and I don't want to be incapacitated by the door.

"Hello, Princess." Disgust rolls through me at the Russian accent.

"Maxim." He must feel the hatred in my voice because he kicks the stall door in.

"I don't have to hurt you, Princess. Come with me willingly, be my wife, and I won't have to force the decision on you." His almost black eyes rake over me as he runs his fingers through his blonde hair, a creepy smile on his face.

God, he's an idiot. "What, you're going to rape me to get me to say yes? I'm not a virgin. I don't have to marry the man I choose to sleep with."

He takes a step closer to me as he undresses me with his eyes. "Would it be rape if you enjoyed it in the end?" Yes. Yes, it would.

"If you have to force women into sex then the answer is yes. Plus, would I enjoy it?" I hold up my pinky. "I bet your pinky dick can't make any women come."

Maxim storms to me, pushing me up against the wall with his hand around my neck. "Why can't you see that with you being the Clan princess and me being the Bratva prince that us together could give me so much power."

"I'm never giving my power to anyone. Especially you."

I take that moment to hit his hand away from my neck and throw my other fist into Maxim's face. He takes a couple steps back, shaking off my punch and the shock on his face feels great. He has no idea who he's messing with. Not taking a second to breathe, I continue to go at him. He's not down yet, so I'm not leaving.

Maxim recovers faster than I thought and while I go for another face shot, he takes a swing at my ribs. There is a crunch of bone when our fists connect and my breath is knocked out of me as I stumble back, hoping the crunch wasn't my ribs. His hit had more power than I expected for a tall, skinny man that has never worked for anything in his life. Looking up at Maxim, I see him holding his nose as blood runs down his face. Good, I broke his nose. Tears start pooling in his eyes and I bet he's never broken his nose before. Such a pansy prince. He wants all this power, but he's never worked for it.

Pride washes through me and I charge at him again with one last punch, knocking him out. Standing over his unconscious body, it takes everything in me not to kill him. Instead, I bend down next to him with disgust. "Next time I see you, I'll kill you."

Leaving him on the floor, I head for the sink. As I wash my hands, I look at myself in the mirror, making sure I don't look rattled. After drying my hands, I situate my romper and hair and leave Maxim for someone to find. Not caring who I piss off, I push my way through the dance floor to where our group is. When I finally get to Mike and Simon, I instantly look for Aisling and Killian, but they aren't there. "Where's Aisling?" I ask Simon.

He shrugs his shoulders. "She hasn't come back since going to find her man."

Dread instantly sinks in my stomach. Something isn't right. Pulling out my phone, I hit her name as I make my way to the front of the club. Aisling's phone just rings without her voicemail picking up and I hang up and call again as I step outside. Looking left and right, I try to spot them. They better not be fucking in his car. When she doesn't answer, I hang up and start calling out her name as I walk down the sidewalk.

Clicking my brother's contact, I curse silently because something isn't right. Killian answers on the second ring. "I know. I'm late. I'm just around the corner."

"You mean you're not here? Aisling isn't with you?" I turn in a circle looking for her.

"What are you talking about? No, Aisling isn't with me."

"Killian. You texted that you were here like ten minutes ago. She came out to meet you."

Worry fills his voice. "I haven't texted her since before you left."

"Killian, get here now." I hang up on him and yell out for Aisling. I try her phone again, but this time I hear her phone's ringtone. "Aisling?" I run toward the sound of her ringtone. At the edge of the alley, a car comes to a screeching stop next to me and I brace myself for a fight, but then Killian steps out of the driver's seat.

"Have you found her?"

I shake my head frantically. "Her phone was ringing down the alley." Killian pulls a gun from behind his back, and I point at it. "You got one for me?"

Killian hands me a gun as we meet in front of his car. His headlights light up the alley as we walk down it with our guns in front of us. Aisling's ringtone echoes throughout the alley. With each step we take down the alley, my stomach sinks further. There is no way Aisling would willingly go into a dark alley by herself. "Killian."

"I know. I've already called Father."

We find her phone behind the third dumpster, with her clutch, but Aisling isn't here. "Fuck," Killian yells out and punches the side of the dumpster. "You were supposed to stay together, Riona. Why weren't you with her?"

"She was coming to get you. Don't blame me. I was being attacked by the Bratva asshole in the bathroom."

"Kids, that's enough." Killian and I shut our mouths instantly at the sound of our father's voice. We both turn to him, and he looks me over. "What happened? Briefly."

"Aisling received a text from Killian saying he was here and to meet him outside. She left to meet him while I went to the bathroom. Maxim attacked me in there. After I knocked him out, I went back to where we were supposed to meet and they weren't there. I came out here to find her, while trying to call. When I didn't reach her, I tried Killian." No need to say anything else. Aisling isn't here.

"Okay, I'll handle this and Maxim. Go home, Riona."

What? I'm not going. I can find her. "But..."

"Go home," he orders with a glare, telling me to not question him right now. Bowing my head, I walk out of the alley, past my father's men, to the waiting Mercedes with Steve holding the back door open. "Miss Murphy."

"Steve." I give him a nod and slide into the backseat.

I hate being dismissed but at least once I get home, I can start my search for Aisling. I'll burn this city to the ground to find her and I know Killian will be at my side.

Acknowledgements

This past year has been such a wild ride venturing into the dark reverse harem romance world. I'm so thankful to all my readers for their support and excitement for the stories I'm creating. I feel like I've found my group of book besties.

I also want to give a big shutout to my friends and family because they happily listen to my wild and disturbing plot ideas. Without their support I wouldn't be able to pursue this crazy adventure.

About the Author

E. Molgaard was born and raised in North Carolina. She currently lives in Raleigh, NC with her dog Mia. When she isn't writing you can find her curled up with her dog watching her favorite shows or hanging out with her friends and family.

She became an avid reader after college, which inspired her to start writing down the stories she imagined.

Connect with E. Molgaard

Instagram
Tiktok
Author Profile on Goodreads
Amazon Author Profile
Facebook Author Page
Etsy Shop

Also by E. Molgaard

Hockey Romances

Love on Ice Series

Checking for Love
Saving My Heart
Fighting Attraction

Skate With Me Series

Wake Me Up
Talk to Me
Return to Me

Police Officer Romances

Forever Us Series

Wanting Us
Secretly Us
Wonderfully Us

Reverse Harem Romances

Set the World on Fire Duet

Ignite the Fire
Watch it Burn

Stained with Ash